The Rise to Godhood

The Zetan Chronicles, Volume 1

Martin Lundqvist

Published by Martin Lundqvist, 2022.

Sign up for Martin Lundqvist's Mailing List

Also By Martin Lundqvist

Chapter 1: An Awakening.

She woke up feeling dizzy and confused. It wasn't time, yet she had a foreboding feeling she had never felt before. Despite existing for a trillion years, she feared that her death was drawing closer. Close was a relative term, which could mean countless millennia, yet it would only be a blip on her timeline. She thought of going back to sleep, but she couldn't. The True Maker had awoken, and her curiosity was too much for her to ignore.

True Maker made up her mind. She needed to investigate what was going on in the Milky Way Galaxy, and to do that, she needed a form. In her natural ethereal form, she suffered from sensory overload. Thus, the only way to experience the world was to take a mortal form.

An image of a tall, slender blonde woman filled her mind. Why did she see this human? *"Sabina..."* echoed as a faint whisper in her mind. The woman's name was Sabina, and she existed in two separate timelines. She was the one who stood to save True Maker and the Milky Way from certain doom.

'Why am I depending on a human?' True Maker thought and took Sabina's form to feel what she was feeling. She felt nothing. The empty shell she wore had no soul attached to it, which meant one thing. Sabina hadn't existed yet.

Seeing that her future saviour would not exist for 70,000 years, True Maker thought of a more suitable name for the clone of her coming redeemer. True Maker closed her eyes and tried to attune to the humans on earth. Humanity was praying to the deity Gaia, who was the personification of the planet itself. *'Gaia...'* True Maker mumbled the name a few times, and her human body agreed with her. *'Gaia it is.'* True Maker decided.

Inhabiting a human body, True Maker felt emotions that she never felt otherwise. She felt hunger and thirst. She understood how living species filled these needs, but she didn't know what humans used to quench their thirst. She would have to find out.

True Maker imagined a virtual computer screen, and she looked at the chemical makeup of a human. The four primary elements by weight in a human body were Oxygen, Carbon, Hydrogen, and Nitrogen. Thus, she deduced that her body needed these elements in the largest quantities to quench her thirst. At the moment, she lacked oxygen, hydrogen, and carbon.

'Hmm. I should eat solid-state methane, while liquid oxygen would be my best guess for a drink.' True Maker speculated. She conjured a container filled with liquid oxygen. At -183 degrees, this would be a cool, refreshing drink, perfect for quenching one's thirst.

True Maker lifted the container and poured the content into her mouth. She felt immense pain as the freezing liquid caused frostbites to the body's digestive system and went into shock.

True Maker looked at the lifeless body of the blonde woman. So little did she know about the lives of living beings that her attempt at quenching the body's thirst had ended up killing it. While this was tragic, it also served as a reminder. It was better to combine observations with logic rather than blind faith in reason.

True Maker decided to revive the body. She liked the beautiful human form, and it would be interesting to learn about humans by living a short lifetime. How long was a human life anyway? A few millennia? That was nothing, and it would be over as soon as it started.

When True Maker had manifested in Gaia's body, she felt hungry and thirsty. She needed to find a better way to sustain her body than trial and error.

True Maker focused her attention on Earth, and she found a similar yet dissimilar species. Those creatures were Gaia's forebears, yet they were too different for their genome to be related. She needed to investigate why this was the case, but first, she needed to find out how to quench her thirst and still her hunger.

True Maker watched the humans for a while, and she learnt that they used liquid water to quench their thirst while eating berries and nuts to still their hunger. As she conjured the water, the berries, and the nuts, she felt a lot better as she fulfilled her needs. To be a satisfied human was a nice feeling, and she would spend the coming years experiencing the perfect human life. Learning about the human body was her new project, and she forgot about the foreboding feeling that had awoken her from her sleep.

Chapter 2: The Thirst for New Experiences

"The lowest of servants, the daughter of the false prophet Kheera Allahan will become the Dina Wibb and give birth to our next Messiah. Whoever sires this child is bound for greatness. These are my dying words. Make me proud, my son...."

These were the last words of Grand Seeress Ahana Anchalan on her deathbed in the Year 9998 of 5th Age (71202 years before present day). Two years have passed since the prophecy.

"AREELA, WAKE UP."

Areela Kheeran shook her head in disapproval at her brother for waking her up. Today was her birthday, but as her birthday coincided with midsummer at Zetani, this hardly made her unique. In Zetan culture, it was a virtue to only engage in procreation during the midsummer holiday. As the gestation period for the Zetan species was a year, most people had their birthdays on or around the holiday.

Areela looked at her brother, Kailow, whose blue skin glittered from excitement. "Happy Birthday, sister." Kailow Voltrom chirped.

"Cut it out, Kailow. You only woke me up, so I would wish you happy birthday as well." Areela snapped.

"Yet, you only turn 200 once. How does it feel to reach adulthood?" Kailow teased.

Areela paused to think. What did she feel? She felt that Zetan society wasn't enough to quench her thirst for new experiences. She wanted to experience something different, a community that wasn't inhibited by the strict adherence to ancient laws, a society where you could celebrate birthdays any day of the year.

"I feel that I would enjoy my birthday more if I didn't share it with half the people in our capital," Areela exclaimed.

"Shh, that's blasphemy. What you are saying is that people should have sex on forbidden days. You know how bad that could end." Kailow replied.

Areela didn't know, at least not from personal experience. The justification for the rule was to avoid overpopulation, as this would drain the Zeto Crystal and force the Zetans to use unclean energy sources. The overpopulation had happened 10,000 years earlier and had led to planetwide wars and wanton ecological destruction. The planet and the Zetans had recovered since then, but the myths of that terrible period were crucial for the Zetan civilisation.

"I know what happened at the end of the fourth age, but the grand clerics' solution is dumb. Why don't we find a way to enjoy sex without causing overpopulation?" Areela asked.

"What are you talking about? Copulation without the probability of conception is against the natural order." Kailow objected.

"What about lowering the probability? Would that be outside the natural order?" Areela asked.

"I don't know. I am not as obsessed with sex as you are. At least you'll get to experience sex today since you have reached adulthood." Kailow teased.

"Shut up, Kailow. This is not what I want. I want the freedom to choose who I am with and when I am with him!" Areela exclaimed and stormed out of the room.

AREELA WAS SITTING by a waterfall in the wilderness overlooking the Zetan Capital of Ronesia. She felt ambivalent. Today was the first day she was allowed to experience sex after a century of abstinence. The Zetan species had a lifespan of a thousand years, with the fertile period being between 100 and 600 years of age. The law stated that only individuals aged 200-500 years could procreate, and only during the midsummer eve. This rule ensured that the population remained constant so that Zetani could remain a pristine paradise.

While there was no penalty for having sex outside the allowed period, conceiving at the wrong age or time of the year was a crime that led to banishment. Areela's friend Podixa had fallen to the temptation a century earlier, and she was now living with her son on Disyerto-2, a barren world, 50 years travel away. Would she risk this for the fleeting pleasure of physical contact?

When thinking of Podixa, Areela wondered why there were no other beautiful worlds like Zetani in the Milky Way Galaxy. The Zetan lore stated that only planets that had Zeto Crystals could host naturally occurring life, which was the reason for Zetani's uniqueness. Zetani was the only planet with a natural ecosystem in the known universe. Yet, the Zetans had only explored worlds within a 50-lightyear radius of Zetani. As the diameter of the Milky Way Galaxy was 200,000 lightyears, there were bound to be other planets with rich ecosystems in the galaxy. However, how would she ever reach them in her lifetime?

Areela didn't know the answer to this question, but she did know one thing, she wouldn't lose her virginity tonight. As she was single, the Zetan genome masters had matched her with a 398-year-old Zetan man called Xialiab. While the masters claimed they would be compatible, Areela felt nothing but disdain for the old and uninteresting fellow.

'I am not sleeping with him; I'd rather wait another year.' Areela thought and messaged Xialiab via a hologram. "Xialiab, I am sorry, but I feel ill and cannot make it to Mancin Island tonight. I hope you'll have an enjoyable summer solstice."

Having sent this message, Areela went home to sleep through an uneventful midsummer.

Chapter 3: An Instant Attraction.

Areela was in the library when Xialiab approached her. Although she had never trained her innate telepathic abilities, she sensed his emotions and thoughts. Xialiab was furious, and this would lead to a tricky confrontation.

"Areela, why did you reject me on Midsummer Eve?" Xialiab questioned angrily.

"I told you already. I felt sick and nauseous on that night." Areela lied.

"Don't lie to me. I have trained my telepathic abilities. I can read your every thought." Xialiab warned.

Areela didn't like his tone. If he knew her every thought, why had he even bothered showing up to confront her?

"Well, then. What do you want?" Areela snapped at Xialiab.

"I want you to reconsider your rejection. Only a few days have passed since midsummer. If you choose to be mine, we can lay as husband and wife, and I can support you. I am a successful professor at the Ronesian Science Academy, so you'll have a good life." Xialiab replied dryly.

"You're not fooling anyone. You used your status at the Academy to convince the genome masters to match your DNA with someone half your age. I want to choose my partner. Goodbye, Xialiab." Areela replied and turned around.

"This is not over yet, Areela. I will find something you did and use it to bring you down. I will use my position to crush you." Xialiab threatened.

'Oh no. Xialiab is serious about his threat,' Areela thought, and she panicked. She was of the servant class, and she had offended a successful man that the genome masters had appointed her to be one of his concubines. Although she hadn't broken any laws, she feared that her decision would come back to bite her.

"Leave her alone, Xialiab."

Areela looked towards the stern yet calming voice. It belonged to a handsome fellow around her age. He had a chiselled physique and pastel blue skin, indicating that he was from the highest caste in the Zetan society. She wished that the genome masters had picked him as her partner for the Midsummer holiday.

"Don't involve yourself in this, Zelinko. The seers chose her to be my midsummer bride, and she dishonoured me." Xialiab replied.

"Yes, she was your chosen partner, but she was also free to abstain from having intercourse. The servant class are not our sex slaves." Zelinko replied.

"Be careful, Zelinko. While your father's position might protect you, it won't protect this girl." Xialiab threatened.

After saying this, he clasped his temple, blasted Areela with a psionic blast, and left the library.

Zelinko ran up to Areela and nudged her gently. He worried that Xialiab had murdered the poor girl, but he felt relieved as she opened her eyes and gasped. "What happened?"

"Xialiab blasted you with a psionic blast. He controlled his outburst. You should make a full recovery." Zelinko said and wiped off Areela's nosebleed with a handkerchief.

"I don't understand. What happened, and who are you?" Areela asked in confusion.

"Oh, I am sorry. We haven't got introduced. I am Zelinko Siblexom, son of Siblex Valzom, the mayor of Ronesia. Let me help you with your headache." Zelinko said, put his hand on Areela's head, and used his psionic powers to heal her.

Areela stared at Zelinko in amazement. She had suffered from nauseating migraine a moment earlier, but she felt better than ever after a touch from his hand.

"Wow, how did you do that?" Areela asked.

"I used my innate psionic powers. All Zetans have them." Zelinko replied.

"No, we don't. I can't do what you did." Areela protested.

"That's because you never received the training to unlock your abilities. Every Zetan has telepathic, psionic, and prophetic powers. The powerful classes hide these abilities from common people like you." Zelinko revealed.

"So, is this a conspiracy against the servant caste?" Areela asked.

"No, we hide the powers for the greater good. Psionic powers are a double-edged sword. Imagine living your life knowing that someone could kill you from afar with the power of their mind if you let your guard down. Surely, you would prefer ignorance?" Zelinko asked rhetorically.

"No. I have been longing for knowledge all my life. That's why I am at the library." Areela replied. "Very well. Then you'll be happy to know that our seers have foreseen that your progeny will lead our civilisation to a new golden age. This prophecy is why Xialiab was keen to marry and impregnate you." Zelinko revealed.

"And what about you?" Areela asked.

Zelinko clasped his cranium, leaned towards Areela, and whispered. "I have seen you in my visions. Together we will achieve something that many believe to be impossible. We will find other worlds that have Zeto Crystals. Sentient beings like us inhabit these planets."

Hearing Zelinko's words filled Areela with purpose. A few days ago, she had been a servant who had rejected the dreadful Xialiab's hand to marriage. Yet now, she had a purpose, having learned about the world's secrets, and encountered a handsome fellow with a prophetic vision. This vision was more significant than Zetani and the ancient Zetan traditions.

Sweeeeesh

A Xylo bird flew towards Areela, landed on her hand, looked at her with its luminescent green eyes and chirped a beautiful melody. Areela looked at the bird in amazement. How could this happen? Xylo birds were rare and reclusive, yet the bird had chosen her.

"Behold the Xylo bird, the symbol of our city; this mystical bird has chosen you. This confirms that you are the Chosen One." Zelinko exclaimed.

A group of bystanders approached them and marvelled at the rare appearance of the beautiful mystical bird. Areela felt awkward with the sudden attention. She had been a humble servant for 200 years, and now her life had changed overnight.

"Come with me; I know a place where we can be alone," Zelinko whispered into Areela's ears. He turned to the bystanders and spoke with a confident voice. "Move along, citizens. There is nothing to see here."

The bystanders dispersed, as it would seem, in a single wave. As the bystanders left, the Xylo bird took to the sky, and Zelinko led Areela to his tower overlooking Ronesia.

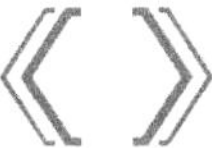

AREELA SAW THE SAME Xylo bird later the same day when she came back to her senses after waking up from the many waves of pure pleasure she had experienced for the first time. Areela had been longing for sex, but she had never imagined that it could be this amazing. While she had enjoyed Zelinko's chiselled physique, glowing pastel blue skin, and the sweet smell of his masculinity, it faded compared to the spiritual journey they had embarked on together. They had been to other worlds through feelings of ecstasy and timelessness that felt like paradise.

As Areela opened her eyes, she noticed that Zelinko was drinking wine at a table. He wore an intricate outfit worthy of a high-ranking official. But how had this happened? They had been making love moments ago, and an outfit like that would take time to put on. Areela decided to ask. "How did you get dressed so quickly? We had fantastic sex just moments ago."

Zelinko put down his wine chalice, chuckled, and replied. "The physical part of our lovemaking ended three hours ago."

"I don't understand. What about the many orgasms I just had?" Areela asked.

"It was orgasms of the mind. I have trained myself to higher consciousness. I used my mind to take you on a journey to the most amazing places of our galaxy, including the most important place of them all, Dihawara Densi, the Divine Dimension." Zelinko revealed.

"The Divine Dimension? What is that?" Areela asked.

"It is the home of the creator of the universe, The True Maker. She has taken a form. A human form. This must mean something." Zelinko revealed.

Areela paused to think. She had heard about the True Maker in the past. Zetan lore stated that the True Maker had imbued the Zeto Crystals with her soul, and that these crystals enabled advanced life on Zetani. However, she had never heard about humans before.

"What are humans, and why would True Maker take a human form?" Areela asked.

"Humans are a semi-sentient species on a faraway planet called Earth. It is a beautiful planet, which is almost as beautiful as Zetani. I would love to go there someday. As for True Maker's actions, your guess is as good as mine!" Zelinko replied.

"Why haven't you travelled there?" Areela asked.

Zelinko flipped a switch, and the entire Milky Way Galaxy came up as a three-dimensional hologram, which covered the whole room. A tiny section was blue, while the rest was black except the white stars.

"This tiny segment is Zetan territory. It has a cross-section of 50 lightyears from one end to the other, with Zetani in the middle. This is the only part of the Milky Way Galaxy that we have explored. Earth is over there, 4,000 lightyears away." Zelinko said.

"So, is it out of reach?" Areela asked.

"The scientific consensus would say so, but I have seen us visiting earth in my visions," Zelinko revealed.

Bang

There was a loud bang as soldiers broke the door to Zelinko's room and swarmed the residence. The last person to enter was Siblex Valzom, the Ronesian mayor.

Siblex walked up to Zelinko and scolded his son. "My son, what is this insignificant servant doing here? Was a rumble in the hay with her worth risking my standing with the City Council?"

"She is more than a rumble in the hay. She is the prophesied mother of our future chosen one." Zelinko replied.

"The nonsense you tell yourself to justify your outrageous actions. You had no problem inserting your member into your fiancée two days ago, yet you couldn't stay away from Xialiab's property." Siblex scolded.

"That's different. I procreated with Shauwana to fulfil my duty to the council. Areela is my destiny." Zelinko replied.

Furious with his son's defiance, Siblex rumbled, and his facial colour shifted to a silvery dark blue colour. He picked up a vase, slammed it into the wall, and exclaimed. "That's enough. Guards, escort the servant out of this building. I will confront my son."

The guards grabbed Areela and hurried to leave the room. The room got darker before the unavoidable mental confrontation between father and son.

Chapter 4: Gruesome scenes on Earth.

The True Maker felt concerned as she tried to decipher the feelings she experienced while inhabiting Gaia's body. Despite having food, beverages and comforts adapted to human preferences, she felt how her sadness worsened. While True Maker could always return to her ethereal form, she wanted to know why she felt depressed while inhabiting Gaia's body. Gaia was destined to save her and the Milky Way Galaxy from an unknown evil in the coming millennia. However, True Maker couldn't comprehend how such an unremarkable creature could impact the future.

True Maker studied a group of humans through her omniscience. Humans lived in small communal groups leading a nomadic lifestyle on earth. Perhaps Gaia felt depressed because she was alone, which conflicted with her human needs? But how would she test this hypothesis? It wasn't suitable for True Maker to involve herself in human development, as it was a breach of her role as a passive force in the galaxy.

True Maker used her premonitory powers to find a solution. She found a tribe in Africa that would die in a sandstorm in three days. By interacting with this tribe, Gaia would experience human interaction without changing the timeline. Having made up her mind, True Maker teleported Gaia to Lake Turkana in Kenya in 69200 BC.

GAIA SHIVERED FROM the cold as she arrived in Kenya. Despite being close to the equator, the skies were grey, the landscape arid, and the winds freezing. Gaia felt confused. She knew that she was in Kenya, the birthplace of humanity. Yet, how could her species' home be such a horrible place?

Gaia walked through the depressing landscape where the carrion eaters were having a field day, unaware that the good times wouldn't last. As much as carrion eaters feasted in times of death, they needed life to sustain themselves.

Gaia kept walking until she found a few malnourished and starving humanoids who were digging the soil for edible roots. Gaia pitied them, but she couldn't feel any connection to them. They were not of the same human consciousness that she was.

As the natives saw her, they ran towards her, threw themselves at her feet, and pleaded, "Goddess. Please clear the skies and give us food. We are starving."

"What is happening here?" Gaia transmitted to True Maker.

"I wanted you to see your species. I understand that you have been lonely." True Maker replied.

"But why are they starving. What is happening?" Gaia asked.

"You are witnessing a volcanic winter due to an eruption at Mount Toba. The eruption will last for six years and cover the planet in ice. Most humans will die, but the few survivors will make your species stronger." True Maker revealed.

Gaia was about to answer when a shocking event took place in front of her. A shaman slit the throat of an infant and chanted. "We sacrifice to you. Please help us."

Gaia acted instinctively and pushed the knife-wielding shaman away from the bleeding infant. She put her hand on the baby's throat, and the wounds healed. The humans threw themselves to the ground and chanted as they witnessed the miracle.

"You must help them. You can't let them die like this." Gaia whispered to True Maker.

"I must let it happen. My role is that of a passive observer. Terrible things can happen if I alter the intended timeline." True Maker replied.

"Then I will help them myself." Gaia dissented.

"No, you won't." True Maker replied and teleported Gaia away from Earth.

"WHY DID YOU SHOW ME this? What do you want?" Gaia cried as she was back in the exquisite palace True Maker had created for her in the Divine Dimension.

"I showed you the fate that had befallen humanity in every iteration of the Milky Way Galaxy. Countless times, your branch of humanity has gone extinct because of the ice age caused by the Mount Toba eruption. Starving and desperate, they slit the throats of their newborns in last-ditch attempts to plead to higher powers for redemption. It's the cruelty of human nature." True Maker stated.

"Why did you not save us from this cruel fate?" Gaia sobbed.

"Us? You are not like them. You are very different." True Maker replied.

"What do you mean?" Gaia continued to cry.

"I saw you in a vision that awoke me from my deep slumber. I don't know how, but you will save me and this timeline from obliteration. As I recreated you, I realised something unique. Something that has never happened in any timelines that I have foreseen." True Maker revealed.

"What did you realise?" Gaia asked.

"I realised that you are the first human with a Zetan genome. I haven't seen this in a trillion years. This is so exciting. I must know how this came to pass." True Maker replied.

"So, humanity's suffering means nothing to you?" Gaia exclaimed.

"I am sorry, dear child. I am omniscient, but not omnipotent. My role is that of an observer, seeing and making tweaks between each version of the universe. When the scope and time are endless, one cannot obsess about saving single species on single planets." True Maker replied.

"I see. What can I do to help my species?" Gaia asked.

"I do not yet know your part in this current timeline. Only time will tell. I will leave you for a while. I need to deal with an urgent matter in the Andromeda Galaxy. However, if you need me, I'll be here." True Maker whispered, and her ethereal spirit teleported away from Gaia.

Gaia picked up a vine of grapes and got seated in a hot bath while munching on a delicious grape. Despite having a beautiful house, delicious food, and all the comforts in the Divine Dimension, she felt unhappy knowing that her fellow humans were suffering on Earth. However, she could do nothing about it, so she had to trust in True Maker's visions that everything would turn out for the best. Unconvinced by her decision, Gaia leaned back into the bath, closed her eyes, tried to forget the horrific events she had witnessed on Earth just moments earlier, and dozed to sleep like an innocent child.

Chapter 5: A Prophetic Pregnancy.

"Sister, don't sit there daydreaming! Let's row to Mancin Island."

Areela looked at her sweet and child-like brother Kailow. He was not yet in his 2nd century, and he hadn't faced the tiring responsibility of growing up to be a full adult yet. While he was biologically an adult, as the Zetans reached puberty at around the 100-year-mark, Kailow was still the equivalent of a human teenager at the age of 175.

"I am coming! Don't stress me." Areela shouted while hoping that she would have more time to think. Her affair with Zelinko three months earlier had led to a conception, which worried her. While it would be a dream to raise a child with the mayor's son, the fact that he hadn't been her appointed partner was an insurmountable issue.

Areela remembered what Xialiab had said in fury when she rejected him. If he found out about her pregnancy, she risked deportation to some barren world. She would linger in darkness and forever miss out on the outstanding beauty of Zetani autumn.

Thinking of the risk of deportation, Areela wanted to contact Podixa on Disyerto-2. The city council had deported Podixa for illegal procreation many years earlier, and so, if they were to send her away, she wanted to join her friend. However, since Disyerto-2 was 50 light-years away, she couldn't communicate with Podixa. The only way to transmit faster than light was to use Zetan telepathy, and they were both novices in that art.

"You're slower than a turtle. Hurry up; we don't have all day." Kailow teased.

"Not as slow as you," Areela chirped, got up and sprinted towards the boat.

Kailow got up, sprinted past Areela, and teased her as they reached the boat, "Damn, sister. You became so slow when you reached adulthood."

'You would not run fast either if you were pregnant,' Areela thought, but she didn't want to share her troubles with her younger brother. Since their mother had passed away, she had raised him. What would happen to her brother if the city council sent her away? Was he mature enough to look after himself?

"I am having a slow day. I'll beat you next time." Areela said and got on the rowboat.

"Cool. Oh, I can't wait to watch the double sunset at Mancin Island. It will be amazing." Kailow chirped.

The double sunset was an event that only happened twice per year at Zetani. It happened at the spring equinox and the autumn equinox. During those days, both the suns in the star system set simultaneously. The double sunset was magnificent when the red dwarf Zetani Sol merged into the blue giant Zetani Maximus at the horizon, creating the illusion of a purple sun setting.

"Oh, I don't know. I am not feeling it this year," Areela said and sighed.

"Wow, you have become a downer since you became an adult. Let go of your worries. We will have so much fun on the island. Mayor Siblex Valzom will be handing out food, drinks, and money to everyone." Kailow enthused.

She almost had a panic attack when she heard about the mayor's presence at the autumn equinox fair. What if he saw that she was pregnant? What would she do then?

'They'll find out eventually. I need to find a way to avoid deportation,' Areela thought while remaining silent for the rest of the boat ride to the island.

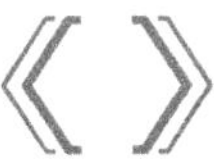

AREELA ENJOYED THE food, the drinks, and the circus performances when she saw something that broke her heart. She saw Zelinko, together with his father and Shauwana. Areela studied her rival for Zelinko's love, and what she noticed made her feel sick. Shauwana was also pregnant. This was so unfair. Shauwana's tryst with Zelinko would help her rise to prominence, while Areela risked deportation to some desolate hellhole!

"Stop staring at the mayor's son, Areela. A man like that would never want someone like you," Kailow teased.

"Shut up. I don't want to hear a single word from you." Areela shouted loud enough for everyone at the fair to stare at her.

"Whoa, relax. I get it. You got a serious crush on him. I'll be at the archery range. Meet me there when you have calmed down." Kailow said and rushed off.

Feeling how everyone stared at her, Areela hurried to her rowing boat and left the island.

"I KNOW THAT YOU FEEL upset, but don't worry. Everything will be alright. I am glad that our intercourse had its desired result."

Areela was crying in solitude when Zelinko suddenly appeared like a mirage in front of her. She didn't know how to feel about his appearance. If he was aware of her condition, why had he abandoned her?

"What about you and Shauwana. I could tell that she is also pregnant." Areela replied.

There was a short silence, and Zelinko's mirage was flickering in front of Areela. She didn't like that he used telepathy instead of showing up in person, and the flickering was a sign that he was lying.

Zelinko re-emerged and replied, "Shauwana is my betrothed, and she will be my lawful wife. However, you are my destiny."

"Then be with me. At least claim me as your concubine. Don't abandon me to my fate." Areela sobbed.

"I will save you and our unborn child. However, I must lay low. I stole you from Xialiab, and my father punished me. I cannot defy him until my plan comes to fruition. Have faith in me, Areela."

As the mirage of Zelinko faded away, Areela felt heartbroken. The father of her child was to marry another woman, and he refused to even look at her. Areela's only hope was his vague telepathic promises.

"True Maker, please give me a sign," Areela sobbed as she sat all alone when the rest of the city was celebrating the autumn equinox.

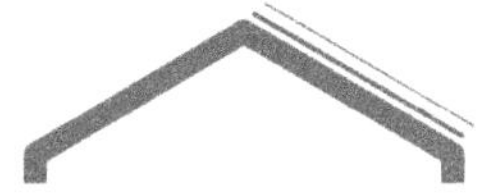

Chapter 6: The Abduction.

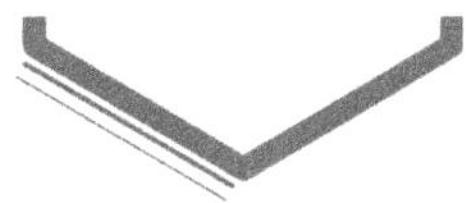

"Aowww!"

Areela grimaced in pain as she bent down to pull some lint away from the filter of a cleaning robot. Being a servant, she maintained the array of robots that did most of the cleaning and maintenance in Ronesia. Under normal circumstances, this was an easy enough job, but her pregnancy was giving her complications. Worse yet, she hadn't dared to visit a medical professional out of fear that Xialiab would denounce her and request her deportation.

A colleague rushed over, got seated on the floor next to her, and spoke, "Are you okay, Areela? Why haven't Supervisor Nimbin given you easier tasks since you are pregnant?"

"I am okay, Saronka. I haven't asked Nimbin for easier tasks as I don't want special treatment." Areela replied.

"Don't be silly. You are not asking a favour for yourself. The favour is for your future baby. Our society wants every baby to have the best gestational period possible. So if you work too hard, you might harm the child." Saronka replied.

"I guess..." Areela mumbled.

"Come on. Don't worry. I'll ask Nimbin to give you easier tasks because of your condition." Saronka replied.

Hearing this, Areela froze. She feared that Xialiab would find out about her pregnancy if Saronka spoke to Nimbin. But then again, she was six months pregnant and half-term, so it would be impossible to hide her pregnancy for much longer in any case.

'Please, help me, Zelinko.' Areela thought and held back her impulse to cry.

Saronka hugged Areela and soothed her, "You don't seem happy about the pregnancy. Do you have a bad relationship with the man the genome masters appointed to you?"

"It is complicated," Areela said and sobbed.

"So, so, my dear. It is natural to doubt the man the genome masters appoint you, but it will work out for the best." Saronka replied.

"Do you think so?" Areela asked.

"Yes. I wish I had followed the genome masters' advice. I gave up on them when I found my husband. We have been together for 98 years without a conception taking place. It has been a long and sad time." Saronka revealed.

'Perhaps you could solve the problem by having sex more than once per year.' Areela thought, but she held her tongue. Conceiving outside of the allowed period was a severe crime on Zetani, and she was a fool to even think about it. 'At least I didn't break against that law,' Areela thought in a desperate attempt to be optimistic.

"I am sorry to hear that," Areela said.

"Don't worry about me. Go home and get some rest. I'll talk to Nimbin for you." Saronka said and forced a smile.

"Thank you, Saronka," Areela said, got up from the floor, and left the facility.

"COME ON, SISTER. LET'S go to the midwinter celebration."

Areela opened her eyes and looked at her brother Kailow. He seemed as happy as ever, unbothered by the worries of the world. And why wouldn't he be? Kailow was still young and excited about living. She had felt the same in her youth, which had ended less than a year ago.

"Uh, what's the point?" Areela moaned.

"The point is for you to get out of bed. You are not sick; you are pregnant with a successful man. It should be a cause for joy." Kailow replied.

Hearing her brother's enthusiasm, Areela knew she had to tell him the truth. She couldn't lie to her closest friend in the world. She could only imagine the shock he would feel if she didn't prepare him for the dark times ahead.

"Brother, I need to tell you something," Areela said solemnly.

"Don't warn me about the dangers of having a good time. I can look after myself." Kailow teased.

"I am not pregnant with Xialiab," Areela replied.

"What? Does he know this?" Kailow exclaimed.

"Since we didn't sleep together, I'd say so," Areela replied.

"Tell me what happened?" Kailow replied.

"I rejected Xialiab. A few days later, he confronted me. Zelinko protected me against him, and we had an instant attraction." Areela revealed.

"Zelinko Siblexom? The mayor's son?" Kailow asked.

"Yes," Areela replied.

"But he is getting married to Shauwana Xiblenkan tonight," Kailow replied.

"Yes, I know. That's why I am so depressed." Areela replied.

"Don't be. The wedding day is the perfect day to confront Zelinko. If you bring your fling to public knowledge, he has no choice but to take you in as a concubine." Kailow exclaimed.

"But he told me to lay low and that he would look after me," Areela whispered.

"Bullshit. Those rich pricks are all the same; Zelinko will send you away unless you publicise your relations." Kailow replied.

Areela considered Kailow's words. Her brother was correct. Six months had passed, and Zelinko hadn't taken any actions to protect their unborn child. Clearly, he was waiting for her to give birth so he could send her away to a fringe world. After all, Zelinko had said that she was to give birth to the chosen one. Thus, it was the child, not her, that he worried about.

"You're right. We need to confront Zelinko today. This has gone on for long enough." Areela said.

"Good. Let's get dressed and hurry to the venue." Kailow said and helped Areela out of bed to head to the wedding ceremony.

AREELA AND KAILOW WORE conspicuous clothes as they headed to Mancin Island, where Zelinko's wedding took place. They needed to hurry as it was close to midnight, and the ceremony would begin soon. Areela needed to reveal the truth before it happened, so there could be an amendment to the marriage contract that allowed Areela as a concubine.

They were almost at the ferry crossing when Xialiab approached them and spoke, "Areela and Kailow, where do you think you are going?"

"We are going to Zelinko's wedding. We need to set things right." Kailow exclaimed.

"That's not going to happen. The two of you are coming with me." Xialiab replied.

"No, we are not. Come, Areela." Kailow replied and turned in the direction of the ferry crossing.

Pow

Xialiab blasted Kailow with a psionic blast, who collapsed and broke his nose in the landing. Kailow groaned as he tried to get up, with silvery-bluish blood streaming from his nose.

"Uh, what happened?" Kailow mumbled.

"You were being disobedient, and I punished you for it, servant!" Xialiab taunted.

"I'll tell the others. You won't get away with this," Kailow replied, closed his eyes, and passed out.

"No! What have you done?" Areela exclaimed.

"His pain will be passing. He should survive." Xialiab stated.

"Why are you doing this?" Areela sobbed.

"To look after my unborn child. What kind of father would allow the mother of his child to act irresponsibly? I am the one the Zetan genome masters chose for you. Therefore, it is my right to take you to protected custody." Xialiab said and smirked.

Areela looked at Xialiab. He had a cold unemotional gaze, and she feared his intentions. She could have tried to appease him if he had acted in anger. However, his current mindset indicated a calculated move by the prominent scholar.

"Okay, I am coming with you," Areela said.

"Good. I am glad you came to your senses." Xialiab replied.

"Can I please put my brother in a recovery position? I don't want him to choke on his own blood." Areela pleaded.

"Yes, your brother is worth more to me alive," Xialiab said.

Areela nodded, got down next to her brother, moved him into the recovery position and whispered. "Be strong, brother; everything will be alright. I love you."

After that, she got up and followed Xialiab to a nearby vehicle without resisting. As she got into the vehicle, she heard how the wedding bells rang for midnight. Her love interest was now a married man, her brother was unconscious, and she was the captive of a psychopath. What an awful winter equinox!

Chapter 7: The Science Academy Stabbing.

As Areela opened her eyes, she found herself strapped to a bed. She was in a strange medical ward, unlike any medical room she had ever visited. Since her job was to clean and maintain the service drones, she had seen many medical wards, yet most of the science appliances in the room were new to her.

Areela felt dizzy, and she had a burning thirst. What had happened? Areela remembered that she had passed out while in Xialiab's vehicle. Had he drugged her or used his psionic powers to knock her out? Areela knew one thing. Her thirst was killing her.

"Water, I need water." Areela wheezed.

An electronic airlock opened, and Xialiab entered the room. He smirked at Areela and spoke, "Welcome to my private laboratory at the Ronesian Science Academy; I hope you enjoy my hospitality."

"Water. Give me water." Areela gasped.

"Oh, but I cannot serve an ungrateful servant. That would be below my standing." Xialiab taunted. "Please, I am begging you. May I have some water." Areela whispered.

"That's better. I guess I need to ascertain your survival by providing water." Xialiab mocked as he fetched a large plastic bottle and poured water into Areela's mouth.

At the end of the waterboarding, Areela vomited and whispered. "Why are you doing this? Why did you abduct me?"

"I didn't abduct you. I used my legal right to detain you as you are mentally unstable." Xialiab taunted and showed Areela a 3D hologram of a document.

'The Ronesian Family Court gives Xialiab Sandrom the right to detain Areela Kheeran to protect his unborn child from coming into harm's way. Supervisor

Nimbin Saronkan confirms that Ms Kheeran is mentally unstable and that she tried to conceal her pregnancy.'

"But it's not your child. So why are you doing this?" Areela sobbed.

Xialiab slapped Areela and exclaimed, "Because you've denied me my destiny. My mother, the Grand Seeress Ahana Anchalan, proclaimed with her dying breaths that you, a simple servant girl, would bear the chosen one. You'll give birth to the prodigal son that will help us shape the future of this galaxy. It was my destiny to father that son, but you stole my purpose from me."

Hearing Xialiab's confession, Areela felt terrified. A vengeful lunatic had kidnapped her, and he had the legal right to treat her at his whims. She needed to get out of here and bring the issue to the magistrates. As much as Areela feared deportation for her illegal procreation, that was a preferable outcome to whatever Xialiab had in mind.

Xialiab smiled wickedly and spoke again. "Now that you know why you are here, you might wonder what I plan to do?"

Areela nodded and looked at Xialiab in paralyzed terror, unable to get a word out.

"I thought you'd never ask. I took the freedom to sample the DNA of your unborn child. The computer predicts that he will have the following physical appearance." Xialiab said, smirked, and pressed a switch on his hologram watch.

A hologram appeared in the room, showing a beautiful baby boy. The hologram showed the baby growing and reaching adulthood. He was the most beautiful and perfectly symmetrical being Areela had ever seen.

"Is that the future appearance of my beautiful baby?" Areela said and wept tears of gratefulness while forgetting about her precarious situation.

"Well, he was. But the baby these holograms depict will never come to pass." Xialiab stated.

"Are you going to kill my baby?!" Areela shrieked and tried to break free from the straps.

"Tsk, tsk, tsk. I am not going to kill him. I am going to change him. Every time you look at your child, you'll remember the terrible cost of betrayal. Behold what your son will look like after I alter his DNA." Xialiab exclaimed and pressed his watch again.

A hologram of a hideous creature appeared in the room. The creature was more beastly-like and mean-spirited than a good looking Zetan, and it had a lizard-like skin, sharp fangs and claws, and glowing purple eyes.

"Aaargh! You must be bluffing. That thing isn't even Zetan." Areela said.

"You shall see, Areela. You shall see." Xialiab said and took out a scalpel.

With the scalpel, he started cutting up Areela's stomach. She screamed in agony until she passed out from the excruciating pain. As her stomach was cut open, Xialiab took out a prototype DNA modifying device, used it on the fetus, and closed the wound. It was time to push the boundaries of science and nature.

AS KAILOW WOKE UP FROM his confrontation with Xialiab, he knew where he needed to go. He needed to tell Zelinko that Xialiab had abducted Areela. Kailow had no chance against the wicked scholar on his own, so getting the mayor's son on his side was the only way to save his sister.

Kailow ran to the boatshed. The wedding festivities were in full swing on Mancin Island, but he needed to crash the party.

As Kailow got seated in a rowing boat, he felt dizzy and noticed that blood was free-flowing from his nose. He needed to seek medical attention, but his sister needed him more. Kailow rowed the boat as quickly as he could, and a short while later, he stumbled onto Mancin Island. Kailow rushed to the centre stage. Everything was blurry due to his concussion, and there was only one way to find Zelinko. He needed to address him via the microphone.

Kailow rushed onto the scene and spoke into the microphone, "Zelinko Siblexom, I need to speak to you about Areela. It is urgent."

Having said this, Kailow collapsed and passed out.

"WHO STRUCK YOU WITH a psionic blast, and why are you here, servant?"

As Kailow opened his eyes, he was in the first aid room on Mancin Island, and Zelinko was holding onto his head. Kailow took a breath and noticed that his nose was clear of blood. It was a miracle.

Zelinko released his grip on Kailow's head and shouted. "Answer me, Kailow. Why are you here? I don't appreciate it when people crash my wedding and cause a scene."

"Xialiab knocked me out, and when I woke up, he and my sister were gone," Kailow revealed.

"Wait, who is this young man, and why should we care about his sister?" Shauwana interjected.

Zelinko looked at his newlywed pregnant wife. It wasn't ideal that he hadn't told her about Areela, but this forced his hand. "I engaged in intercourse with Kailow's sister. She is now pregnant with my child and a prisoner of my rival Xialiab." Zelinko stated.

"Are you joking? Why are you telling me this on our wedding night?" Shauwana exclaimed in shock.

"I don't have time to explain, as I must stop Xialiab from kidnapping the mother of my future child. So keep calm, and I'll be back in no time."

Shauwana stared at Zelinko, but she didn't say anything.

Zelinko turned to Kailow and spoke. "Kailow, since you ruined my wedding day, I hope you are willing to help me save your sister."

Kailow nodded, and the two men hurried to leave the island.

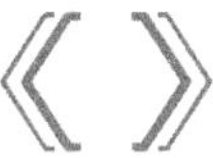

"THE DNA ENHANCEMENT was a success. Please, let me show you to your room." Xialiab said and smirked as he unstrapped Areela from the operation table.

"Fuck you, Xialiab," Areela cried in terror.

"What did I tell you about manners?" Xialiab said and blasted Areela with a mental blast that jumbled her mind and made her unable to respond.

"Let my sister go, asshole!"

Xialiab went into a burst of sinister laughter as he spotted Kailow. 'That foolish brat. He must be so stupid to come here.' Xialiab thought and replied,

"Unfortunately, I cannot let her go, as I am her custodian under Ronesian Court orders."

"I don't care about court orders. Areela told me everything. You are not the father of her unborn child. Zelinko is." Kailow exclaimed.

"Very well. I guess it's time for you to die." Xialiab stated and sent a lethal psionic blast towards Kailow.

Fizz

Xialiab looked surprised as the blast dissipated against a protective barrier surrounding Kailow. Zelinko entered the room and exclaimed, "Let her go. It is over."

"Tsk, tsk, tsk. Look who ran away from his wedding night to steal a woman in my ward. Areela is mine. I have a court order." Xialiab taunted.

"That court order is based on a pretence. She is not carrying your child." Zelinko replied.

"If you say so. I guess I'll see you in court. It would be a shame if she were to die before that, wouldn't it?" Xialiab taunted.

"No! I will kill you for this." Zelinko exclaimed and sent an uncontrolled psionic burst towards Xialiab.

Xialiab had better focus, and he deflected Zelinko's blast. He swatted Kailow like a fly and knocked him out by blasting him into a wall. Then, he turned to Zelinko and overpowered him with his superior telekinetic power. As Zelinko lay subdued on the ground, unable to move, Xialiab taunted, "Tsk, tsk, tsk. Such a shame that you came here. Now I must kill you in self-defence."

Xialiab was about to blast Zelinko out of existence when excruciating pain struck him in his back, and he coughed out silvery-blue fresh blood. He turned around and faced Areela, who said, "How about this for manners? You punk!" Having said this, she slit his throat, thus ending the life of the villainous scholar.

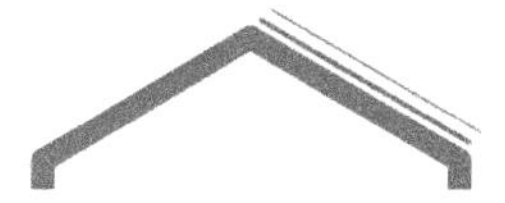

Chapter 8: The Trial.

Areela felt heartbroken as she sought Zelinko among the spectators in the Ronesian Criminal Court. Murder trials were uncommon in Zetan society, and her case was the highest-profile case in a long time. She and Kailow were on trial for murdering Xialiab Sandrom, while Zelinko was not in the courtroom.

Judge Jasper Javonom hit the gavel to silence the spectators and spoke, "Areela Kheeran and Kailow Voltrom. The two of you stand trial for murdering the prominent scholar Xialiab Sandrom. How do you plead?"

"Not guilty," Kailow replied.

"Not guilty," Areela stated.

Judge Jasper turned to Areela, gave her a stern look, and spoke, "Your fingerprints were on the murder weapon. Furthermore, you were covered in Xialiab's blood, and you were in the room when our police officers arrived. So how can you claim innocence?"

Areela drank some water to calm her nerves, and she got teary-eyed when she realised that Zelinko hadn't arrived for the trial.

"I did not murder Xialiab. He was about to murder Zelinko Siblexom when I intervened. So I killed him in self-defence. It was the only way to save the mayor's son." Areela explained.

"Oh yes. You and Kailow came together with an insane story to blame the mayor's son for murdering the head of the Ronesian Science Academy. There is, however, a problem with that story. Zelinko was at his wedding with his newlywed wife, Lady Shauwana." Jasper stated.

"It's a lie. Zelinko was with us at the science academy." Kailow interjected.

Jasper hit the gavel, stared at Kailow, and exclaimed, "Silence, servant. Don't speak unless spoken to first."

After his exclamation, Jasper sent a sublime psionic blast towards Kailow that muddled his senses and made him unable to speak.

Jasper turned to Areela and spoke again, "Here is what happened that fateful night. Xialiab sought a court document to detain you to protect his unborn child. Once you were in his custody, you asked your brother to break you out. You were the one who dealt the killing blow while Kailow was your accessory."

"No, it's not true. Kailow and Zelinko came to save me from Xialiab. The child wasn't his, so he wanted to perform experimental surgery to disfigure it." Areela replied.

"Enough. Admit the murder, and the court will spare your brother and child." Jasper roared.

"No, I am innocent!" Areela said defiantly.

"Silence! I have had enough of your insolence." Jasper shouted, lost control of his emotions, and blasted Areela with a psionic blast that knocked her out.

The onlookers stared in awe at Judge Jasper, and medics rushed to Areela. Jasper flushed, and his cheeks turned silvery from the embarrassment. This was not how a judge should act. He had lost his patience with the insolent servant who had murdered his half-brother, Xialiab. Jasper hit the gavel many times and shouted, "Court adjourned, please leave the courtroom."

Guards entered the courtroom and escorted the onlookers out of the building.

ZELINKO COULDN'T ENJOY his time on the luxurious space yacht, which orbited the beautiful pink gas planet Seralius. He was on a honeymoon with his wife Shauwana, yet another woman's fate occupied his mind. Moreover, Zelinko felt terrible for not protecting Areela as she stood trial for murdering Xialiab.

After the Ronesian Science Academy confrontation, Zelinko had been too weak to move. Finally, after an undisclosed time, he had opened his eyes when his father Siblex and his wife Shauwana had helped him away from the scene. They had dragged him onto a space yacht to leave for his honeymoon the following day. Two weeks later, he had recovered from his fight with Xialiab, and he was cruising the Zetan star system with his newly-wedded wife.

Zelinko turned on the hologram TV and watched Areela's trial. It was a foregone conclusion. Areela belonged to the servant caste, and the judge was Xialiab's half-brother. Nothing except for his intervention could save the mother of his future child.

Zelinko struggled with his conscience. He wanted to save Areela, but admitting what happened would destroy his marriage and his father's career. What would he do?

Shauwana entered Zelinko's room, turned off the TV, and spoke gently. "Don't worry about that trial, my dear. Areela's conviction will be for the best. If your unborn child means so much to you, we can adopt him. He will, after all, be an orphan otherwise."

"But this is not right. This is all my fault. I seduced Areela as I wanted to be the one fathering the chosen one. She never stood a chance." Zelinko said and sighed.

"Don't be silly. Who cares about prophecies uttered by a delusional seer on her death bed? Think ahead, my dear. I forgive your transgressions, and we can rule Ronesia after your father's retirement. That's a goal to strive for." Shauwana said.

Zelinko nodded. He didn't want to argue with Shauwana about his problems. It served no purpose, and besides, there was no way he would be able to get back to the trial in time to save Areela.

Shauwana smiled at Zelinko, unzipped her dress, and spoke. "So, so, my dear. Do you know what's the best part of being pregnant is?"

"Um, no, please tell me," Zelinko said and stared away in the distance.

"The best part is that we can enjoy as much sex as we want without the risk of breaking the conception laws. I cannot get pregnant if I am already pregnant," Shauwana seduced.

Zelinko gave in to Shauwana's advances and kissed her. If he couldn't get rid of his mental anguish, he could at least enjoy Shauwana's body.

"AREELA KHEERAN, THE court finds you guilty of murder. You will be executed on the autumn solstice eight months from now. Kailow Voltrom, the court finds you guilty of being an accessory to murder, and the court sentences you to deportation to Disyerto-2. You'll remain in prison until the next spaceship is ready to take you away. Case closed."

AREELA COVERED HER face and sobbed in silence as Judge Jasper Javonom hit the gavel and handed her the final sentence. Only a miracle could save her now.

Chapter 9: The Birth of Thorax Zelinkom.

The summer solstice was approaching, and in the best of worlds, Areela Kheeran would have enjoyed the prospect of motherhood together with her love, Zelinko Siblexom. Unfortunately, the 1999th summer solstice of the fifth age on Zetani was not the best of worlds for any of them, and she was chained to a hospital bed in the detention centre. Her lover had abandoned her, and her jailors kept her alive solely as she was the vessel of her unborn baby.

A female doctor approached her and spoke, "Would you like to be awake for the Caesarean procedure? It is your only chance of seeing your child."

Areela hesitated. She wasn't sure what would be more depressing: never seeing her child or seeing him once and then losing him?

Areela remembered the threat that Xialiab had made that fateful night at the science academy. She needed to know whether her child was a beautiful baby or the terrifying freak that Xialiab claimed it would become.

"Keep me awake; I want to see my baby," Areela replied.

"Understood," the doctor said and injected Areela with a moderate amount of sedative so she would be awake during the procedure.

The surgical team appeared in the room, and they covered Areela with a curtain so that she wouldn't see them performing the caesarean section. Next, a surgeon cut the first incision on Areela's belly. It was uncomfortable, but the discomfort wasn't the big issue due to the sedatives—instead, the fear of how the baby would turn out terrified her.

Areela felt fearful when she heard the surgeons mumbling amongst themselves in horror.

"Is my child alive? Is something wrong?" Areela shouted in panic.

The surgeons went silent, and one of them exclaimed. "Get Director Samirom! He must decide how to handle this atrocious creature."

Areela grabbed the female doctor she had spoken to earlier and exclaimed. "Show my child, please! You promised me that you would."

"I don't think that is possible, unfortunately. We have to decide whether to abort or keep this baby." The female doctor replied.

"You promised me that I would see my child!!" Areela exclaimed in an outburst.

The doctor sighed, grabbed the atrocious creature, and showed it to Areela. It was a sight to behold. As Xialiab had mentioned, the baby had a lizard-like thick, scaly skin, sharp devil fangs, and glowing purple eyes. The newborn stared at Areela as she screamed in horror at the sight, and he replied by giving out a terrifying roar.

"We must sedate her now!" The doctor said to one of the nurses, who injected Areela with potent sedatives. The room turned into a blur, and the last thing Areela heard was Zelinko's voice. "Don't worry, doctors. My wife and I will look after this prophetical child. We will name him Thorax Zelinkom."

Areela tried to call Zelinko for help, but she was too weak, and the room slowly faded to complete blackness.

THE TRUE MAKER EXITED Gaia's body as she became aware of a new existence in the Milky Way Galaxy. A Zetan baby had been born, and that baby was unlike anything that had ever existed.

This birth intrigued True Maker. Most timelines were unremarkable, but she noticed two unique individuals during this one. Gaia, whom she had spent the last few years inhabiting and observing, and now this new and strange Zetan being.

True Maker studied the DNA of the baby. The baby was a hybrid between the Zetans and Xenos, two completely different species. One was a sophisticated humanoid-like being with silvery-blue skin and telekinetic powers, and one was a beast-like creature that ate raw flesh and drank fresh blood. But how had this happened? Large swaths of space in the Milky Way Galaxy separated the two species, and they had never interacted with each other.

True Maker looked back in time along Thorax's timeline. She saw how Xialiab altered the baby's genome. Such a strange twist of fate. True Maker reflected on the progress she had been through in the last few years. As it would seem, enough iterations of the Milky Way Galaxy had run for some truly remarkable things to happen!

True Maker took a closer look at Thorax, and she felt the same connection she felt with Gaia. Was it possible to inhabit his body as well? True Maker focused her powers. A short while later, she flashed through time and space and saw a chaotic hospital ward, where tensions were high. She looked at the man who held her naked body. "Papa?" she babbled before the connection severed.

Chapter 10: The Patricide.

Zelinko Siblexom was looking at the beast-like ugly creature, the outcome of his affair with Areela. The 3-month-old was a hostile and fearsome animal who grunted with an unpleasant roar whenever something upset him. Even more sickening was that the creature seemed to prefer raw meat over milk. What kind of baby was this?

Zelinko looked at the baby, whom he had named Thorax Zelinkom. As much as he wanted the child to reflect on his greatness, he could not admit fatherhood to the child. Yet it was the baby that Seeress Ahana Anchalan had foreseen as the chosen one while on her deathbed.

As Zelinko studied his progeny, Thorax's eye colour changed from dark purple to glowing blue, the same colour as the primordial Zeto crystal. This transformation had happened a few times, and the baby would utter a word or two in a Zen state before regressing to his beastlike behaviour.

"Zelinko... Zeto Crystal... Save Areela..." Thorax said, in an echoing sound, as if he was receiving messages from a faraway source.

Zelinko massaged his temple. Was he going insane, or had the animal-like baby given him a prophetical message from the True Maker? He knew one thing. If he were to save Areela Kheeran, he needed to hurry up as she was due for execution by sunset.

'I need to find the truth.' Zelinko thought to himself, grabbed Thorax, and headed towards the underground vault where his father Siblex hid the primordial Zeto Crystal.

AREELA WAS RAVING MAD in her prison cell. She had lost everything, and the city council would execute her for a crime she committed in self-defence. Although she had tried to reveal the truth about Xialiab's experiments and that he used his power of attorney to alter her unborn baby's DNA, no one had listened to her. Quite the opposite. During the mock trial, Judge Jasper Javonom had been inside her head and blasted her with psionic energy every time she was about to say something. These actions had made her words come out as incoherent nonsense.

The secret telepathic and psionic powers that the Zetan leadership possessed were terrifying forces they used to dominate their subjects. Areela had lived in ignorance for the first 200 years of her life, and the last year had been an endless nightmare.

"Let me out, you bastards! I am innocent. Judge Javonom was inside my head during the trial to discredit me." Areela shouted and kept banging on the cell door. No one came to answer the door, and she collapsed to the floor with tears flooding down her cheeks. She was inconsolable as she was due for execution and had given birth to a monster.

"KAILOW, I HAVE SOME good news."

Kailow looked at Jasper, who approached him in his prison cell. Why had the judge who sentenced him to imprisonment and exile come to talk to him?

"What is it?" Kailow asked.

"I am giving you permission to participate in today's autumn equinox celebration," Jasper replied. "Why is that?" Kailow asked.

"As Areela will face public execution today, I want you to be in the front row. I want the two of you to suffer for what you did to my brother." Jasper taunted.

"Fuck you. I am not going anywhere." Kailow exclaimed.

Jasper blasted Kailow into a wall with his powers and mocked, "Oooh, did that hurt? Learn to respect your betters, and it will happen less often."

Having said this, Jasper left the room, and two guards entered. They handcuffed Kailow and dragged him away.

"ACCESS DENIED."

Zelinko swore as he failed to open the electronic lock to the secret bunker where the Zetan leadership kept the Zetani Zeto Crystal. Officially, the primordial Zeto Crystal was on display at the top of a sculpture in central Ronesia. However, that crystal was a worthless prop. Society could not allow every Zetan to unlock their inner potential because that would make a master and a servant indistinguishable.

"Please let me try."

Zelinko looked at baby Thorax, whom he held in his arm. The baby's eyes were glowing blue, and the baby looked wise beyond his years.

"Uhm, okay," Zelinko said as he moved baby Thorax closer to the touchpad and the biometric lock of the bunker.

Thorax put his hand on the biometric scanner and typed in the code. 'Access granted' appeared on the display, and the heavy vault doors slid open.

"Put me down. We'll move quicker on foot." Thorax said and rushed ahead as Zelinko put him down.

Zelinko stared in amazement at the lizard-like baby. What kind of devilry was this? Why could his three-month-old baby walk and talk?

"Hurry up, we don't have all day," Thorax exclaimed, which got Zelinko to spring into action.

They rushed down a corridor and reached the inner vault, where the city council kept the Zeto Crystal and other priceless treasures. "Lift me; I cannot reach the control panel," Thorax instructed.

Zelinko did as instructed, Thorax opened the door to the vault, and they both entered the inner sanctum. Zelinko felt mesmerized when he looked at the primordial Zeto Crystal.

It was the second time that he had seen the beautiful crystal. He first saw it during his Bar Zhadung adulthood ceremony when he had turned 100 years old. He had touched the crystal, and it had unlocked his innate abilities. It was the initiation ceremony to become one of the few members of the Master caste. Anyone who had their innate telepathy, premonitions and psionic powers unleashed had an enormous advantage on other Zetans in their day-to-day lives.

"Grab those sapphires," Thorax instructed and pointed to some beautiful gemstones.

"Why?" Zelinko asked.

"She has shown me the way. When our consciousnesses linked, I found a way to replicate the power of the Zeto Crystal. Those sapphires should suffice as vessels for its power." Thorax revealed.

Zelinko hesitated. It was insane that he considered taking instruction from the three-month-old freak next to him. But, then again, he had dreamt of fathering the chosen one, which had to have a higher purpose.

Zelinko picked up a few sapphires and spoke, "I got the sapphires; what now?"

"Now hold the sapphires close to the Zeto Crystal and utter the following phrase, 'Gong Dau, Gong Dia, Gong Undung. Mua Zetani. (For the past, for the present, for the future, my Zetani.)'"

Zelinko did as his son commanded, and the room lit up as immense energy streamed from the Zeto Crystal to the sapphires, making them shine almost as bright as the crystal.

"Zelinko Siblexom. What are you doing in our sacred vault?"

Zelinko turned around, and he saw his father, Siblex Valzom, accompanied by two security officers. The strict looks on their faces indicated that this could lead to a confrontation.

"Thorax told me to come here. I needed to power up these sapphires and save Areela." Zelinko replied.

"Thorax? Have you lost your mind? There is no way your freaky son would tell you anything. He is only three months old." Siblex replied.

"You tell him, Thorax!" Zelinko exclaimed.

"Frrr, graoww, graah?" Thorax replied in confusion.

Zelinko turned to his son. The shining blue light in his eyes was gone, and he had reversed to his beast-like purple eyes.

"He spoke to me before; I promise," Zelinko mumbled.

"Son, everything is going to be okay. Come with me, and we will take you somewhere outside of public view until we have resolved this nasty Areela business." Siblex replied.

"No, you cannot execute her. She saved me." Zelinko mumbled.

"Who cares? She murdered a council member, and his brother took his place. We cannot pardon this criminal or admit your crimes. Her life is forfeit." Siblex stated.

"No!" Zelinko exclaimed and released an uncontrolled psionic blast in front of him. The shockwave was strong enough to slice his father and the security officers in half. Zelinko stared in shock at the scene. What had he done?

He kneeled next to his father and exclaimed, "Oh no. Father, I am sorry. I didn't mean to hurt you." Siblex opened his eyes and wheezed, "Zelinko.... You have doomed us all."

Those were the last words of Siblex Valzom, the 21st mayor of Ronesia during the fifth age.

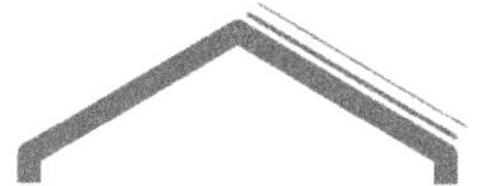

Chapter 11: The Revolution

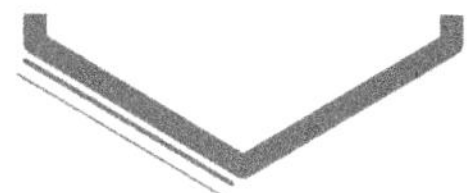

"Oh no, what have I done?"

Zelinko was shaking with tremors as he kneeled beside the corpse of his father and the two security officers. He had lost control, but he could never have imagined that he was so powerful. Could the contact with the Zeto Crystal be to blame?

"The fifth age has ended. Revolution has begun."

Zelinko stared at Thorax. The child had yet again luminous blue eyes.

"Who are you?" Zelinko asked.

"I am Thorax Zelinkom, your son. The True Maker is speaking through me." Thorax replied.

"The True Maker? But you are meant to be dormant?" Zelinko stuttered.

"I have been dormant for countless iterations of the Milky Way Galaxy. However, this time is different. The Zetan race must reach its true potential. It is the only way to save humanity from extinction." Thorax replied.

"Humanity?" Zelinko asked.

"A sentient race on a faraway planet. Yet, our present focus must be to start the Zetan revolution. Bring the Zeto Crystal to the main square in Ronesia. Let the masses see the guiding lights that their elites have stolen from them," Thorax replied.

"It will lead to war, and many will die," Zelinko replied.

"Yes, but it is the only way for the Zetan race to achieve true greatness. I have seen you wither and die in countless iterations of the Milky Way Galaxy. Setting you free and unleashing your true potential is the only way to save you." Thorax stated.

"By making us kill each other? How is that setting us free?" Zelinko asked.

"In less than 100 millennia, the Zetani Maximus star will go supernova and destroy Zetani and its surrounding star systems. I have seen this happen 999 times in a row. The only way to get a different outcome is to get the Zeto Crystal out of this vault and unleash chaos. You wanted to father the chosen one, and this is your chance." Thorax replied.

Zelinko looked at his beast-like offspring. He sensed immense mental powers from the baby boy, powers that were magnitudes greater than he could imagine. He realised that there would be one problem if he carried out the divine plan, he would lose his own life. He had committed patricide, and if he freed the people from their mental servitude, they would repay him with violence. Moreover, he had hidden the truth about Zeto Crystals for centuries, and they wouldn't appreciate him revealing it.

"Why do you need me to do it? You are much stronger than I am." Zelinko asked.

"I cannot make decisions that alter the outcome for the Zetan species; only a Zetan can," Thorax replied.

Zelinko nodded, grabbed the Zeto Crystal and left the vault.

THE SKY WAS ROARING with thunder as Zelinko left the secret bunker in the mountains outside Ronesia.

'This is strange. The weather is always pleasant on public holidays,' Zelinko thought. Then, he remembered that Areela was due for execution on Mancin Island within the next hour. This exposed him to a dilemma. The True Maker had told him to take the crystal to the main square and reveal the truth, but he couldn't allow the mother of his son to die. She was priceless as she had helped him to create a new destiny.

"Thorax, should I head to the Ronesian Main Square and reveal the truth, or should I save your mother?" Zelinko asked.

Upon receiving no answer from his son, he turned around and saw the baby crawling on the ground, screeching unpleasant baby roars, acting like his usual self again.

Zelinko picked up the baby. He knew what Thorax's silence meant. The True Maker had left the decision to him. 'Areela, I am coming for you.' Zelinko thought, strapped the baby to his body, and ran as fast as possible to reach Mancin Island.

"AS THE TWIN SUNS SET, they will purge the sin from your body with holy fire."

Areela Kheeran felt terror as the setting suns were getting closer to the point where they would merge into one. When that happened, a large prism would amplify its rays to scorch her with concentrated sunlight.

Although public executions were rare at Zetani, she had attended a few in her life, as the tradition was to carry out executions during the autumn and spring equinox celebrations. She remembered the terrifying screams that the afflicted shouted as the concentrated sunlight slowly burnt through them, like the cuts of an old and rusty knife.

"Let her go. She is innocent."

The crowds gasped, and Judge Jasper Javinom stared at Zelinko as he came rushing while clutching his baby to his chest.

"What is the meaning of this nonsense? You cannot spare this woman; only your father can." Jasper replied.

"My father is dead. I killed him an hour ago." Zelinko replied.

Zelinko's revelation stunned Jasper and the crowds. Jasper spoke after a few seconds of tense silence, "Zelinko, do you realise what you are saying? Did you confess patricide to our Ronesian citizens?"

Zelinko turned to the crowds and spoke, "Yes, and I have an even bigger revelation. Citizens of Ronesia, the ruling caste has lied to you for millennia. The crystal on display is not the real Zeto Crystal. I have the real one in my pocket, and it belongs to every Zetan. It will unlock your innate abilities."

"Guards, arrest this traitor at once," Jasper exclaimed, and several guards moved towards Zelinko.

"Auch, my legs, uh!"

Zelinko turned towards Areela, who was chained to the altar. The concentrated prismatic sunlight was burning her feet, moving towards her body. He needed to act. "Areela, catch!" Zelinko exclaimed, and he threw the Zeto Crystal to her.

As Areela caught the crystal, she felt strange. Her body was surging with energy, and it seemed like time was slowing down. She flexed her muscles, and the chains that bound her broke.

The crowds gasped in shock as Areela's chains broke, and the guards took a few steps back.

"Do I have to do everything myself?" Jasper exclaimed and blasted a psionic shockwave towards Areela that pushed her backwards while holding the Zeto Crystal. As she fell to the ground, the colourful light from the two suns hit the Zeto Crystal and revealed a tear in the space/time continuum. As spacetime tore open, Jasper stepped back from the altar and didn't dare to intervene.

"Hurry through that tear in space," Thorax commanded and rushed towards the gap.

As Areela saw her son in action, her spirits returned. The prophecy proved correct, and her son was the chosen one! She rushed towards the portal when Thorax grabbed her and spoke, "Mother, the crystal needs to stay on Zetani, but we need to leave."

Areela nodded, threw the crystal to Kailow, and hurried through the portal. Seeing this, Kailow and Zelinko rushed toward the portal. However, before entering the portal, Kailow followed his sister's example and threw the Zeto Crystal toward the crowd.

Thus, ended the fifth age on Zetani. Enraged with the masters' deceit, the servant caste stormed the ruling council, and with the help of their newfound powers, they slew them all. And thus, the sixth age of the Zetans started, an era of innovation and exploration, where an individual's abilities meant more than his heritage. Neither my father Zelinko Siblexom nor any of the other liberators were ever seen on Zetani again.

The End of the Fifth Age, by Kian Zelinkom, 71200 years before the present time.

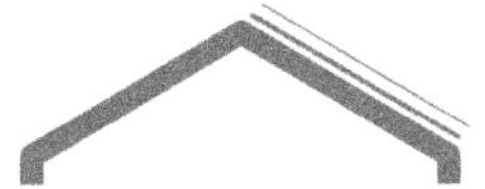

Chapter 12: Another World

Areela was freefalling through a tunnel of light. It was so beautiful and yet so eerie. She hadn't considered her options when she chose to jump head-first into the rift in space-time that the Zeto Crystal had opened.

Areela stopped abruptly, and it surprised her that the instant deceleration didn't injure her. But where was she? As she looked around, she saw an endless featureless white plain. Despite the place being so visually unappealing, it still mesmerized her. She closed her eyes and recalled her one day of passion with Zelinko. He had used his mental powers to take her to the place of the ultimate pleasure, Dihawara Densi, also known as the Divine Dimension. Areela looked around. Being here in person felt different, as her mind could no longer fill the place with meaning.

*Swoosh, swoosh, swoosh! *

Areela felt relieved when Thorax, Kailow, and Zelinko appeared. Whatever this place was, it was good that she hadn't arrived here on her own.

"Wow, what is this place?" Kailow exclaimed.

"This must be Dihawara Densi. I recognise it from my meditation sessions. I could never have imagined that I would ever come here." Zelinko speculated.

"That is correct, father. This place is the Divine Dimension, the realm of The True Maker. It is a hidden dimension that intersects hundreds of versions of the Milky Way Galaxy." Thorax stated.

"What do you mean? How can there be hundreds of versions of our galaxy?" Kailow asked. "Hundreds, thousands, millions... The exact number is irrelevant as your bodies can only exist in the galaxy you were born in." baby Thorax replied.

"Why is that?" Kailow asked.

"Because every galaxy has its set values for the four fundamental forces of physics. The atoms in your body would go haywire in any other dimension, and you'd face instant destruction." Thorax replied.

"So, are there infinite versions of our galaxy with different gravity, electromagnetism, strong nuclear forces, and weak nuclear forces?" Zelinko asked.

"Not infinite. Only certain settings for these forces correspond with a stable, functional universe. But enough of the science lesson. We'll need to move. People will follow us through the portal, and it is impossible to determine their intentions." Thorax stated.

"Where do we need to go?" Zelinko asked.

Areela decided to speak up. She was sick of others seeing her as a pawn, so this was her chance to change her destiny. "We should go to Disyerto-2. My best friend got deported there, and her partner is a scientist. They can help us." Areela said.

"I am sorry, Areela, but I was waiting for Thorax to speak," Zelinko said dismissively.

"Thorax is a baby, and I am his mother. I will speak for him." Areela stated.

Zelinko turned towards Thorax and waited for the baby to reply. After a few seconds of tense silence, Thorax spoke, "Disyerto-2 is a good option. We should heed my mother's advice." "But how would we travel 50 lightyears on foot?" Kailow asked.

"Distances are compressed in this dimension. Fifty lightyears are only 500 kilometres in here." Thorax revealed.

"Yet, 500 kilometres is a multi-week trek, and we didn't bring any provisions."

"Time works differently here, as does your need for sustenance. Disyerto-2 is that way; you'll know when you are in the right spot to open a portal to get there. I need to direct my focus elsewhere; make sure to look after this baby for me." Thorax said, pointed towards a direction, and slumped to the ground as True Maker's spirit abandoned the baby.

Areela picked up the baby, pointed in the direction he had given them and enthused, "Let's go; the only way is to move forward." The others nodded, and the three refugees left the portal they had opened to their home planet.

JASPER JAVONOM STARED in awe as the servant class freed themselves from their mental chains by touching the primordial Zeto Crystal, thus unlocking their inner potential. He hadn't prepared for Zelinko's coup. It had been unthinkable to him that a fellow member of the ruling caste would give the Zeto Crystal to the unwashed masses.

"Soldiers, kill them all, and bring me that Zeto Crystal!" Jasper commanded.

His lieutenant Hadib Nabilom replied, "Are you insane? We cannot murder our citizens."

Jasper slapped Hadib with his mental forces and exclaimed. "Silence, Hadib. What would happen with you and the enforcer caste if the servant caste were to rise? They won't spare you."

Hadib nodded, turned to his troops and commanded, "Soldiers, disperse these civilians. Use your non-lethal psionic capabilities from training."

The troops lined up and prepared to knock out the protesters using the abilities they had learnt from their secret training sessions. Jasper didn't like Hadib's approach. The enforcer caste had weak psionic capabilities as their abilities stemmed from training and not exposure to the Zeto Crystal. Yet, he didn't want to command mass murder before Hadib had tried and failed with his approach.

The soldiers lined up and tried to disperse the protesters by sending a collective psionic shockwave. The shockwave was enough to knock out those civilians who hadn't touched the Zeto Crystal. However, those who had, stood unmoved by the enforcers' weak magic.

"Use your ballistic weapons. Shoot to kill." Jasper commanded.

The enforcers pulled up their pistols and shot at the protesters. Many fell to the bullets, but a group led by Saronka Nimbinkan formed a protective telekinetic barrier, which caused the shots to hang stationary.

"Come on, ladies, let's give these oppressors hell for what they did to our friends," Saronka exclaimed and waved her hand in the direction of the troops. Her group followed her lead, which caused the bullets to return to the guards who had fired them, killing and maiming several in the process.

Seeing this, Jasper knew that he had lost. Ronesia had fallen, and the revolution would spread across Zetani. He would, however, not allow these servants to kill or capture him.

"Soldiers, retreat through that portal!" Jasper commanded and hurried to jump into the portal to save himself from the angry mob.

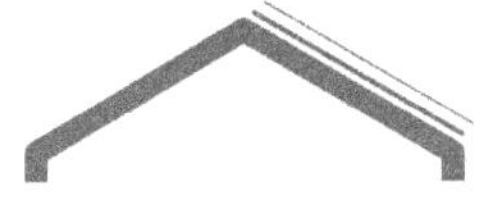

Chapter 13: The Pursuit

Podixa Sairan was overlooking the vast desert of Disyerto-2 from her bedroom window. Despite living in comfort in the high-tech space colony that she and her husband Arish Kisherom oversaw, something was missing. There was nothing to see outside the forcefield barrier that protected the Pustinja outpost. No life except microbial life existed on the planet, and although it was survivable, it wasn't a nice place to live. She had preferred to be a servant on Zetani rather than a leader at Disyerto-2. At least a servant on her home planet could enjoy the bliss of living on a beautiful, biodiverse planet.

Podixa thought about her husband, Arish Kisherom and smiled. There was one good thing about living on Disyerto-2. On her planet, the laws allowed contraceptives, and she could have as much sex as she wanted. Thinking back on her time at Zetani, banning contraceptives and conceptions outside the Midsummer celebration was insanity. Why did the leadership of her home planet come up with such an absurd doctrine? As the prefect for the Pustinja Outpost, she would not uphold those ancient laws. They had been deported to Disyerto-2 for breaching the procreation laws, so why would they embrace the rule that had condemned them?

As she was thinking of her home planet, Areela Kheeran showed up as a hologram in front of her. However, Areela's appearance didn't make any sense. No deportees were meant to arrive for another two years, so how could Areela transmit to her?

"Hi Podixa, I am coming with a group of friends. I have urgent news." Areela transmitted.

Podixa struggled to reply. No one had taught her telepathy when she was a servant on Zetani. Although her husband, from the science caste, had taught her some Zetan abilities, she had not been very interested in the topic. Moreover, Pustinja was a small place, and she preferred talking to people in person rather than using ancient techniques.

"What is your news, and where are you? There are no long-distance ships inbound." Podixa replied. "I am in the Divine Dimension. Judge Jasper Javonom and a group of enforcers are pursuing us." Areela replied.

"What are you talking about, dear Areela?" Podixa replied.

"Jasper sentenced me to death for killing his brother Xialiab in self-defence. Zelinko Siblexom started a revolution to save me, and we escaped. Because of this, Jasper and his enforcers are pursuing us." Areela replied.

Areela's revelation put Podixa in a tough spot. She hated Jasper as he was the one who had sentenced her to deportation. However, she was the prefect of this outpost, and she didn't want to stir the ire of the Ronesian Council. Although she was 50 light-years away from Zetani, nothing stopped their leaders from sending robotic armies to destroy her.

"Sorry, but I cannot help you. Defying the capital would doom this outpost. You know that." Podixa replied.

"No, it wouldn't. Zelinko started a revolution in Ronesia when he revealed that the master caste had kept the Zeto Crystal away from the other castes. All Zetans have amazing innate capabilities that the masters have hidden from us. If you stop Jasper, no one will avenge him." Areela revealed.

Podixa reflected on Areela's claims. Perhaps the reason Disyerto-2 was a lifeless wasteland was the absence of a Zeto Crystal?

"Did you bring the Zeto Crystal with you?" Podixa asked.

"No, doing so would destroy our homeworld. But we found out that there are other Zeto Crystals and a way to reach them. Finding the other crystals could lead to a Golden Age for our people." Areela stated.

Podixa smiled. As crazy as it sounded, this could be the way for her to have freedom while living on a beautiful planet. If she found a world with a primordial Zeto Crystal, she could create the ultimate Zetan society.

"Lead Jasper and his enforcers to the Grand Square in front of the Pustinja Palace. We'll organise our defences there." Podixa said.

"Thank you, I will be there in seven days," Areela said and ended the transmission.

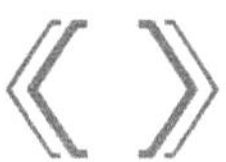

JUDGE JASPER JAVONOM looked at the dozen enforcers who followed him through the portal. Most were wounded after escaping from the angry mob, and one was dead. That enforcer was cut in half as the portal ran out of energy at the halfway mark. The portal's closure left his lower body on Zetani, while the upper body had dropped out in this mysterious world.

Lieutenant Hadib Nabilom dragged himself to Jasper and spoke, "What is this place, sire? Where are we?"

Jasper studied his lieutenant and reflected on the question. Hadib and most of his men would be fine. As reluctant as Jasper was to use his mental powers to heal lesser Zetans, it served him better to treat his men rather than letting them die from treatable conditions. As for the location, he recognised the place from his meditation sessions. He was in the Dihawara Densi, the land of the gods.

"We are in the Divine Dimension. We need to pursue the rebels that escaped here. We might not be able to save Ronesia, but we will avenge the fall of our capital to the rebel scum." Jasper stated.

"But we cannot initiate a pursuit as we carry injuries from the fight," Hadib objected.

'Why is he stating the obvious? Does he take me for a fool?' Jasper thought, but he decided to hide his irritation. There was no point in showing his disdain for his subordinates, and besides, it was dangerous. He was alone with them in this faraway land, and they could kill him in his sleep if he weren't careful.

"I will heal you. Come here, Hadib." Jasper instructed, and Hadib got seated on the ground next to him.

Jasper concentrated and used his telekinetic powers to drag the bullets out of Hadib's body. Precision was crucial as he didn't want the procedure to increase the size of the bullet wounds. Unfortunately, while his powers enabled him to increase the body's natural healing rate, he couldn't heal the unhealable.

"Judge Jasper!"

Jasper twitched as one of the enforcers exclaimed his name without warning. The sudden noise made him lose focus, and he threw his arm backwards as he turned. His sudden movement accelerated the bullet and struck the noisy enforcer in the head. As the man dropped dead to the ground, Jasper urged,

"Can you please be quiet and not startle me. I am performing a very sensitive procedure."

"What about Adnan?" Another enforcer asked.

"He is dead. I am not a god. I can't resurrect people. So please stay silent while I treat your ailments." Jasper stated.

The enforcers adhered to Jasper's instructions, and an hour later, he had removed all the bullets and fragments from their bodies. However, a problem remained; he would need to help his men into a guided meditation session to help spike their immune system and natural recovery. This session would take days and give his enemies a big head start. It was, however, the only way to beat them in the long run.

Jasper gathered his followers in a circle and chanted to initiate a round of group meditation.

"Om mani padme om mani padme om........"

"HOW MUCH LONGER? THEY are getting closer."

Areela looked at her brother, who was whimpering about the approaching enforcers. At first, she had felt terrified when the enforcers arrived not far behind them. However, as the enforcers hadn't taken up the pursuit, Areela, Kailow, and Zelinko had slowed down. Walking for weeks without food or water was strenuous and mind-numbing, although it seemed survivable in this realm. A few days ago, the enforcers had picked up their pace, and the soldiers kept a lot higher pace than Areela, who was weak after spending six months on death row.

"I am moving as fast as I can, Kailow. I am weak from traumatic childbirth and spending six months on death row." Areela exclaimed.

"We cannot fight amongst ourselves. We need to get to Disyerto-2." Zelinko interjected.

"But it's 100 kilometres ahead of us, and our pursuers are only 10 kilometres behind us. I cannot walk that fast." Areela replied.

"I'll face them. You keep moving ahead. If I defeat Jasper, I can get the others to follow me. If not, I aim to stall them to give you enough time to save my child." Zelinko stated.

"Thank you," Areela exclaimed and hugged Zelinko.

"Here, take these sapphires. I have charged them with the energy from the primordial Zeto Crystal. I hope they'll be able to open a portal to Disyerto-2 once you get there." Zelinko stated.

"Thank you, Zelinko. I'll meet you at the Pustinja Outpost." Areela replied.

Zelinko nodded and turned around. He had been running for too long. Today would be the day he stood up for what was right. With determined steps, he marched to face his enemy.

Chapter 14: The Confrontation

"Jasper Javonom, this ends here."

Jasper gave Zelinko a curious look. As it would seem, the man who had betrayed the ruling council had returned to face him. There had to be a reason why his rival had returned to confront him.

Hadib Nabilom took a step forward, pulled out his pistol, and exclaimed, "Freeze, Zelinko! You are under arrest for betraying the city of Ronesia."

Jasper gave his lieutenant a stern look and instructed, "Keep your pistol down, you fool. Have you forgotten what happened at Mancin Island? Zelinko is much more powerful than the servants who threw your bullets back at you."

Hadib put down his pistol and backed down while Jasper smirked, advanced towards Zelinko, and spoke, "So, tell me. Why have you returned to face me? Were you afraid that I would hurt your lover in the confrontation?"

"I'd rather face you than flee," Zelinko replied.

"Is that so? Then you should have faced me at Mancin Island instead of fleeing through that damn portal." Jasper exclaimed, swung his arm, and sent a psionic shockwave towards Zelinko.

Zelinko deflected the wave, which returned to strike Jasper in the face, and broke his nose.

'I must stay calm. A calm mind is the only way to beat this traitor,' Jasper thought and took a deep breath.

"Jasper, it is over. Surrender to me, and I will let you join me on a glorious quest. There are other Zeto Crystals out there. Beautiful worlds like Zetani await us in the Milky Way Galaxy." Zelinko proclaimed.

'Bloody fool letting his guard down, I'll show him.' Jasper thought and took a psionic stranglehold on Zelinko's windpipe.

Seeing that his boss had subdued the usurper, Hadib got overconfident and fired his pistol toward Zelinko. Zelinko used a waving motion which caused the bullet to reverse and hit Hadib in the chest.

"Bloody idiots, this is how you do it!" Jasper stated and squeezed his fist to crush Zelinko's windpipe.

Zelinko collapsed to his knees, and blood was pouring from his mouth.

"For treason against the Ronesian Council, I sentence you to death," Jasper said while squeezing Zelinko's cranium until blood poured from Zelinko's eyes, and he dropped dead to the ground.

"Hurry up, men. We need to catch those elopers before they escape." Jasper commanded and marched as fast as possible with his severe nosebleed.

"OH NO! ZELINKO HAS fallen. I can feel it."

Kailow looked at his sister, who had a sudden meltdown at this very unlucky moment. They needed to hurry up, but the only way to move was to get his sister out of her current emotional state—what a mess.

"What are you talking about, Areela?" Kailow said.

"Jasper killed the father of my child. I cannot move on." Areela sobbed and dropped to the ground while shaking and wailing in misery.

"But Zelinko sacrificed himself to help our escape. Giving up now would dishonour his sacrifice." Kailow pleaded.

Areela didn't listen to her brother. She was paralysed from losing her lover, who had sacrificed himself to save her.

Kailow tried to assess the situation. Jasper was less than 5 kilometres away and approaching quickly. The teleportation place was 50 kilometres away, so he could take the child and make a run for it. However, there was an issue. Even if he took Thorax to get himself and the child to safety, he didn't know how to open a portal to Disyerto-2.

"Don't worry, Kailow. Zelinko is still alive." Thorax whispered before he reverted to his natural beastly state.

Chapter 15: The Resurrection

Zelinko's life was flashing in front of his eyes when the course of the images reversed. "You're not ready to die yet," A soft ethereal voice said.

He opened his eyes and felt a burning sensation from something in his pocket. He had forgotten to give Areela one of his charged sapphires, and it had discharged its energies to bring him back to life. Zelinko took out the sapphire from his pocket and studied it. It had reverted to a regular crystal, but it still had a faint glow.

"Help me, please."

Zelinko turned to the voice and saw the wounded Hadib Nabilom, bleeding from a bullet wound in his stomach. Watching the man who had tried to kill him moments earlier, Zelinko felt pity for the enforcer lieutenant. He had known Hadib for many years, and he had always been a good man, so would he let one mistake be Hadib's undoing, or would he save the lieutenant?

"I'll save you. Hold tight." Zelinko said and used telekinesis to remove the bullet from Hadib's body. After the shell was gone, he placed the sapphire on Hadib's bullet wound, and its energy healed the enforcer.

"Wow, how did you do that?" Hadib said in awe.

"It's the power of the Zeto Crystal, stored into this sapphire. It belongs to all Zetans." Zelinko said. "Thank you, Master Zelinko. I owe my life to you." Hadib replied.

"Good. Then come with me. We must stop Jasper from murdering my family!" Zelinko exclaimed and hurried to intercept Jasper's group before his family came to harm.

"GET UP; THE ENEMY WILL be here soon." Kailow urged and shook his sister.

"It's too late. Jasper is here," Areela replied, shed a tear, and pointed toward their enemy who approached them.

"Rebel scum. Zelinko is dead, and you need to tell me how to open the portal back to Zetani." Jasper commanded.

"We are not helping you. Your brother brutalised my sister, and she killed him in self-defence. You didn't even let her defend herself in court." Kailow replied.

Jasper had no desire to debate the merit of Kailow's accusations, so he sent him flying with a psionic blast that hurled him hundreds of meters.

Jasper laughed and taunted. "Worthless vermin. It feels good to unleash my unmasked powers now that I no longer need to hide behind the law."

"You monster! Why did you kill my brother?" Areela exclaimed.

"Oh, did I? We can't know that until we find his body." Jasper mocked.

"Kailow, I'll avenge you," Areela shouted and blasted Jasper with her new-found psionic powers. Unfortunately, Areela was no match for Jasper, so he deflected her attacks and knocked her into submission.

"Silly woman, you shouldn't have done that. I better get physical with you." Jasper said and approached Areela.

"Leave her alone."

Jasper froze when he heard Zelinko's voice. 'How can this be? I am sure that I killed him moments ago.' Jasper thought, turned around and spoke with fake confidence. "Look who is here. You shouldn't have called me out, Zelinko; you would have a better chance if you stabbed me in the back."

"This madness must end. I am offering you a chance to cooperate for the good of our species." Zelinko urged.

"I will do something even better. I will kill you, Zelinko!" Jasper exclaimed and sent a psionic bolt towards Zelinko.

Zelinko deflected the bolt, but he felt weak. Coming back from the dead had convinced him that his purpose was to defeat Jasper. Yet, when he took the heat of the initial blast, fear started creeping back into his mind.

Jasper unleashed a flurry of bluish bolts from his hands while Zelinko tried to deflect them. Their fight deflected psionic energy bolts everywhere, and the enforcers threw themselves to the ground to take cover. After deflecting a dozen bolts, Zelinko missed one and got hit in the face, which caused 3rd-degree burns.

Jasper walked up to Zelinko, grabbed a mental stranglehold on his throat, chuckled, and taunted. "Ha-ha. You might wonder how I beat you twice in a day. The trick is repeated exposure to the Zeto Crystal. I attuned myself to the crystal more than you did. That's why I am far more powerful."

Zelinko had an epiphany. His father's presence in the secret Zeto Crystal vault wasn't a coincidence. His father had also been there in secret to increase his powers. Yet he had kept his son in the dark. So great was the allure of power and the fear of losing it.

Jasper squeezed Zelinko's windpipe and spoke again. I'll kill you slowly this time, and I'll make sure you are dead!

Pow, pow, pow

Jasper gasped in shock and collapsed as three bullets from a pistol struck him from behind. Then, he saw Hadib, whom he had left to die with his last dying breaths.

Zelinko got up and shook Hadib's hand. His decision to show mercy to a fallen enemy had paid off, as Hadib had extended the same compassion to him.

ZELINKO WAS OUT OF breath, and he felt severely unwell. The aftereffects of death and resurrection were catching up with him. Furthermore, it didn't help that he had walked 490 kilometres in 7 days without food, water, or sufficient sleep. He needed to get up and make his way to the teleportation spot, which was less than 10 kilometres away, yet it was too difficult. So close, yet so far!

"Kailow, you are alive!"

Zelinko opened his eyes, and he saw Areela hugging Kailow, who also had experienced a rough day, as silvery bruises covered the young man's body.

"Yes, I must be stronger than I thought," Kailow replied and smiled.

"I am so glad to hear that," Areela said and hugged her brother.

"So, what are we waiting for? Disyerto-2 is less than 10 kilometres away, and I can't wait to have a drink." Kailow enthused.

Hearing Kailow's enthusiasm raised Zelinko's spirits. Why would he allow himself to die here when he was so close to reaching his goal?

Zelinko got up, cleared his throat, and spoke, "Our target is 8 kilometres that way. We should be able to get provisions once we reach Disyerto-2."

The enforcers nodded, and two of them helped Zelinko on the last stretch of his lengthy trek. A couple of hours later, they reached the teleportation spot.

Chapter 16: The Reunion

Podixa Sairan studied the defences she had set up at the main square in front of the Pustinja Palace. She was nervous about the occasion. Although they had weapons, none of her settlers had battle experience. There was no need as the outpost had a limited population, and there were no other species outside of the perimeter.

Podixa looked towards the horizon, where an approaching sandstorm covered the orange sun. It looked like a massive storm, and she hoped that the nanotechnology barrier would keep the sand out and the atmosphere in. Unfortunately, this wasn't always the case when a large storm hit.

"Prefect Sairan, a group of outsiders are approaching." A flying sentry drone reported and beamed towards a rift in spacetime in the town square.

"Ready yourself!" Podixa exclaimed as Areela, Kailow, Zelinko and the enforcers came crashing through the portal. Podixa looked at the new arrivals, who had all collapsed. What was going on?

"Medics, approach them with medical scanners to look for life signs. We cover you from here." Podixa commanded.

The medics complied, and they approached the unconscious arrivals with health scanners while wearing hazmat suits.

"No foreign pathogens detected. All the foreigners suffer from severe dehydration." The medic stated.

"Send them to our medical wards at once. Put them on a silver saline drip and guard the corridors until we have determined their intentions." Podixa commanded.

More medics arrived with stretchers, and they wheeled off the new arrivals to the medical ward.

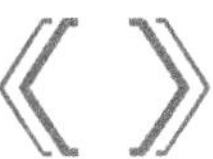

AREELA KHEERAN WATCHED the sparks that fizzed as the sandstorm clashed with the nanotechnology forcefield that protected the Pustinja Outpost from the elements. It was a terrible spectacle to behold. Although there were some deserts on Zetani, she could never have imagined that anyone would be living like this.

'I better drink some water,' Areela thought, and she was thankful for being alive. She remembered the burning thirst she had felt as soon as she arrived through the portal. It was as if one week of dehydration struck her at once!

As Areela put the glass to her mouth, the water almost burned against her tinder-dry throat. 'Slow and steady.' She thought as she drank the water, which caused her pain and renewed energy.

Podixa entered the hospital room, smiled at Areela, and spoke, "Areela Kheeran. I thought I would never see you again. At least not like this."

"I am glad that you saved me. Is everyone in my group okay?"

"I am sorry, but two members in your group were too far gone when they got here. We couldn't save them." Podixa revealed.

Hearing this, Areela was close to having a panic attack. She couldn't bear knowing that two of her companions had perished, and the worst part was that she didn't know who the survivors would be.

"Take me to the morgue. I need to see them so I can get closure." Areela said.

"I am sorry, but you still need to rest from your arduous voyage. You were close to dying from dehydration." Podixa replied.

"How am I going to rest fearing that those that I love could perish? Podixa, I need to know." Areela urged. Podixa nodded and replied, "Okay. Please come with me."

Areela nodded and followed Podixa to the morgue while walking down the most anxiety-ridden steps of her life.

"BLESS THE TRUE MAKER!" Areela exclaimed as she entered the morgue at the Pustinja Outpost.

"What is wrong with you? Why are you happy about deaths among your entourage?" Podixa said. "Those two men were among the enforcers that pursued us. They didn't swap sides until Zelinko defeated Jasper. I rather see my enemies among the fallen than my child or brother." Areela replied.

"I understand. I am sorry if I made you worry for nothing. I didn't know who was in your entourage," Podixa replied.

"That's okay. So, can I see my child and my brother now?" Areela asked.

"Yes, please have dinner with my husband and me tomorrow night. I am sure that he is keen to know our unexpected guests." Podixa replied.

LATER THE SAME NIGHT, Areela entered the private dining room in the Pustinja Palace. The table had an assortment of dishes that Areela hadn't seen before, but they had one thing in common. They didn't seem at all appetizing.

Kailow arrived while holding Thorax in his arms. He approached his sister, handed her the mutant baby, and spoke. "So, sister, it must feel good to be safe with your baby?"

"Yes, how do you feel about all this?" Areela asked.

"Well, it's a bit ironic. If I had done nothing, I would be cryogenically frozen and arrive here in 50 years. So, it seems like my actions did not affect my outcome." Kailow said with an afterthought.

"Don't say that. We still have a few Zeto-charged sapphires. We can get supplies and vehicles to travel to the other six prime planets in the Milky Way Galaxy. Together, we can find the planet where the humans live." Areela replied.

"Only if we can convince your friend Podixa to help us," Kailow replied.

"What can I do to help you?"

Kailow and Areela stared at Podixa, who appeared in the room while wearing a tight, low-cut yellow dress that emphasized the beauty of her slender body. When seeing the beauty of Podixa's complexion, Areela understood how her ex-slave friend had seduced the successful scientist Arish Kisherom and had born his son. This act of seduction had taken her to the top of society, albeit she was at the top level on a much less beautiful planet.

"So, as I said a week ago, we found a way to travel through Dihawara Densi, to reach any place in the Milky Way Galaxy within weeks," Areela replied.

"Yet, your method of travel seems dangerous. Two of you perished, and the rest of you would have faced the same outcome if you hadn't received urgent medical attention." Podixa remarked.

"We had to leave without supplies for the trip. Dehydration almost killed us, not the trip itself." Areela replied.

"I see. I'll need to discuss this with my husband. If anyone could develop a suitable engineering solution, it would be him. But for now, please help yourself to the food." Podixa said and pointed towards the food platters.

Kailow and Areela looked at each other in hesitation. Who would be brave enough to try the food first?

Kailow filled a plate with grilled worm larvae, off-green and slimy algae, and black rotten fungi. As he ate the unappetising food, he struggled to swallow.

Podixa gave him a cold stare and said, "When the master caste decided to use this planet as a prison colony, they provided us with almost inedible food to make our punishment worse. Since the trip from Zetani is a one-way trip, and there is no ecosystem on this planet, or anywhere else in this star system, this is what we have for sustenance."

After her statement, Podixa left the room, while Kailow and Areela realised they would have to sustain themselves on food like this.

Chapter 17: Thorax Reveals the Zeto Crystal Locations.

Areela and Kailow were sitting at the town square in the Pustinja Outpost, overlooking the desert outside. The sandstorm had subsided, and life had gone back to normal with the clearing skies. The clear skies made the outpost livelier, with more people going out and about with their daily lives.

As Areela looked at the desert, she felt like she was holidaying on the Parchus planet in the Zetani system. While Zetani was the only liveable planet in this star system, several planets existed where powerful Zetans could travel for a holiday, and Parchus was similar to Disyerto-2.

Areela closed her eyes and imagined what life could have been if Zelinko had taken her as his wife and Xialiab hadn't messed everything up. She could have lived in peace on her beautiful home planet while raising her beautiful child with her good-looking husband. Instead, she was on a desert planet, her now one-year-old toddler was a mutant freak, and the local government hadn't allowed her to meet Zelinko, her most beloved.

A tall man accompanied by a few government officials approached Areela and spoke, "Good day. I am Arish Kisherom, and I am the governor of Disyerto-2."

"It is a pleasure to meet you, Arish. I had hoped to see you at the dinner with Podixa." Areela replied.

"There was a problem that needed my attention. As a matter of fact, we have had many problems recently. As unexpected as it is, your arrival could save our people from destruction." Arish revealed.

"What problems do you have?" Kailow asked.

"Severe malnutrition and dangers from the harsh elements in the desert. But the worst problem is apathy." Arish replied.

"Apathy?" Kailow asked.

"Depression. Imagine living on a condemned desert planet without hope for the future. It does things to people's minds. My wife and I have tried to inspire hope, but it is fading." Arish said and sighed.

'Hope. The invisible force that could make or break a person,' Areela thought and said, "There is hope. There is a bright future ahead of us. We found that distances were shorter when we travelled from Zetani via Dihawara Densi. A light-year is only 10 kilometres in the Divine Dimension. So if we have supplies and fast vehicles, the whole Milky Way Galaxy is within our reach."

"Yet, there are billions of stars and planets in the galaxy. How would we find the good ones?" Arish asked.

Areela couldn't answer this question, but she knew Thorax could. If she could start his connection with the True Maker, she could find out where the other suitable planets were.

Areela grabbed one of the charged sapphires from her pocket, and she placed it on Thorax's temple. At first, the child was restless, but it wasn't long until his eyes shone with the same blue colour as the charged sapphire.

"Grraah...... Yes, you have summoned me. How can I help you...?" Thorax said.

"I need to know where the other Zeto Crystals are. Can you please tell me?" Areela replied.

"The closest Zeto Crystal is at Zetani, to where you are never to return during your lifetimes. The second closest crystal is at Zetani Nova, 450 lightyears to the southwest, based on a 2-dimensional map of the Milky Way Galaxy. Zetani Nova is a beautiful planet that is very similar to Zetani. I, the True Maker, created Zetani Nova to ascertain Zetan survival after the Zetani Maximus star goes supernova. However, the Zetans have never reached the planet in the 999 iterations of the universe that has existed so far. If you manage to settle in Zetani Nova, your next goal is to save humanity on Earth. Earth is 10000 lightyears to the southwest of Zetani Nova, and humanity is due for extinction in four years due to a supermassive ice age. Thus, time is of the essence. Other important planets are Elvonia, inhabited by the Elves; Goldonia, inhabited by the dwarves; and Grashdung, inhabited by the orcs. Whatever you do, stay clear of Xenora, which is 50 lightyears to the east of Zetani Nova. The planet and its native sentient species are hostile to Zetans." Thorax replied.

Hearing the toddler's lengthy explanation awed Arish. There was no scientific explanation of how the mutant baby knew all these things. Thus, the only possible reason was that the True Maker had awoken from her slumber. Arish bowed in front of Thorax, turned on a 3D hologram star map of the galaxy, and spoke. "Oh, exalted one, praise be Thee. Can you please show us where these fantastic worlds are?"

Thorax nodded, marked the locations on the map, and spoke, "Best of luck, Arish, son of Kisher. May you lead your people to safety, and may the light from the Zetan civilisation spread across the galaxy."

The True Maker left Thorax's body, and the baby was again back to grunting and drooling with beast-like mannerisms.

A FEW WEEKS LATER, Areela and Kailow explored the surrounding Disyerto-2 environment. Once the sandstorms had ended, Areela realised that the planet wasn't as horrible as she first thought. They could have had another outcome if the master caste had funded the expedition for free settlers instead of convicts. Alas, she understood why the local population was angry with the master caste. However, the age-old rivalry was a shame since she missed the father of her child, who was currently locked up.

Areela looked up and stared in awe at the purple salt crystal formations inside an abandoned cave when Podixa called her via a teleprompt device. At first, using a communication device felt strange for Areela as she had grown accustomed to telepathy.

Areela stared at the hologram while Podixa spoke, "Why are you staring in silence, Areela? Is your telecommunication device broken?"

Areela shook her head and replied. "I feel so silly. I thought we were having a telepathic discussion." "Ha-ha. Is that why you look like you are having a stroke?" Podixa teased.

"Uhm, I guess," Areela replied.

"In any case, please hurry back home," Podixa urged.

"Why? Is there another sandstorm approaching?" Areela asked and looked towards the desert outside the cave.

"No, my husband is making an announcement today. He is setting up an expedition to find the planets that Thorax told us about."

'Why hasn't my friend told me anything about this until now? Why keep me in the dark?' Areela thought, but she replied, "We'll be heading back straight away. We'll be back in the Pustinja Outpost as soon as possible."

Having said this, Areela and Kailow got on a hovercraft and hurried back to the meeting.

Chapter 18: The Expedition

When Areela arrived at the Pustinja Outpost, she noticed many people had gathered in the main square. Tensions seemed high, and many of the locals were holding guns. There was a small group in the centre of the square, which consisted of Zelinko and the surviving members of Jasper's enforcers. Areela rushed towards Zelinko, but the local militia held her away.

Governor Arish Kisherom spoke from the balcony of the Pustinja Palace. "Citizens of the Pustinja Outpost. Today we are witnessing a remarkable milestone. For the first time in history, we will visit other planets with sentient species. We will grant these former enemies from Zetani the chance to travel to the world of Grashdung, where the fearsome orcs live."

Arish's statement broke Areela's heart. Why did he insist on separating her and Zelinko? This separation wasn't meant to be, as the True Maker had tasked them with colonising Zetani Nova together. She needed to reach Arish before it was too late!

Areela sent a weak psionic blast towards Arish, which he deflected easily. When he searched for the perpetrator, she gave away her mental signature and telepathed, "Governor Kisherom. You cannot send Zelinko away. We need him."

"I am sorry, but I cannot oblige to your request. Zelinko belongs to the Master Caste, which has spent millennia oppressing the lower-caste-Zetans on Zetani. He will try to usurp power if we bring him to Zetani Nova." Arish replied.

"Yet, if you don't bring him along, you will not know how to charge sapphires with the force of the Zeto Crystal. That will end your expedition before it begins." Areela replied.

There was a moment of silence. Eventually, Arish contacted one of his militiamen, who led Zelinko away from the others. There was a moment of protest before Zelinko understood why they took him away. Then, as he understood their purpose, he smiled at Areela as the militiamen led him away.

Podixa gave Lieutenant Hadib Nabilom a charged sapphire and inserted another sapphire into a large-scale scaffolding. After that, the Zetans directed a ray of concentrated sunlight into the Zeto-charged gemstone, which opened a dimensional rift. Hadib and the other enforcers entered a hovercraft, and they flew into the portal. They were gone in the blink of an eye, to the gathered onlookers' amazement.

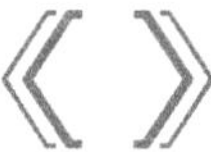

AREELA FELT STRANGE as she was alone with Zelinko for the first time since their passionate night almost two years earlier. She felt conflicted, and she didn't know what to do. On the one hand, Zelinko was the only man she had ever been with, and he was the father of her child. He had also abandoned his child and wife to save her. Yet, he had left her in the prison cell and allowed Jasper to sentence her to death for killing Xialiab. Areela had spent a year in prison because of Zelinko's cowardice. How would she be able to forgive him?

"Thank you for saving me from going to Grashdung. I owe you my life." Zelinko said.

"Well, I guess that makes us even...." Areela said and looked at Zelinko with a cold gaze. As much as she wanted to love him, she couldn't. The worst part was that she couldn't stop loving him either.

"I should have been there for you. If I had protected you from the start, Xialiab wouldn't have dared to hurt you, and none of this would have happened." Zelinko stated.

"So, why didn't you?" Areela asked.

"Because I was betrothed to Shauwana, and her pregnancy complicated things. Before Xialiab snapped and disfigured Thorax with his experiment, I hoped to make a deal with him to protect everyone." Zelinko revealed.

Areela turned her gaze to the toddler, who was munching on some maggots while growling and babbling in exhilaration. He seemed happy to eat the disgusting food on the outpost, and he was the only one who felt that way. Areela had an insight. What if Xialiab's experiments enabled Thorax to be a host for the True Maker, to become the Chosen One? If everything had happened the way she wanted, Thorax would have become an unremarkable baby.

Areela smiled at Zelinko and spoke, "As crazy as it sounds, everything worked out as it was destined to be. Thorax is special, and we are fulfilling our destinies."

"I guess you are right. Everything happens for a reason." Zelinko pondered.

"As is this," Areela said, pulled Zelinko closer, and kissed him under the moonless night sky.

AREELA WAS WALKING the streets of the Pustinja Outpost when she saw Podixa argue with a local Disyerto-2 woman. They argued in a local language, which had diverged from the Zetani language as the planets were 50 lightyears apart. At the end of the argument, the woman handed Podixa a tiny sapphire and stormed off in anger.

Areela approached Podixa and spoke, "What did you argue about?"

"She didn't want to give up her sapphires as they were her only memory of her mother. Yet, we need to gather all our sapphires before our trip to Zetani Nova. How else will we have enough sapphires to charge once we get there?"

Areela nodded with an afterthought. She had never considered how to find the necessary sapphires or how many they needed. However, if they aimed to charge sapphires and travel forth, Podixa's plan made sense.

"So, how is everything coming along?" Areela asked.

"Good, we have set up 100 hovercrafts and gathered enough supplies to feed 500 people for two months. If your claims are correct, we will have enough supplies to travel to Zetani Nova and back."

"That won't be possible. We don't have enough energy to power the portals for that many people." Areela replied.

"So, what do you suggest?" Podixa asked.

"Come with me and bring only your closest allies. Then, if we find the Zeto Crystal on Zetani Nova, we can charge our sapphires and bring the rest of the population. If not, we might perish." Areela stated.

Podixa pondered on Areela's words. She didn't like going to an alien planet with only a small group. What if the locals were hostile?

Yet, Areela was correct. Podixa had seen how the portal had closed after they sent the Zetani enforcers to Grashdung. They had only six charged sapphires left, and they would not be able to get their whole group through the dimensional rift twice with that limited energy.

"You are right. I will speak to my husband. We'll come with you to explore this new world together. We'll find a way to bring the rest of the population later." Podixa said.

"Thank you," Areela replied.

Podixa pointed in the direction of a small tea shop and chirped, "Come with me. I know you don't like our food, but you'll love this tea."

Areela nodded, and as she tasted the spiced tea that consisted of fermented sand bacteria, her mind transcended time and space. While the tea wasn't as potent as the Zeto Crystal, Areela imagined how this tea could have a similar effect on another species in the future. Finally, her vision faded, and her mind felt at peace as she closed her eyes and passed into blissful sleep.

"MAY THE TRUE MAKER keep you safe and reunite us before a long time has passed."

It was early in the morning, and Arish Kisherom looked at his assistant Amela Andelan, who would lead the Pustinja Outpost in his absence. It was an emotional moment. In the search for a better world, he would have to leave the planet that had been his home for the last 30 years. Arish and Podixa had left their youngest two children in Amela's ward. They had only brought the 31-year-old Besim Arishom, whose birth was why Judge Jasper had deported them to the Pustinja Outpost.

Podixa picked up Besim and strapped him to a seat in the hovercraft. The young boy was both excited and nervous over the adventure ahead, and he couldn't keep his eyes away from his younger siblings, who were staying with Amela.

When the time was right, Amela placed a charged sapphire in the portal frame and directed a beam of concentrated sunlight into it. As the interdimensional portal opened, Areela and Podixa looked at each other. Who would be the first to set forth on the perilous journey?

Areela drove through the portal first, relieved she wasn't running from something this time. Instead, a higher purpose motivated her. She was on the way to her destiny.

Podixa stared as the hovercraft that held Areela's entourage evaporated into thin air. She hesitated for a bit but pushed herself to press down the accelerator. She and her husband were the leaders of their people, leading them to a better future.

Chapter 19: Teleportation Problems.

F^izz Podixa Sairan stared in disbelief at the hovercraft's dashboard as it came to a standstill in the Divine Dimension. The interdimensional trip had been vivid, and she was happy that she and her family had come out on the other side in one piece. Yet, why didn't her vehicle respond?

Podixa got out of the hovercraft and inspected the hovercraft's motor. It wasn't there. Instead, there was an empty gap where the engine had been. What was going on?

Podixa realised that she had been lucky when she saw a corpse of a Zetani enforcer. The man had been cut in half.

Seeing the dead man, the young Besim Arishom screamed in terror while Arish calmly tackled the matter and reflected, "Hmm. The Zeto-charged gemstones seem to have enough energy to teleport a certain mass. This is an issue that we need to resolve."

"So, what do we do?" Podixa asked.

"Well, according to the True Maker, Zetani Nova is 450 lightyears/ 4500 kilometres to the southwest from our current location. That is not something we can traverse on foot." Arish replied.

"Okay, I'll contact Areela, and I'll ask her to pick us up," Podixa said and telepathed to her friend.

Arish exited the hovercraft and examined the dead enforcer with a medical scanner. The cortisol levels in the dead man's blood were normal, which indicated that his death was instant and painless. Yet the enforcer was dead nonetheless, so how would he avoid facing a similar outcome?

Arish reflected on a suitable experiment to determine the exact amount of energy he could send through the portal risk-free. To find out the energy in one Zeto-charged sapphire, he needed to push weight from the ordinary world through the portal while a man on the other side measured if the object had lost mass. That was the safest way of figuring out the carrying capacity of one charged gemstone.

Arish picked up his phone. While it was useless for communications as he had no phone connection, it had another use. As he was a prominent engineer on Zetani before his exile, he could use his knowledge to create 3D sketches of an improved portal structure. If he could connect many Zeto-charged gemstones into one superstructure, he would minimise the risk of a power failure mid-travel that would kill a Zetan or lose cargo.

After sketching his portal designs, Arish concluded that a pyramid formation was the best shape for the portal superstructure. With a prism at the top of the pyramid, he could split the sunlight into seven powerful rays. These rays would pass many Zeto-Charged sapphires on the way, concentrating the energy and causing a drift of time and space and thus opening a portal in the middle of the pyramid. If he connected enough crystals, he could transport large space carriers. His idea amazed him; with a bit of luck, this could start a new era of space colonisation.

Arish let go of his dreams and got back to reality. These schematics were only dreams for now. He was stuck in a void between the dimensions, and he didn't even know whether they would make their way to Zetani Nova. He felt even less confident that he would find a Zeto Crystal on the planet.

Zelinko approached Arish and spoke, "What happened? How could we have lost most of our supplies through the portal?"

Arish nodded and said with an afterthought, "The problem is that our teleportation devices are unstable. So, to make the process stable, we need to have several arrays with charged sapphires, which we organise symmetrically."

"That doesn't help us now. So, what do we do?" Zelinko asked.

"We must press ahead. We have four charged sapphires left, so if we return to Disyerto-2, we will run out of sapphires, and our plans will fail." Arish replied.

"Agreed. Pack everything that we need in our hovercraft. We will need to get to Zetani Nova as quickly as possible." Zelinko stated.

The group hurried to repack their hovercrafts to make room for themselves and only pack what was essential for the way ahead. An hour later, they were all heading for the teleportation point to Zetani Nova.

TWO DAYS LATER, THE group had arrived at the teleportation spot that linked the Divine Dimension to Zetani Nova. They had planned for a week-long trip, but since the Divine Dimension was empty, they had set the hovercraft on autopilot, which had cut travel time. They exited their hovercraft and tried to open the portal to Zetani Nova.

"It's strange. I don't remember how we opened the portal to Disyerto-2?" Areela reflected.

"The portal activated by itself when we stood in the right spot," Zelinko recalled.

"Wait, so don't you know how to open the portal from here? Are we stuck?" Podixa exclaimed.

The blue light returned to Thorax's eyes, and he spoke, "Don't worry. The portal to Zetani Nova will open when the sun rises on the planet if you leave a charged sapphire in the right location."

"The True Maker, are you watching us?" Podixa exclaimed.

"Always and forever. As am I watching the rest of my creation in this galaxy," Thorax replied.

"So, why didn't you warn us about the instability of the portal? We lost one of our hovercrafts, and the Zetani enforcers lost one of their men." Podixa complained.

Thorax stroked his chin, sat in silence for a while, and spoke with an afterthought, "Please tell me, Podixa... How does an infant learn to walk?"

"Through progressively learning to use his or her body?" Podixa replied.

"Exactly. If I had stopped you from falling by warning you of the portal, would you still have travelled, or would you have stayed on Disyerto-2? Because of your partial failure, Arish started working on a solution to the problem. This wouldn't have happened if you had averted the original problem." Thorax revealed.

"My son, will we be okay if we travel to Zetani Nova?" Areela asked.

"I cannot tell you your destinies without changing them. But I can reveal that the Divine Dimension is at a higher energy level than the Milky Way Galaxy. Alas, a trip there will cause a massive exotherm reaction. Good luck, my friends." Thorax said and reverted to his usual self.

As True Maker's spirit abandoned them, the Zetans reflected on the message they had received. It was a relief that they would not die from teleporting to the surface of Zetani Nova, but the rest sounded foreboding. Then again, it was an age-old reality that one could not anticipate one's death.

Eventually, Areela spoke, "It's good to know that we will reach Zetani Nova. But what did he mean by travelling there being an exotherm reaction?"

"Well, as I understand it, travelling here requires added energy, while travelling from here releases energy," Arish said.

"So, the powerful sandstorm at Areela's arrival was due to the release of energy from the portal?" Podixa asked.

"That would be my conclusion. Of course, this will make travel more difficult, but I'll come up with something." Arish said.

"Mummy, I am hungry," Besim whined.

The Zetans looked at each other. The young child was correct. While waiting for the sun to rise on Zetani Nova, the best way to pass the time was to have a big meal. Podixa prepared soups consisting of freeze-dried maggots, water, and fungi. When they ate the rancid soup, they silently prayed that their next meal would be better!

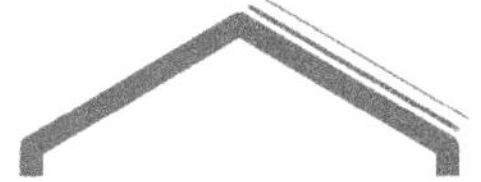

Chapter 20: Trouble in Paradise

As Podixa woke up on Zetani Nova, she opened her eyes and marvelled at what she saw. After spending 50 years in cryogenic sleep en route to Disyerto-2 and 30 years on the planet, she finally experienced beautiful scenery again. The fertile valley reminded her of Ronesia on Zetani, and she couldn't wait to eat the berries and the nuts that would exist in such a lush dale.

Podixa spotted a tree with beautiful fruits, and she was about to grab a fruit and eat it when Arish exclaimed, "Don't eat anything. We are on an alien planet. We need to scan the fruits and nuts for toxins before eating."

Arish scanned the fruit in Podixa's hand, and the health scanner flashed: **'Toxicity level - lethal'.** Podixa threw away the apple-like fruit and got back to her sense. As paradise-like as the planet seemed to be, it was still an alien planet, and carelessness could have disastrous consequences.

The group kept exploring the valley, and a short while later, they found edible banana-like fruits and almond-like nuts. Podixa started a fire, and she made a dessert with the nuts and the bananas. She smiled as she ate her warm dessert and exclaimed, "Praise the Maker. Finally, after 30 long years, I am eating food that is not made of maggots and mushrooms!"

Areela tasted the food and gave Podixa a confused look. Her friend's warm mashed banana and almonds mixture didn't taste good, yet she ate it with such joy and delight.

"Wow, you must have missed our Zetani sweets? This porridge didn't taste that amazing," Areela joked.

"Yes, I do. You never know what you have until it is gone. I have not had real edible food for 30 years." Podixa exclaimed and glared at Zelinko.

Zelinko looked away and didn't say anything. He understood that Podixa, Arish, and the other inhabitants of Disyerto-2 would always hate him for what his caste had done to them. It was inevitable, and the only reason they brought him on this trip was that he knew how to charge sapphires with the power of the Zeto Crystal. If the others found out how to do this, he would no longer have value, and Areela would not be able to save him.

"I'll retreat to my tent," Zelinko said dryly and walked away.

"I am coming with you," Areela replied and brought their child Thorax with her.

As they reached their tent, Areela felt worried. It didn't bode well that Podixa and Arish hated Zelinko. She prayed that they could learn to forgive each other. The future held so much promise, and it would be a shame to dwell on the past.

THEY WERE STILL EXPLORING the valley a few weeks later, and Areela was getting restless. While the dale was a paradise, the disagreements between her husband and her friends were ruining her mood. They needed to find the Zeto Crystal and tell the others; otherwise, they would give up on their goals. The loss of equipment due to the teleportation problems didn't help, and she feared that it would be too late to save humanity if they didn't hurry up.

While humanity didn't mean anything to Areela, saving them was a part of the True Maker's mandate, and she couldn't disobey the supreme deity.

As Areela walked around to gather her thoughts, she saw her brother swimming in a river. Her younger brother looked healthier than ever, as the serene wilderness did wonders to his physique. Yet, upon closer inspection, Areela sensed an immense sadness coming out of Kailow, something she had never sensed before.

Areela walked up to the riverbank and shouted, "Hey Kailow, can you come here, please?"

"Why don't you come here instead?" Kailow asked.

"Because I sense a lot of sadness in you. Is it something you want to talk about?" Areela said kindly. Kailow nodded and swam to the shoreline. He got seated next to Areela and spoke, "Yes, I am sad, and I feel lost."

"Why is that? You are safe, and this place is paradise." Areela objected.

"Zetani was also a paradise, and yet our last year wasn't paradise-like, was it?" Kailow snapped. "Please, don't be angry. Just tell me what is bothering you." Areela suggested.

Kailow took a deep breath, looked away, and mumbled, "Desire... Desire is what is bothering me."

"I don't understand what you mean?" Areela replied.

"I am the fifth wheel in this group. The rest of you hate each other, but at least you also have someone to love. I am an outcast, and my desire for Podixa's luscious body drives me insane." Kailow revealed.

"I see. That's why we must find the Zeto Crystal. Once we have found the crystal, we can bring more people here. That will make it easier for you to find a mate." Areela said.

"I guess we must have faith that things will work out for the best," Kailow replied, jumped into the water, and swam away from Areela.

'At least I pray for things to work out,' Areela thought as Kailow swam in the direction of Zetani Nova's minor sunset.

"NO....! PLEASE DON'T tell me this is our end...."

Gaia kneeled next to a dead boy in a frosty Mesopotamia, while crying silently. The Mount Toba Ice Age was in full swing, and her brethren were dying wherever Gaia walked on earth. She thought of using her powers to resurrect the boy, but what difference would it make. Unless she saved humanity, the life of one boy was inconsequential.

Why was the True Maker allowing this to happen? Although the planet was a frozen hellhole because of the volcanic eruption, it had the potential for life and beauty. Humanity was supposed to keep living.

Gaia had a vision of a different outcome. With the power of the primordial Zeto Crystal, she could save one tiny area of her planet and turn it into a lush paradise, isolate it from the biting cold outside. She had seen the Garden of Eden in her vision, and it would save humanity. Yet time was running out. She would not find the Zeto Crystal unless True Maker allowed her to, and even if she did, she lacked the technical knowledge to build this garden.

The Zetans... The Zetans were far away, yet they were her only hope to save humanity. Gaia used the innate powers she had gained from having the True Maker inhabit her body, opened a portal, and left the frozen earth.

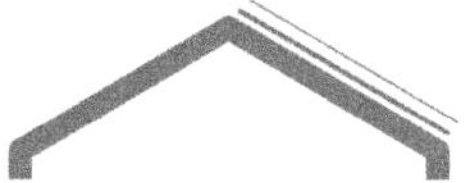

Chapter 21: The Discovery of the Zetani Nova Crystal.

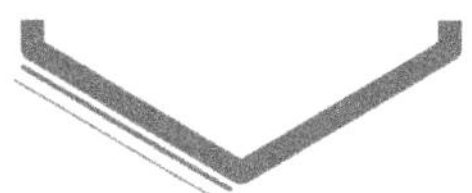

Kailow was walking along a lake when he heard water splashing around a bend on his path. He couldn't see anything because of trees and shrubbery blocking his view, but he sensed a solid psionic presence. This presence was much stronger than he felt while around someone in his entourage. Were there other sentient species on the planet?

He snuck closer to the splashing sound. He didn't know the intentions of the native inhabitants, and he wanted to find out more about them before initiating contact. Kailow snuck up to a viewing spot to overlook the gorge below. What he saw mesmerised his eyes. A stunning humanoid female was bathing by herself while humming on a beautiful and melodic tune in the waist-deep crystal-clear water. The woman had a light tan, a tall, slender body, and long luscious blonde hair. She was unlike anything Kailow had ever seen, and she instantly overtook Podixa's place as the object of his desire.

Kailow felt shameful about his sudden sexual desire. This woman belonged to another species, yet he couldn't keep his eyes off her. He missed his old life on Zetani, where he had other activities to keep his mind occupied. After leaving the Zetani culture and its strict adherence to sexual abstinence, his mind had been trapped in an unending cycle of desire to fornicate.

Kailow decided to head back and tell the others about what he had seen, as it wasn't his place to make the first contact with the native inhabitants. But, as he got up, he stumbled on a sharp rock and spun down the hillside.

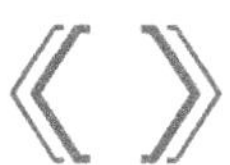

GAIA FELT BLISSFUL while bathing in the beautiful lake on Zetani Nova when the noise from a rockslide startled her. Yet, after the initial shock, she felt curious, so she walked towards the foot of the lake. She was about to get dressed when she heard a moaning under the rubble.

Gaia rushed to the hillside, and she saw a silvery blue hand sticking out under the rocks. Gaia started digging through the rocks, and she faced an unconscious, blue-skinned humanoid being. She had never seen a being like this before. Could this be the Zetan she was looking for, the one True Maker had instructed her to find?

She sensed the man's good aura, and she felt more familiar with him than she had ever felt with humans on earth. Although she was a human, she felt close to this Zetan, as they both had a close affinity to the Zeto Crystal and the True Maker. She looked at the roughed up but handsome blue gentleman. He looked close to her relative age, and he had a large gash on his forehead, which leaked a stream of silvery-blue fresh blood.

Gaia listened to the man's breathing. He was injured, and she needed to save him. However, True Maker had warned her of using her supernatural powers to alter events, and she had warned Gaia about teleporting to Zetani Nova.

'I'll try to save him without using my healing powers,' Gaia thought and lifted the wounded man towards the riverbank. She placed the man in a flat position and fetched her clothes. She tore her clothes as a bandage and cleaned the man's wounds.

Once she had done the bandaging, she sat close to the man. She put her hand on his temple, using her empath abilities to read his mind, to learn about him and his people. She felt at peace while connecting to Kailow, learning about the ancient Zetan prophecies and why he was on Zetani Nova. She felt hungry and went out to look for food while leaving Kailow in a safe location.

"UGH.... MY HEAD... What happened?"

Kailow felt confused as he returned to consciousness and heard the familiar sound of something grilling over a campfire. He remembered falling after seeing a beautiful humanoid bathing, but how had he gotten back to his camp?

"Areela, what happened?" Kailow moaned.

"I am not Areela; I am Gaia," Gaia replied.

Kailow opened his eyes, and Gaia's ultimate sophistication and magnificent beauty took him aback. Her face had a perfect symmetry, and she was the guardian angel who had saved him. Yet, while admiring Gaia's beauty, he also felt afraid. Gaia had the same glowing blue eyes as Thorax had whenever True Maker inhabited his body. Was he facing the embodiment of the supreme deity?

"Don't be afraid, Kailow," Gaia said, and her blue eyes stopped shining.

"How did you do that?" Kailow asked.

"Do what?" Gaia said.

"How did you stop your eyes from glowing?" Kailow asked.

"My eyes glow because of my deep connection with True Maker. But don't be afraid. I am not her." Gaia replied.

"I am not afraid; I am fascinated. So, who are you?" Kailow asked.

"I am a clone of someone who will save True Maker and the Milky Way Galaxy in the future," Gaia replied.

"I don't understand. How can you be a clone of someone who has no physical embodiment?" Kailow asked.

"I am the embodiment of the True Maker in a human form. True Maker saw my form in a vision. She created me as an exact copy of what she saw. We live in the 1000th iteration of the Milky Way Galaxy, and things will turn out differently this time. In all the 999 iterations that have passed, humanity went extinct during the Mount Toba ice age, while the Zetans stagnated and went extinct when Zetani Maximus turned supernova. You are the first Zetan to ever set foot on Zetani Nova, the haven planet for your species after the inevitable destruction of Zetani." Gaia revealed.

"So, are we stuck in a time loop? Is the universe a simulation?" Kailow asked.

Gaia reflected on Kailow's question. It wasn't a farfetched conclusion. It was plausible that True Maker was the controlling software of the simulation. However, if that were the case, did True Maker keep this detail hidden from her, or was True Maker herself unaware of the more comprehensive reality?

Gaia concluded that it didn't matter whether her reality was a simulation. She needed to make sure that humanity survived this iteration of the Milky Way Galaxy. It was her purpose.

"We are not stuck in a time loop. From our perspective, time will be linear and mono-directional. It doesn't matter if True Maker has predicted our actions or not; we have roles to play and lives to safe." Gaia said.

"So, what do we need to do?" Kailow asked.

"This planet's Zeto Crystal lies behind that waterfall over there. Can you save my species on Earth if I show it to you?" Gaia asked.

"I cannot, but my brethren can. Zelinko Siblexom found a way to store the energy from the Zeto Crystal in sapphires. His rival Arish Kisherom invented a nanotechnology dome that protected Disyerto-2's inhabitants from raging sandstorms. If you can get them to work together, we should be able to save your species." Kailow explained.

"Well, follow me then," Gaia chirped, grabbed Kailow's hand, and led him through the secret passageway behind the waterfall.

"HIS DESTINY IS TO MARRY an elven princess on Elvonia. Don't listen to your sexual urges...."

Gaia tried to ignore True Maker's voice that echoed in her head. She was upset that her creator was spying on her, and she felt frustrated by her loneliness and the human need for warmth. Yet, Gaia felt something she had never felt before during her short time with Kailow; she felt a deep connection and purpose. Before meeting him, she had never experienced a normal childhood or had any relationship aside from her associations with True Maker. The True Maker had created her as a young adult, and she had been the physical resting place for the deity during the last three years. Yet she felt she could become more than just an empty vessel for the supreme deity. She was her own person, and that person yearned for Kailow.

"Are you okay, Gaia? What's the matter?" Kailow asked.

"Umm, I am okay. It's just that I have never been in here with someone before." Gaia said shyly.

"Okay. Is it safe to move the Zeto Crystal away from here?" Kailow asked.

Gaia reflected on Kailow's question. Technically, the Zeto Crystal's location didn't matter if it remained on the planet. But then again, what was the purpose of moving the fragment of True Maker's soul out of its beautiful resting place?

"Let's leave it for now, so we can show your kin the crystal in its natural resting place," Gaia concluded.

"Cool. Let's head back to our camp. I am sure everyone will be excited to hear the good news." Kailow chirped.

'Let's hope so,' Gaia thought, nodded, and replied. "Well, lead the way, Kailow."

Gaia held Kailow's hand as they left the sanctuary and felt whole and joyful.

Chapter 22: The Agreement.

Areela felt both fear and excitement as she spotted Kailow walking hand in hand with an alien humanoid. They had come across a sentient alien species, and it was both terrifying and exciting to sense how her brother felt for the human female. As the woman got closer, Areela sensed that she had a Zetan heritage, yet she did not look Zetan. Her head circumference was smaller, and her skin had a strange beige colour, unheard of among the Zetans.

Gaia spotted Areela and spoke, "Hi. My name is Gaia, and I am looking for Zelinko Siblexom and Arish Kisherom."

"Who are you, and why are you holding my brother's hand?" Areela replied.

Gaia reflected on Areela's question. Was she meant to interpret it as a philosophical question or a direct question? She decided to answer the latter.

"I am Gaia, and I am a human with Zetan DNA hidden in my genome. I am a clone of someone who will live 70,000 years from now. Holding your brother's hand gives me comfort as I have been alone for several years." Gaia revealed.

Areela gave Gaia a non-plussed look, and Kailow added in, "Areela, listen to me. Gaia is a friend. We found the Zeto Crystal. We need Zelinko and Arish to work together so we can save her species and ours."

"Okay, I'll find the others. Wait here." Areela said and left the camp.

Gaia and Kailow got seated by the campfire, where a pot was shimmering with a vegetable stew. As the sun was setting behind the mountains that enclosed the valley, it tinted into Kailow's eyes, and Gaia knew one thing. She could not resist the handsome Zetan much longer. She leaned in and kissed him gently, and he instantly returned her kisses with a heated lovemaking passion.

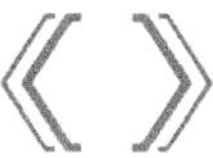

"AHEMMM... EXCUSE ME, both of you should get a room!"

Gaia and Kailow stopped kissing when Podixa teased them. Kailow looked at the former object of his desire. He felt glad that his passion for her had subsided, yet he felt awkward that she walked in on him.

Gaia was unaware of Kailow's unrequited love for Podixa, so she replied, "Hi, I am Gaia. How do you and Kailow know each other?"

"I am a friend of his sister, Areela. You two are beautiful together. I am so glad that Kailow found someone. His solitude added a layer of complexity to the already strained relationships in our group." Podixa replied.

"I am glad that I met Kailow as well. If I may ask, what problems are you facing?" Gaia asked.

Podixa sighed and looked away. Now that she needed to explain their conflict to the alien, she felt silly, and she wished that they had been able to resolve their disputes independently. But unfortunately, old grievances were often the most difficult to resolve.

"Zelinko belonged to the master caste that deported my husband and me to a desert planet for the crime of falling in love," Podixa said.

"How can love be illegal on Zetani? I thought the Zetans were an intelligent species." Gaia said.

"Love itself is not banned. However, conceiving outside of the Midsummer celebration is. We were young and couldn't help ourselves. I am sure that you can understand our predicament."

Gaia looked at Kailow, and she yearned for him. Being 200-year-old as a Zetan was like being eighteen as a human, and she was still merely seventeen. Inhibiting her carnal desire for a whole year would be very difficult, so she understood Podixa's predicament.

"I understand. Was it Zelinko that ordered your deportation?" Gaia asked.

"No, it was Judge Jasper Javonom," Podixa replied.

"Whom Zelinko killed when escaping Zetani. So, you should stop blaming my brother-in-law for what happened to you." Kailow exclaimed.

"I guess you are right. We need to forgive to strive for a common goal," Podixa said.

Gaia was about to reply when something caught her eyes. A beast-like toddler with claws and purple eyes were crawling toward her. The baby's physical appearance was not disturbing, but the realisation that the True Maker had inhabited this body was.

"You never told me that there were others like me," Gaia whispered to True Maker.

I am telling you what you need to know. Other information can set you on a different path. True Maker replied.

"I would prefer if you were upfront and forthcoming with me." Gaia telepathed the True Maker.

It's the basic tenet of this galaxy that all living species have a free will. So, if I tell you about things that will happen, that eliminates your free will, and it will take you on the wrong path. True Maker replied.

"Welcome to Zetani Nova. I am Zelinko Siblexom. I heard you had news about the Zeto Crystal." Zelinko said, which broke Gaia's connection to True Maker. Gaia looked at the Zetan male. He was older than Kailow, and he had an air of authority that the youngish object of her desire lacked.

"Yes, we found it. But you need to promise that you'll help me save humanity if I show it to you." Gaia said.

"You have my word. Yet I cannot speak for Arish Kisherom. You'll need his technical know-how to build a sanctuary for your species." Zelinko replied.

"I am willing to help. If we find a way to Zeto-charge the sapphires, I'll bring my people here, and we'll commit to helping humans on earth." Arish interjected.

Gaia looked at the Zetan scientist who had joined the group. She could tell that the dynamics in the group weren't ideal, yet she wanted to find out about the men's real intentions.

"Zelinko and Arish, please come to me," Gaia commanded while her eyes started to glow blue.

The Zetans hesitated. While they had seen the presence of True Maker when she possessed Thorax's body, it was more awe-inspiring when a beautiful human female commanded them. At the height of her power, Gaia was as terrifying as she was alluring.

Eventually, the Zetans heeded Gaia's command and approached her. She grabbed their arms and formed an emphatic bond with the two men. She sensed that they loathed each other, yet they would work together towards a common goal. Thus, they would do everything they could to fulfil their promise to save humanity.

"I'll lead you to the Zeto Crystals. Let's go tomorrow. It's a long walk, and I would rather not walk in the dark." Gaia said.

"We understand. Please dine with us, Herald of the True Maker, and we'll follow you tomorrow." Zelinko said.

"Thank you, Zelinko," Gaia said and got seated next to Kailow.

As they served her grilled fish and vegetables, Gaia felt happy that she was part of a group. Finally, after years of solitude, she had the chance to achieve her goals and become part of something greater than herself.

Chapter 23: The Departure.

Zelinko stood silent as he absorbed the ambient energy of the beautiful Zeto Crystal, which had a different tint than the Zetani Zeto Crystal. This Zeto Crystal felt purer as if millennia of usage on his home planet had made the Zetani crystal fade.

Zelinko looked at the bag of sapphires he held in his left hand. It was time for him to make a decision. He could share the secret of charging the crystals for the greater good or keep the secret to himself. However, choosing to be altruistic could be dangerous. If the others knew how to charge the sapphires, they had no use for him, and his life would be in danger.

Zelinko turned to the others and spoke, "I must request you to leave."

"Why?" Arish replied angrily.

"Because being the only one capable of Zeto-charging the gemstones is my life insurance. You imprisoned me for two months, Arish. You would throw me to the wolves when I tell you my secret."

Hearing this, Arish flushed with distinct streaks of silver-green anger on his face. He clenched his fists, and a confrontation seemed imminent.

Gaia telepathed to the True Maker, "Should I intervene, mother?"

"No, let them sort it out by themselves." True Maker replied.

"But if Zelinko refuses to share the information, he puts everyone at risk. What happens to Zetan civilisation if he dies?" Gaia asked.

"Well, this is my plan. Don't intervene, Gaia. You'll save humanity and fulfil your destiny." True Maker replied.

Gaia broke the connection with True Maker, grabbed Arish's hand, and telepathed to him, "Let Zelinko win this time. You can find out how to charge the sapphires later." Arish looked in surprise at Gaia, nodded at Zelinko, and left the cave without a word. The others followed suit until only Gaia and Zelinko remained in the room.

"I am sorry, but I need you to leave," Zelinko said.

"I already know the secret chant to charge the crystals," Gaia said to Zelinko.

"That might be true, but I don't want the others to know that you know," Zelinko replied.

Gaia studied Zelinko while waiting for True Maker to say anything. The supreme deity stayed silent, so Gaia said, "When you chant, replace Mua Zetani with Mua Zetani Nova to activate this planet's crystal.

Having said this, Gaia left the cave, so Zelinko could uphold the illusion that he was the only one who knew how to Zeto-charge the sapphires.

ARISH FELT EXCITED when he saw the large haul of charged gemstones upon Zelinko's return. These stones would be enough to power a portal for transporting his people and equipment from Disyerto-2 to Zetani Nova. Such an excellent opportunity to find a new home for his people and become the leader of this new Zetan civilisation.

As for Zelinko, Arish thought of a solution to his rival's uncooperativeness. He would try to insert a nano-robot into his rival in secrecy, which would record his actions. That way, he could learn what he did to charge the sapphires.

The Zetans gathered to discuss the next step.

"So, now that we have bags full of charged sapphires, we need to head back to Disyerto-2 and find as many settlers for this planet as possible. It's the only way to start up this colony, which will be the jewel of Zetan civilisation." Arish said.

"I agree, but who should stay and who should go? I am not willing to risk my child's life on the dangerous crossing through the Divine Dimension." Areela replied.

"Well, feel free to stay then. Besim and I are following my husband back to Disyerto-2." Podixa snapped.

"They all need to go for the ideal outcome to occur." True Maker whispered to Gaia.

"I'll stay. I can look after Thorax for you." Gaia said.

"Hmm, I am not willing to leave my child with a stranger," Areela replied.

"I'll stay as well. We can look after Thorax for you. Zelinko will need you on the journey." Kailow said to Areela.

"Thanks, brother. I feel at peace knowing that you are looking after my child." Areela smiled.

"You need to ascertain that Kailow goes with his sister." True Maker whispered to Gaia.

"That's my choice to make," Gaia replied and blocked out the True Maker.

"So, have we all come to a decision?" Gaia said and smiled at everyone.

"Yes. Zelinko, Areela, Podixa, Besim and I will leave at sunrise. You, Kailow, and Thorax will stay behind and clear an opening in the forest for our new settlers." Arish replied.

"I agree. Let's have dinner and prepare for departure. We have already lost valuable time looking for the Zeto Crystal; the sooner we get moving, the better." Zelinko added in.

Having said this, the group got seated for dinner. They ate in silent anticipation of the days ahead.

THE FOLLOWING MORNING, Gaia witnessed how the other Zetans left Zetani Nova through a makeshift portal. The portal Arish had built consisted of a few metal rods formed together in a pyramid shape with slots for six sapphires. However, he had made plans for building huge portals with hundreds of connected gemstones to enable the teleportation of massive objects.

The building material of the pyramid shape wasn't important, but the symmetry was. The centre of the energy field needed to be in the centre of the structure; otherwise, unpleasant fluctuations could occur. Using a symmetrical pyramid shape, a prism at the top could spread concentrated sunlight to energise the connected gemstones, creating a stronger interdimensional connection.

Gaia noticed that nothing was left behind after the Zetans had left. Thus, Arish's portal worked as intended. Gaia looked at Kailow and felt blissful. She was on a paradise planet with the man she loved. Yet, Gaia also had a slight foreboding feeling. She didn't like that her relationship with Kailow was against True Maker's wishes.

Chapter 24: A Forbidden Attraction.

"I *forbid you from fornicating with Kailow."*
Gaia shook in frustration when the loud voice of The True Maker echoed in the back of her head. She was at her breaking point. For two weeks, she had been alone with Kailow on this beautiful planet, and except for babysitting Thorax, they had plenty of time for themselves. They had been close to engaging in naked yoga on many occasions, but True Maker commanded her to stop when things got hot.

"Are you alright? We can stop if you want to," Kailow said.

"No, I want you. This has gone on for long enough. I have free will, and if True Maker wants to stop me, she can claim control of my body. Enter me, so our souls can become one."

Kailow looked at Gaia. She was as frightening as she was alluring when her eyes shifted from pastel blue to glowing blue while Gaia and True Maker wrestled for control over the body.

'I need to sleep with this woman, even if it is the last thing I'll do in my life,' Kailow thought and entered Gaia.

As they were grinding in ecstasy, a bright flash of pure energy blinded Kailow. He regained his vision and looked at the beautiful woman under him. Her eyes had reverted to pastel blue, and she smiled at him with a blissful look. "Thank you for setting me free," Gaia mumbled.

As Kailow had been a virgin before this encounter, he went full steam ahead, grinding and thrusting like a raging horse, and shortly afterwards, he came, his body quivered in ecstasy. He rolled over next to the sweaty and blissful Gaia, and together they panted in unison.

"Was it good for you as well?" Kailow asked.

"Yes, it feels amazing to be free from her presence, to have free will," Gaia said, feeling wonderful but at the same time also feeling worried. If she lost her connection with True Maker, she would lose her immortality, and she could fail her mission to save humanity from extinction.

"I need to be alone for a bit. I need to reconcile what this means for my life." Gaia said and got up.

Kailow looked at the beautiful female he had made love to just moments ago. He would let her make her choice, yet he hoped they would end up together.

Gaia walked away from Kailow, got seated under a waterfall, and allowed the streaming warm water to carry away the tears that flowed from her eyes.

"I FORGIVE YOU."

Gaia opened her eyes. In front of her stood a woman in her mid-fifties, who looked like an older version of herself. What was going on?

"Are you the True Maker?" Gaia asked.

The woman nodded and replied, "Yes. I realised that you struggled to connect with my spirit form, so I created a form that seems more motherlike to you. I am Ellen Hines, your mother in the 21st century, 70,000 years from now."

Gaia shook her head and replied, "I like your spirit form better as this woman means nothing to me. While her genes match my future mother's, she doesn't exist yet, and we don't have a connection."

"I understand," True Maker replied, snapped her fingers, and Ellen's body evaporated into thin air.

Bzzzzzz

"Woah, why did you kill her?" Gaia said.

I did not kill her. She was never alive as I never gave her a soul. True Maker replied.

"So, what happens now?" Gaia asked.

We stay on track. I have reviewed your timeline. Everything can work out the way I intended. True Maker replied.

"So, are you not angry because of me and Kailow anymore?" Gaia asked.

"Angry? I was never angry about your actions. But as your creator, I wanted what's best for you. Your actions will cause you heartache, but they make no difference in the grand scheme of things." True Maker replied.

"Thank you," Gaia replied and got up.

She felt happy that True Maker had approved her relationship with Kailow. Without the supreme deity's condemnation of her relationship, she would enjoy it as much as possible.

KAILOW WAS ENJOYING a nap in the shade when something awoke him. His nephew approached him with a dead rabbit in his mouth. Yet, Thorax was only a year old; how could such a young toddler be able to hunt for prey?

"Oooncle, Thorax cwaatch rryyaabbit." Thorax chirped while his purple eyes glittered in the sun, and fresh blood dripped from his fangs.

Kailow flinched away from the mutant toddler. He had been babysitting Thorax for three months, and he had never heard the child speak, yet now the child had killed a prey animal and said a complete sentence.

"Is oooncle maad at Thorax?" Thorax asked.

"Umm, no. I am just shocked. I didn't know you could speak?" Kailow said.

"No speeeeaking before fyirst preyy. Thwwat's the law." Thorax replied.

"That's not the law. Who told you that?" Kailow replied.

"Thwwat is the Xeno laaaw." Thorax stated.

"Okay. Good kid, enjoy your catch." Kailow said and got up in a hurry.

Kailow walked away from Thorax as the toddler feasted on the rabbit hungrily. Something was seriously wrong with the 1-year-old freak whom he was babysitting. He hoped that his sister would arrive with the Disyerto-2 settlers soon, as he couldn't wait to leave the freaky child in someone else's care.

Chapter 25: A Flattened Valley

Gaia and Kailow were eating grapes in a cave when Thorax ran towards them on all four and started muttering gibberish. They looked at the child-beast in surprise. After finding out that Thorax could chase prey and speak at the age of 1, they had spent less time minding the baby, as Thorax had a different developmental curve than other Zetans.

"A storm... A storm is coming...." Thorax exclaimed.

At first, they didn't understand what Thorax was talking about. Then they sensed a breeze that increased in intensity, and they heard the faraway noise of thunder and cracking tree trunks. Gaia ran towards a cave entrance, and she looked at the sky. A massive tornado had formed close to the Zeto Crystal's location, and the skies were dark from stormy clouds.

A shockwave is coming. Take cover behind that rock." True Maker instructed.

Gaia picked up Thorax, grabbed Kailow, and exclaimed, "Take cover behind that rock!"

They reached their cover on the brink of time as the shockwave passed above them and flattened the valley.

Gaia looked through her cover after the shockwave had passed. Several Zetan spaceships had arrived.

"Come, let's look for survivors!" Gaia urged, which prompted Kailow to follow her in the direction of the spaceships.

"OH NO! WHAT A DISASTER."

Arish felt heartbroken when he returned with a fleet of settlers from Disyerto-2. His calculations had been correct. Arriving from the Divine Dimension unleashed as much energy as it took to reach the dimension. Since he had come with 10,000 tonnes of supplies and manpower, his arrival on Zetani Nova had unleashed the equivalence of a nuclear detonation in the beautiful valley. It was a shame seeing such destruction in the place where he had spent months looking for the Zeto Crystal.

"What happened to the valley?" Areela exclaimed.

"Our arrival from Dihawara Densi started an exotherm reaction equalled our tonnage's potential energy," Arish replied.

"What do you mean?" Areela asked.

"We crashed from heaven. Somehow the environment had to take the hit instead of us. I think this is because the energy burst comes before our arrival instead of simultaneously," Arish explained.

"Why didn't you warn us about this? Kailow and Thorax were somewhere in the valley. We must find them." Areela exclaimed.

"We are alright."

Areela took a deep breath of relief when Gaia, Thorax, and Kailow came running toward her. As demoralising as the destruction of the beautiful valley was, she felt relieved that her kin was unharmed.

"What happened? Why did you blow up the valley?" Kailow asked.

"Ask Arish. Apparently, he forgot to mention that coming here with a large spaceship would set off a massive energy burst." Areela sniped.

"Uhm, don't blame me. I can't know what will happen with new, untested technology." Arish replied.

"What are you talking about? You ran several tests on Disyerto-2." Areela replied.

"Never on this scale. I couldn't risk flattening our city." Arish replied.

Gaia zoned out from the Zetans argument. As sad as the destruction of the valley was, it was temporary. Besides, the settlers would have cut down a large part of the forest to build their settlement in any case.

A more urgent problem reached Gaia's mind. What had happened to the Zeto Crystal when the shockwave flattened the valley? They needed the Zeto Crystal to get this colony up and running.

"We need to hurry to the Zeto Crystal's resting place. I sense that the crystal might have gone missing."

Having exclaimed this, Gaia grabbed Kailow and hurried to Zeto Crystal's resting place with the others in tow.

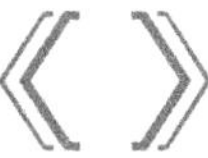

"OH NO! THE MOUNTAIN collapsed from the shockwave."

Gaia felt heartbroken when she saw how the shockwave from the explosion had collapsed the cave that hid the Zeto Crystal. While the crystal itself was indestructible, it would take a lot of time to excavate the mountain to find it. Time was of the essence, as there were less than two years until humanity would go extinct.

Fearing that she wouldn't be able to save her species, Gaia collapsed, and she was inconsolable for the rest of the day.

Chapter 26: Gaia's Dilemma.

Kailow was looking at Gaia, who slept next to him. She had been moody in the last few weeks as they lost track of the Zeto Crystal. The crystal was missing deep below the mountains that collapsed when the Zetans landed in the Arishome Valley. Kailow found it ironic that Arish had named the valley after himself as his actions destroyed it. However, the name of the valley was the least of his concerns.

Kailow pitied Gaia as she was losing hope to save her species. Yet he didn't blame his fellow citizens for not prioritising her needs. They were settling on a new planet, and their needs were more important than the prospect of helping an alien to look for a magical artifact. Besides, wouldn't it be better if humanity were to go extinct? If they stalled for two more years, no other sentient species would remain on earth. In that scenario, the Zetan colonisation of the planet and the appropriation of the Zeto Crystal would be a victimless affair.

'Come on, Kailow. You are better than this,' Kailow thought and slapped himself. It was cruel and selfish to consider letting another race go extinct to make room for his species. "I am sorry, Gaia." He mumbled, but she didn't reply as she was in a deep sleep.

Did she know about his inner thoughts? Kailow was in awe of Gaia's empath abilities. Although other Zetans had similar abilities, he could counteract them. Although he wasn't as powerful as others, they could not use him like a puppet.

However, Gaia was different. Her powers stemmed from True Maker and were far beyond anyone on the planet. Yet, she had an inner conflict that terrified him. He didn't know if he admired Gaia's persona or connection to True Maker. He was a mere mortal; was he worthy of loving the embodiment of a deity?

"You are great, Gaia. I just wish there weren't two souls within your body," Kailow mumbled, tucked Gaia in, and walked to a lookout to watch the stars. The night sky was beautiful on Zetani Nova, and it was so different from the sky he had grown up with on Zetani. In the distance, he spotted Zetani Maximus, the blue giant star that his home planet orbited. As he thought about his home planet, which was 500 lightyears away, he felt bittersweet and wished that he could turn back time and re-live his youth.

GAIA SAW A BEAUTIFUL humanoid who admired her reflection in a Zeto Crystal. Watching the attractive female made Gaia feel overwhelmed by jealousy. At first, she did not know what caused her anger. Why did the sight of a beautiful woman and a Zeto Crystal anger her? Seeing a Zeto Crystal was a good sign. If she could pinpoint the location of the crystal, she could convince Zelinko and Arish to visit the planet. Once they were there, they could Zeto-charge enough sapphires to run a conservatory for her fellow humans on Earth until the Mount Toba ice age got milder.

"Princess Imogen. Your father is summoning you to the throne room."

Hearing the dialogue in her vision, Gaia knew who the woman was. She was an elven princess of Elvonia. True Maker had stated that Kailow would marry an elven princess; thus, Imogen must be Kailow's future wife. Seeing her future rival in a dream, Gaia uttered a high-pitched scream and woke up.

"ARE YOU OKAY, GAIA?"

Gaia looked at Kailow, and she felt angry. How could he dump her for that royal skank? Why would this happen?

She bit her lip and replied, "Yes, I am fine. It was only a nightmare."

"Are you sure? You have seemed so distant lately." Kailow replied.

"You would also act distant if the survival of your species was hanging in the balance while everyone is abandoning you!" Gaia exclaimed and rushed off.

Gaia sought solace. She hated this place for what it had become. What had been a paradise was now a blown-out valley where construction work was going on around the clock. Why couldn't the Zetans fulfil their promise? She had helped them, so why did they refuse to grant her the same favour?

"Tell Zelinko and Arish about the Zeto Crystal on Elvonia. They will help you charge enough sapphires to create a conservatory on earth." True Maker said.

"I don't want to lose Kailow. You told me that Kailow will marry an elven princess." Gaia protested. *"You have already lost Kailow. The seed of doubt in his mind is growing stronger every day, and there is nothing you can do to reverse the course."* True Maker replied.

"Nonsense. I am beautiful, and I have been great to Kailow. So why wouldn't he love me." Gaia objected.

"Because it isn't your destiny to be loved. Look into his mind if you don't believe me." True Maker replied.

"I don't care about destiny. I have free will, and Kailow will love me." Gaia exclaimed.

"That is your ego talking. Farewell, for now, Gaia." True Maker replied and ended the connection.

As the True Maker disappeared, Kailow approached Gaia and spoke, "Your eyes were flashing. Were you talking to her?"

"Yes," Gaia replied.

"What did she say?" Kailow asked.

"I don't want to talk about it," Gaia said.

"I understand," Kailow said and gave Gaia a sympathetic look.

Gaia hesitated for a second, but she couldn't resist the urge to reveal her genuine emotions. If she didn't trust Kailow, then who else could she trust?

"She said that I wasn't destined to be loved." Gaia sobbed.

"So, so. Your mother is only telling you what you need to hear. That is all she ever does." Kailow replied and hugged Gaia.

Gaia enjoyed the hug, and she would have loved it if Kailow's words were sincere. Yet they weren't, and she knew she had accelerated the inevitable. Yet she wouldn't give up on her love. Although the supreme deity conspired against her relationship, she would do anything to save it.

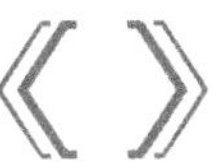

THE FOLLOWING DAY, Gaia entered the newly erected town hall for the Podixania colony, named after Podixa Sairan. While it was bemusing that Arish had named the valley after himself and the settlement after his wife, Gaia had a more important matter to attend to. She needed to convince Arish and Zelinko to fulfil their parts of the bargain. They had promised her that they would Zeto-charge sapphires and help her save her species. They had blamed the delays on the disappearance of the Zeto Crystal, but with an available Zeto Crystal on Elvonia, they had no excuse for not going.

Gaia got seated in a meeting room, and the two leaders approached her with a carafe of wine. "Behold the first vintage of Zetani Nova, cultivated in the regions of Arishome valley," Zelinko said and poured three glasses of exquisite red wine.

"How is this possible? You arrived three months ago, and you flattened the valley." Gaia asked in bewilderment.

"We sent scouts surveying the landscape. As a result, we found vast amounts of wild grapes to the south, which were perfect for our first vintage." Zelinko replied and smiled.

Hearing this infuriated Gaia. The Zetans had claimed to be too busy to excavate the mountains to look for the Zeto Crystal, yet they had wasted a lot of time and effort finding a way of making alcohol. How was that a sensible priority?

Gaia hid her anger, tasted the wine, and spoke, "Elvonia, which is on the way to earth, has a Zeto Crystal in a temple close to their Royal Palace. I would appreciate it if we went there, charged our sapphires, and headed to Earth to save my species."

Arish and Zelinko looked at each other. Neither of the Zetans was keen to leave while the other stayed on Zetani Nova. Despite cooperating while establishing Podixania, they didn't trust each other.

"Unfortunately, we cannot take a spaceship to Elvonia. We haven't established a safe way to land through the dimensions, and we would hate to cause collateral damage to the elves." Arish said.

"I know, and we don't need a spaceship," Gaia said.

"How are we to build a large dome on earth if we don't have enough materials?" Arish asked.

"We don't need a large dome anymore. Because of your stalling, there won't be many humans left. So, we need to find the few humans remaining and bring them to a smaller facility where we provide food and shelter." Gaia ranted.

"Gaia is correct. We should help her save her species." Zelinko said.

"Bah, that's easy for you to say. You'll need my expertise to build the facility on earth, and I have a planet to run. I plan to link up all the former Zetan penal colonies in Disyerto-2 and turn Zetani Nova into something marvellous." Arish stated.

"If you let me help Gaia, I promise to stay on earth. That will be the end of our rivalry." Zelinko stated.

Arish reflected on Zelinko's promise. It could be a great way to get rid of his rival without dishonouring himself by resorting to violence.

"We have an agreement. If you make a public proclamation that you will not return to Zetani Nova, I will help you." Arish said.

"We have a deal," Zelinko said, skolled his wine, shook Arish's hand, and left the meeting room.

Gaia took a deep sigh of relief. Finally, the first part of her plan came to fruition. Now she needed to convince Kailow to follow her to earth while staying away from Elvonia. If she could pull that off, she could fulfil her purpose while staying in a relationship with the man she loved.

Chapter 27: Farewell to Zetani Nova.

Areela Kheeran was packing her bags for the upcoming trip to Elvonia and Earth. It felt bittersweet to leave the paradise planet Zetani Nova such a short time after they found it, but they needed to move on. She had promised to help Gaia do everything they could to save humanity, as requested by True Maker. What kind of person would she be if she backed down on that promise? Besides, breaking promises to the supreme deity seemed dangerous, although True Maker had never explicitly warned what would happen if Areela didn't keep her promise.

As Areela was planning on her trip, Thorax walked up to her. Areela looked at her beasty son. He had grown to be as tall as a 10-year-old child, despite being only a year and a half. Areela felt fearful when she was in Thorax's presence, which pained her. What kind of mother felt this way around her child?

Thorax's eyes were shining blue, which indicated that True Maker was talking through him. True Maker's presence in him was foreboding, and it was now a rare occurrence, as True Maker had used Gaia for communicating since their paths crossed a year earlier.

"Mother, I have come to bid thee farewell," Thorax said.

"What are you talking about, my son? You are coming with us to Elvonia and Earth." Areela replied. "No, I cannot come with you. My destiny will take me elsewhere." Thorax replied.

Areela looked at Thorax and struggled to look happy. She couldn't smile while bidding farewell, yet she felt this was for the best. "So, what is your destiny, my son?" Areela asked.

"My destiny is to stay here until she instructs me otherwise. True Maker doesn't have many heralds in this galaxy; it's a waste to keep us in the same place," Thorax replied.

"But my son, you are less than two years old. Who is going to look after you?" Areela objected.

"Podixa will look after me. I have already spoken to her. This is my farewell," Thorax said, and his eye colour reverted to purple.

As Thorax reverted to himself, he looked at Areela in confusion and said, "Mamma? Hungry?"

Before Areela had answered, Thorax spotted a rabbit. He sprinted on all four and slashed the rabbit with his sharp claws. After that, he carried the dead rabbit between his teeth and dropped it at Areela's feet.

"Thorax loves mammma. Thorax brought a present for mummy." Thorax said and smiled with blood dripping from his mouth.

"Thanks. Mummy loves you as well." Areela replied and patted Thorax on the head while she secretly thought, 'I better follow True Maker's instructions and leave this beast child here.'

LATER THE SAME DAY, Areela spotted Gaia and Podixa at the public baths. They were submerged in the warm water from a thermal spring, drinking wine while listening to meditative Zetan music. Areela entered the rockpool, and she decided to discuss the dilemma she faced with her son.

"Podixa, Thorax said you promised to look after him while I am away?" Areela said.

Podixa put down her wine chalice. She sensed hostility from Areela, but she couldn't pinpoint why. "Yes, he approached me while he was under the influence of the True Maker and asked whether I would look after him in your absence. I wasn't going to argue with the supreme deity, so I accepted."

"Why didn't you discuss this with me? I am his mother!" Areela exclaimed.

"I assumed that he had discussed it with you. No one is happier than me if you bring that freaky kid on your journey." Podixa replied.

Hearing this, Areela was about to burst into anger, but Gaia intervened, grabbed her arm, and soothed Areela's mind with her empath powers. Areela broke down and cried, "I feel like such a terrible mother. I am relieved that Thorax is not coming with us. I am terrified and disgusted by him." Areela sobbed.

Gaia held Areela's hand, looked into her eyes, and spoke. "Don't feel terrible. The truth is that Thorax has the genome of the Xenos, a fierce and proud species, which are dissimilar to the Zetans."

"The Xenos? I have never heard about them. How could Xialiab turn my child into a monster!?" Areela exclaimed.

"Xialiab wanted to make your child as disfigured as possible from the Zetan perspective. So, when he altered Thorax's DNA, the result became a Xeno/Zetan hybrid by chance." Gaia explained.

"But Thorax's destiny was to be the Chosen One. So why did True Maker allow Xialiab to disfigure him?" Areela sobbed.

"The disfigurement turned him into the Chosen One. Without Xialiab's intervention, you would have given birth to a normal child. In that scenario, Zelinko wouldn't have acknowledged the child as his, and you would have ended up on Disyerto-2 with Podixa." Gaia revealed.

Hearing this, Areela sighed, poured some wine, and drank it blindly. Then, Podixa spoke, "If True Maker gives us free will, how can she know what choices we will make?"

"Because True Maker doesn't only have power over time, she is time. So, she knows what choices you'll make." Gaia replied.

"But she won't tell us what will happen?" Podixa asked.

"If she did, you would no longer have free will," Gaia replied.

"What about you? Do you know what will happen in your life?" Podixa asked.

"No, because that would invalidate my free will. However, the most interesting thing in this iteration of the Milky Way Galaxy is that True Maker doesn't know what will happen to herself...." Gaia replied.

"How can that be?" Podixa asked.

"Because no one, not even the True Maker, can see events that take them past their own death," Gaia replied.

"Wow, this got dark very quickly. Let's drink some wine and focus on what we can do now, and let's enjoy our last day on Zetani Nova together." Areela said and raised her chalice.

"Cheers to the present," Gaia replied, and they drank their wine while letting the healing springs rejuvenate their bodies.

ARISH KISHEROM WAS making the finishing touches for the future inter-dimensional landing facility on Zetani Nova. Six months earlier, when they had landed and flattened Arishome Valley, they had unleashed an enormous energy burst as they arrived from the Divine Dimension, as they didn't have a proper landing facility. Arish had thought of a theoretical solution, but he hadn't been able to put it to practical use because of the difficulties of setting up a new colony.

Arish looked at the plans. The ideal landing platform would be inside a vacuum in an underground bunker with the shape of a pyramid. If the landing from Dihawara Densi took place in a vacuum, it couldn't create a destructive shockwave. But where would the excess energy go? The laws of thermodynamics stated that energy couldn't disappear; it could only turn into other forms of energy.

'Hmm, the Zeto-charged sapphires break against the laws of thermodynamics,' Arish thought. If he left the sapphires in a vacuumized bunker, they should attract the excess energy that the landings released.

Arish summoned his assistant Amela Andelan to the landing site office in the Karmena Mountains, 100 kilometres north of Podixania. She looked displeased as she arrived and spoke, "Master Arish, I heard that you left Podixa Sairan in charge of Podixania during your expedition to Earth."

"Yes, my wife is loyal and a fitting ruler in my absence," Arish replied.

"But why is she not coming with you? Wouldn't you rather have her by your side?" Amela replied.

Arish studied Amela. He knew what his assistant was after, and yes, she was more competent than Podixa, whose main strengths were her sexy body and her capability of giving him healthy offspring.

"Podixa is staying in Podixania to look after my children. I do not wish to drag them along on a dangerous mission to Earth in the middle of an ice age. Besides, I am giving you a more important mission than my wife." Arish said.

"I don't understand. What are we building here?" Amela asked.

"We are building the future of interstellar travel. For eons, our species have travelled through space to reach other worlds. Our generation is the first to travel through the dimensions instead. This reimagining of space travel will change everything, and I am leaving you in charge of figuring out better ways to travel in the future." Arish said and handed Amela a device with blueprints on it.

Amela opened three-dimensional blueprints, studied them for a while, and spoke, "These blueprints are impossible to build. Your plans defy the laws of physics."

"Yet here we are, 450 lightyears from home, travelling through the dimensions while breaking the known laws of physics. If anyone could build these designs, it is you." Arish said and kissed Amela.

"I will not fail you, Master Arish," Amela replied shyly.

"Good. I am returning to Podixania now. I will see you when I return. Sooner rather than later, I hope," Arish stated.

Amela licked her lips and seduced, "Master Arish, would you mind giving me a proper farewell before you go."

Arish smiled and unbuttoned his pants; he wouldn't mind that at all!

GAIA LOOKED AT THE temporary pyramid-like structure that Arish had built on the Karmena Mountains. While the makeshift portal structure looked unimpressive, Gaia had visions of the future when such buildings would become massive interdimensional portal platforms. A colossal pyramid covered in gold and gemstones flashed before her eyes. At some point, the Zetan civilisation would be powerful and wealthy beyond measure, thanks to Arish.

Gaia approached the hovercraft where Zelinko, Areela, Kailow, Arish, and a dozen other Zetans were waiting for her.

Kailow walked up to Gaia and teased, "Good morning, sleeping beauty. Are you excited about our expedition?"

Gaia felt silly that she was the last to arrive for the briefing and replied, "Yes, I am sorry I am late."

"All good. We hoped that you had changed your mind so we wouldn't need to travel 100,000 kilometres to visit your icy home planet," Arish taunted.

Gaia didn't reply to Arish's provocation. She knew that he was too fearful of True Maker to betray his promise, so it was just as well if he handled his disapproval by taunting her.

Instead of arguing with Arish, Gaia looked at the vehicles he had constructed for the expedition. They were impressive. The primary vehicle was a hovercraft spaceship with sleeping pods for 50 people and storage space for a two-year expedition. In addition, there were four smaller hovercrafts, spacesuits, and respirators for different thermal conditions inside the large hovercraft.

Arish pointed towards the hovercraft and spoke, "Behold the Terra-1 hovercraft, the first hovercraft powered by Zeto-charged sapphires. It will take us to places where we have never been before. Our first destination is Elvonia, where we will contact the Elves to seek an alliance. For the new Zetan empire! Mua Zetani Nova!"

"For the new Zetan empire! Mua Zetani Nova!" The men chanted and boarded the hovercraft.

Hearing their intentions made Gaia sad. She had hoped that the Zetans would traverse the galaxy to help save humanity, but they seemed more intent on other reasons.

"Everything will happen as it is meant to happen," True Maker whispered.

True Maker's words made Gaia forget her objections. Instead, she entered Arish's hovercraft and left Zetani Nova, never to return.

Chapter 28: Stuck in the Gravity Well.

Gaia woke up as she was thrown out of bed when the hovercraft spaceship struck a hard object, hitting her head against the wall. At first, she was clueless about what had happened. The hovercraft had crashed, but how? The Divine Dimension was an endless flat plain, so how could one crash a vehicle under such circumstances?

She tried to get up, but she couldn't. Although she had a small gash on her chin, she didn't feel injured. However, she felt too heavy to move.

"Someone, please help me...."

Gaia froze when she heard an agonising voice coming from the sleeping pod. Someone was injured, and she needed to save the person immediately.

"Mother, what is going on?" Gaia shouted.

"You are stuck in a gravity well coming from a black hole. It is nothing to worry about." The True Maker replied.

"What do you mean!? How can being stuck in a black hole not be a problem?" Gaia exclaimed. *"Since you're in a higher dimension than the Milky Way Galaxy, you are not thorned to shreds by the gravitational force. You are just too heavy to move."* True Maker replied.

"But if we are stuck here forever, we'll die, and we won't be able to save humanity," Gaia exclaimed. *"You won't be stuck forever. The black hole is moving at 10 per cent of the speed of light. It will move away from your location in a couple of hours, and you'll be free to move."*

"I understand. Thanks for telling me." Gaia replied and closed her connection with True Maker.

True Maker's words calmed Gaia, but another thing frustrated her. Kailow and the other crew members were screaming in panic, and she hated her inability to help them. Their screams tormented Gaia, and she felt hopeless, unable to save her friends. 'I hope these hours will go fast,' Gaia prayed as she closed her eyes to meditate.

"GAIA, WAKE UP. ARE you alright?"

When Gaia opened her eyes, Kailow was on the floor next to her, and his silvery-blue skin was drenched with drops of silvery sweat, perspiring from the exertion of pushing himself. Gaia looked at Kailow; she had never seen him this tired before. She tried to get up, but the gravity from the black hole was still too strong.

"Yes, I am fine. We are on top of a black hole tearing through the galaxy. Once it moves past us, gravity should restore to normal, and we'll be able to move." Gaia replied.

"When will this happen?" Kailow asked.

"True Maker said it will take a couple of hours," Gaia replied.

"A couple of hours? We can't stay like this for a couple of hours. What if someone is hurt?" Kailow exclaimed.

Gaia realised that Kailow was correct. True Maker had a chilling indifference to individual life. It was understandable for an eternal supreme deity to feel that way, but Gaia valued life more as a mortal. Unfortunately, she had accepted True Maker's assurances without finding out for herself. Would she be able to forgive herself if her complacency caused the death of one of her companions?

"Okay, I will get up," Gaia said and rolled over to a crawling position.

"I heard that Nayanika was screaming for help before, but she has been silent. We better hurry." Kailow urged and pushed himself towards Nayanika's quarters.

Gaia followed Kailow, and she felt annoyed that her mother didn't lend her a fraction of her power, as she only had the strength of a regular human without it.

As they approached Nayanika's sleeping pod in slow-motion, they discovered that the female crew member was dead. A railing had fallen unto her, and it had crushed her under the enormous weight it had due to the black hole's gravity. Nayanika's death filled Gaia with guilt. She had settled for doing nothing when her fellow crew members needed her; this was her fault!

"Kailow, we must help her. Please fetch one of the charged sapphires from the engine room." Gaia shouted.

"Why do you need it?" Kailow asked.

"It is my fault that she died, so it's my responsibility to bring her back," Gaia exclaimed.

"Okay, I'll do my best," Kailow replied and hurried to fetch a Zeto-charged sapphire.

Moments later, Kailow returned with a sapphire. Gaia was about to resurrect Nayanika when True Maker interrupted her. *"Gaia, I cannot allow you to resurrect this Zetan. Her death was how the timeline was meant to play out."*

"What are you talking about? You caused her death to happen. You told me that everything would be okay in a couple of hours." Gaia ranted.

"No, I did not cause her death. I didn't run your hovercraft into the gravity well of a black hole. That was Arish's fault." True Maker replied.

"No, but your actions stopped me from saving her. I will undo the damage you did." Gaia said and slammed Nayanika's chest with a Zeto-charged crystal.

"No! This is not how I intended the timeline to be!" True Maker shouted and severed the connection with Gaia.

Moments later, Nayanika opened her eyes and gasped, "What happened?"

"We had a collision, but everything will be alright," Gaia soothed, but deep down, she felt terrified. She had defied the supreme deity; what consequences could this have?

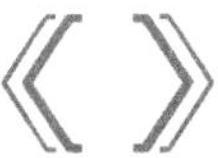

LATER THE SAME DAY, Gaia looked at the Milky Way Galaxy below. The black hole was moving away, and it had left dozens of ruined star systems in its wake. It was both terrifying and beautiful at the same time.

As Gaia watched the beautiful destruction, a blonde woman in her forties approached her. The True Maker had once again taken the form of her future biological mother, Ellen Hines.

"Sabina, I am sorry that I screamed at you," Ellen said.

"Why have you retaken a human form, and why are you calling me Sabina?" Gaia asked.

"Sabina Hines will be your name in one distant timeline, where I will become your future mother. I appeared as Ellen because I wanted a physical connection with you. Creating a temporary body is less intrusive than possessing your mind. Hug your mother, Sabina." Ellen replied.

Gaia hesitated for a moment. She wasn't keen to hug the True Maker's impostor body, but she didn't want to offend her creator either. She got up and hugged True Maker. It was a lengthy hug, and at the end of it, Gaia sobbed and whispered, "I am sorry that I defied your will, mother."

True Maker nodded and replied, "It is alright. I have seen what happens next; Nayanika's unintended survival won't affect the outcome of your mission or the future of our galaxy."

"So, why is it wrong for me to save people?" Gaia asked.

"Because you cannot see the full consequences of your actions. Let's say that Nayanika survives and moves on to raise a happy family. Then one of her descendants commits genocide and destroys entire planets 5000 years later. Was it still the right choice to save her?" Ellen asked.

"Yes, because there wasn't any direct causality between my choice to save Nayanika and things that happened eons later. We can only judge an action by the consequences and facts known at the time." Gaia replied.

"I see. While your morality works out on a mortal's event horizon, it is unsustainable on an eternal's timeline. I have learnt from the previous 99 iterations of the Milky Way Galaxy that interventions can have uncontrollable long-term consequences." Ellen replied.

"Hey, who are you, and where did you come from?"

Gaia and True Maker turned to Kailow, who stared at them in amazement. Gaia was the spitting image of the older woman next to her. Could it be her mother?

"I am the True Maker, taking the form of Gaia's future mother, Ellen Hines. It is so nice to meet you, Kailow Voltrom." True Maker replied.

Hearing this, Kailow went down on his knees and kissed the True Maker's feet.

She smiled at him and replied, "There is no need to kiss my feet. I don't strive for worship. Besides, we are practically family."

Kailow got up, shook her hand, and replied. "It's an honour to meet you, True Maker."

"The honour is all mine. It was impressive how you fought your fears and the crippling gravitation pull of the black hole to ascertain my daughter's safety." True Maker replied.

"Thank you, your eminence," Kailow replied.

"You're welcome. I need to leave. Follow your heart, Kailow, and you'll live the life you always dreamt of." True Maker said and evaporated into thin air.

"Well, I guess you finally got to meet my mother," Gaia said and tried to hide her discomfort.

"Wow, she looks almost exactly like you," Kailow replied.

"Yes... Hey, get down on the ground next to me. I want to show you something." Gaia chirped.

As Kailow kneeled next to Gaia, she took his hand and enabled him to watch the beautiful destruction that the black hole caused below them.

"SO, WHAT HAPPENED BEFORE?" Arish asked Gaia as she returned to the hovercraft.

"Our hovercraft came across a gravity well from a black hole in the Milky Way Galaxy below us," Gaia replied.

"Wow, it's a miracle no one died. We decelerated from 90 km an hour to a standstill in no time. It was like driving into a mountainside." Zelinko exclaimed.

"Yes," Gaia replied with an afterthought.

"I need to hurry back to the infirmary to look after our wounded," Areela said.

"I am coming with you," Gaia replied while deciding to follow True Maker's instruction not to use her supernatural powers to save anyone. She would only use the powers her human body had to save lives.

"Okay, I will drive the hovercraft spaceship slow and steady. I don't want that to happen again," Arish said and started the engines for a slow ride to Elvonia.

Chapter 29: A Snakebite on Elvonia.

Gaia was looking down on Elvonia from the Divine Dimension. She felt that another Zeto Crystal was near, and it would be exciting to see the elves in person. True Maker had told Gaia that the elves looked like humans except for their pointy elfish ears, and they were a tad more collectivist and altruistic than humans. These traits made them unique among the sentient species in the Milky Way Galaxy.

The elves' altruistic behaviour was how life on the planet had attuned to the Zeto Crystal. It was the only planet where all life had developed in synergy with the Zeto Crystal. Cooperation was vital in the Elvonian way of life, both for the elves, the plant-eaters, and the meat-eaters. Even the bacteria worked in symbiosis with other life forms so that they helped bodily functions instead of causing disease, perfect harmony in the circle of life.

Yet Gaia wasn't here to learn about the Elvonian lifestyle. Instead, she hoped that her visit would be a short one. The faster Zelinko could recharge their sapphires with the power of the Elvonian Zeto Crystal, the greater the chances of saving humankind on Earth.

"Are you ready to go, Gaia?"

Gaia looked at Kailow, who smiled at her and seemed excited to visit the new planet. If it weren't for True Maker's prophecy, she would have loved to go with him.

Kailow is destined to marry an Elvonian princess, not you.' Gaia recalled True Maker's heed and remembered Princess Imogen, whom she had seen in her visions. However, she wouldn't give up her partner without a fight. Destiny or not; this was her choice.

Gaia grabbed Kailow's hand, looked him into the eyes, and spoke, "Kailow, I need you to stay in the ship while I look for the Zeto Crystal in Elvonia."

"Why? Elvonia will be a beautiful place to visit. We'll have a great time together," Kailow protested and looked at Gaia in surprise.

"I need you to look after Nayanika. I had a bad dream about something happening to her," Gaia lied.

Pow

Gaia felt an intense migraine emerge as she uttered those duplicitous words. She had never lied for selfish reasons before, but what else could she do?

"Are you okay? What happened to you?" Kailow asked and squeezed Gaia's hand.

"I am okay. It was only another vision. Please watch over Nayanika for me." Gaia replied.

"Okay. If that is the will of the True Maker, that is what I will do," Kailow replied.

"The portal to Elvonia is ready. Get ready for departure."

Gaia looked at Arish, who had set up a portal to Elvonia, 50 metres away from their ship.

"I got to go. I'll see you when I get back." Gaia said and hurried to enter the portal for a flight through time and space.

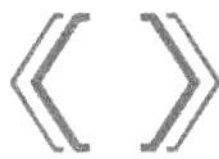

"WOW. THIS PLACE IS amazing." Areela exclaimed as they reached the main temple of Elvonia.

They had been walking for two kilometres, but they had not seen a single elf, although their sensors showed that elves were hiding all around them.

The main temple of Elvonia, the Bracashine Temple, was an enormous stone building carved into the mountainside, covered in leaves and grass. On the side of the temple, there was a sundial that showed the current time. It was presently midday.

"The sensors state that the elves built this temple 50,000 years ago. Yet, if they had such advanced technology back then, why are there no signs of development?" Zelinko pondered.

"Perhaps they've found the technology level that ensured the best outcomes and stayed there?" Areela reflected.

"Yes, that is a possibility," Zelinko said and moved forth.

Gaia didn't reflect on the Zetans' conversation. She needed to rush ahead; she needed to see her rival, who would steal her love.

"Hurry up. We need to get to the crystal." Gaia urged and started running towards the temple.

The others looked at Gaia in confusion, but they followed suit and ran after her.

As they reached the temple, a stunning woman with auburn hair and a beautiful green gown made of leaves and twigs approached them and spoke, "Welcome to Elvonia and the Bracashine Temple. I am Princess Imogen, representing King Concobhar and my people."

"I am honoured to meet you, Princess Imogen. I am Arish Kisherom, the governor of Disyerto-2 and our new colony on Zetani Nova." Arish said and bowed.

"So, if you already have two home planets, why have you come here?" Imogen asked.

"We have come to ask you to lend some of the power from your Zeto Crystal. We have promised to save humankind on Earth." Arish said.

"Save humankind? Why doesn't the True Maker look after them, like she does for all lifeforms on Elvonia?" Imogen asked.

"She does. She is inhabiting my body and speaking through me." Gaia said with her eyes flashing blue from True Maker's presence.

"I see. Please wait here." Imogen said and walked back into the temple.

A few minutes later, Imogen returned with a dozen maidens carrying rainbow-coloured snakes. "Behold the snakes of truth. Nothing bad should happen to you if you are a friend, and their bites should only be a minor nuisance. But if you are an enemy, their bites will be lethal, and you will die instantly."

The Zetans looked at each other. They were not keen to become bitten by snakes to prove their good intentions. Yet, they had come in peace, and how else would they prove themselves worthy?

Zelinko scanned the snakes, and the following message appeared on his health scanner: 'While the unidentified snake species is of a venomous type, it is unlikely that the spike protein in its venom will be harmful to Zetans.'

As he showed the scanner to Areela, she objected, "How can the scanner know if it is venomous if the snake is unknown?"

"It cannot. However, it is the best indication we can get before doing proper testing," Arish stated.

"So, what do we do?" Areela asked.

"We'll find out. I have faith in the health scanner. I'll go first." Arish said and turned to Imogen. "Please allow your Elvonian rainbow snakes to determine my intentions, oh fair, Princess Imogen," Arish said and bowed.

"Of course. May Fíordhéantóir keep you safe." Imogen replied as she directed one of her maidens to take a snake to Arish.

As the snake bit Arish, he felt a bit uncomfortable. He looked at the bite mark, and while it looked like a wasp sting, the pain quickly receded.

"You passed the test, Arish Kisherom of Zetani Nova. Fíordhéantóir blessed you with her mercy." Imogen said, handed Arish a green ribbon, and continued. "Tie this around your head to show that you are a friend of the royal family. That will make the people respect you."

Having said this, Imogen sent the other maidens with the other snakes to bite the rest of the group. Everyone was okay until Gaia got bitten. Being half-human, Gaia reacted to the poison and collapsed to the ground.

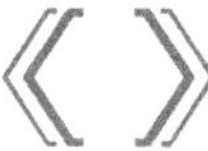

"KAILOW, GAIA IS ILL. She might not make it. You must get here at once."

Kailow felt shocked when his sister contacted him. He had never worried about Gaia's health since they started dating. After all, how could the woman whom the True Maker created herself fall ill?

"I am coming at once. Is there anything I need to bring?" Kailow asked.

"Bring a medical kit and an antidote synthesiser. Gaia fell unconscious from a snake bite during the Elvonian initiation ceremony. The rest of us got bitten, but we are alright."

"I understand. I'll be there as soon as possible." Kailow replied and closed the telepathic connection.

Having said this, Kailow hurried to fetch an antidote synthesiser and a Zeto-charged sapphire so that he could be by Gaia's side in her time of need.

Chapter 30: A Fated Romance.

As Kailow approached the sick ward where the elves kept Gaia, guilt struck him. He should have been there for her. It was unfair that Gaia was unconscious while the rest were in good health. Why had this happened?

"I am sorry about your friend."

Kailow turned around, and he saw the most beautiful woman he had ever seen in his life. It was awful to feel this way when his partner was at death's door, yet he couldn't deny his instant attraction toward this auburn beauty.

"Thank you. I am Kailow, her partner. What happened?" Kailow asked.

"I am Princess Imogen, the heir to the Elvonian throne. Gaia failed our initiation rite. The snake of truth didn't allow her passage to our inner sanctum." Imogen replied.

"So, is this your doing?" Kailow retorted.

"My doing? She chose to partake in the rite. We must be cautious to not allow enemies near our sacred crystal, don't we?" Imogen replied.

"I guess. So, what happens now?" Kailow asked.

"Fíordhéantóir will decide her fate; all we can do is pray for Gaia's soul. Come with me to the temple." Imogen replied.

Kailow looked at Gaia and hesitated. He should stay with his love in this dire time of need, yet there was nothing he could do for her. Even if the antidote synthesiser could develop a suitable antidote against the snake poison, that antidote was unlikely to work on a human.

'Go with Imogen; it is your destiny.' A faint voice whispered into Kailow's head.

Kailow looked around in fright. Who had uttered these mean-spirited words into his ears? Was he losing himself when he needed to be strong? His panic made the room feel stuffy, and what better way to get fresh air than following Imogen to the Elvonian temple?

"Okay. I am coming with you." Kailow said.

"I am happy that you are," Imogen replied, took his hand, and led him out of the medical ward.

HISS

Kailow felt how his heart was racing as Imogen approached him with a hissing Snake of Truth. The prospect of being bitten by a venomous snake was terrifying, and yet Kailow couldn't get past the erotic feelings he experienced. Imogen's perfect symmetry, waist-long auburn hair, and emerald-green eyes made her the most erotic creature Kailow had ever seen.

As the snake bit him, he shivered from sensations of pure pleasure. The Snake of Truth didn't make him ill; it made him horny.

'Snap out of it! You cannot cheat on Gaia when she is fighting for her life.' Kailow thought and fought to regain control of his urges. "I can't do this," Kailow mumbled.

"Do what? I thought you guys came to see the Zeto Crystal. You'll be the first Zetan to see it." Imogen said and smiled.

"What about the others?" Kailow asked.

"Your friends are currently enjoying our royal hospitality at the palace. However, they cannot see the crystal since the Snake of Truth marked Gaia. Such is our laws." Imogen replied.

"What about me?" Kailow asked.

"You are different. Can't you feel how Fíordhéantóir destines us to be together?" Imogen asked. Kailow nodded and said with an afterthought. "I see. It would be an honour if you show me the inner sanctum of your temple."

"Come with me," Imogen said, took Kailow's hand, and led him past the temple guards to the most important shrine of the temple.

The turquoise colour coming from the Elvonian Zeto Crystal illuminated the shrine, and Imogen's eyes glowed as they reflected the crystal's light. Kailow stared at her in awe. He desired Imogen more than anything, yet guilt was tearing him apart.

"This is where we are destined to make love. The fruit of our lovemaking will be King Mellron, the greatest king ever to rule Elvonia."

Kailow stared at Imogen as she dropped her gown to the floor and revealed her ample bosom, accompanied by a slender and tall physique. She was like an electromagnet, which was impossible for the iron in his girdle to resist. Kailow grabbed Imogen's bum and kissed her.

*shock**Pow*

Guilt struck Kailow like a stroke, and he felt sick. Finally, his conflicted feelings broke him apart, and he could not stay any longer.

"I can't do this," Kailow exclaimed.

"I understand. You'll find me here when you can."

Kailow turned around and sprinted away from the temple area.

"I AM SORRY, GAIA. I don't know what flew into me. I would never do anything to hurt you."

Kailow sobbed as he grabbed Gaia's clammy cold hand. She had a weak pulse, and it seemed unlikely that she would make it through the night.

'Hmm, Gaia saved Nayanika with a Zeto-charged sapphire. I can save Gaia the same way,' Kailow thought and touched Gaia's temple with the sapphire. A bright blue light filled the room for a few seconds, and when it subsided, Gaia was still unconscious.

"It's pointless. You cannot save my daughter with a Zeto-charged sapphire. A part of me dwells in her, so she doesn't need the extra energy."

Kailow turned around, and he saw True Maker posing as Gaia's future mother, Ellen Hines.

"True Maker? I am so sorry for almost cheating on your daughter. I don't know what happened to me. I love her." Kailow cried.

True Maker looked at the pathetic Kailow. It wasn't ideal that she intervened to separate Kailow and Imogen. She would have preferred it if the fated romance between Kailow and Imogen happened on its own. For a moment,

True Maker felt guilty. Could she envision a timeline where Gaia and Kailow remained together?

True Maker shook off the notion. Heartache was part of the human experience, and she could not shield her daughter from this against the greater good. "Don't be sorry, Kailow. Your romance with Imogen will give birth to King Mellron, the greatest king ever to rule Elvonia." True Maker stated.

"I don't care about prophecy. I love Gaia. I want to be with her." Kailow said.

"And yet you have had doubts for a long time," True Maker replied.

"I felt terrified in your presence. I am a mortal; imagine loving someone who is a goddess. How can I ever be good enough?" Kailow whimpered.

"You can be good enough by fulfilling your purpose. Gaia knew about your purpose. She lied to you by telling you to stay on the ship to change the path of destiny. Yet these things tend to happen anyway. As the snake bite injected her with a poison that is lethal to humans, you are the only one who can save her life." True Maker revealed.

"So, what can I do to save her?" Kailow asked.

"Make love to Imogen tonight. As your seed fills her, you'll fulfil your purpose. I will reward you by saving Gaia's life. Everyone wins." True Maker replied.

'Not everyone,' Kailow thought and reflected on how terrible True Maker treated Gaia. Why would the supreme deity act like this? Kailow wasn't going to question the True Maker, so he replied, "I will do your bidding, True Maker."

"Call me Fíordhéantóir. That is what the elves call me, and Elvonia will be your new home." True Maker said, smiled, and evaporated into thin air.

Kailow nodded and left the medical ward. Through a cruel twist of fate, the only way of saving the woman he loved was to abandon her.

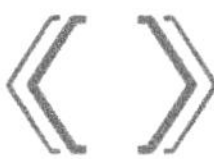

"KAILOW, I WORRIED THAT you wouldn't return."

Kailow looked at Princess Imogen, who had been sleeping next to the Zeto Crystal. Her eyes were teary.

"I had to return to save the woman I adore. Fíordhéantóir told me that the only way to save her life was to make love to you." Kailow replied.

"Did you speak to Fíordhéantóir?" Imogen said in amazement.

"Yes. Let's talk more later. We both know what we need to do to fulfil our destiny."

Imogen nodded and approached Kailow. As Kailow caressed her naked body, he realised that carrying out his destiny did not feel bad at all!

Chapter 31: Leaving Elvonia.

"How could you do this to Gaia?"

Areela felt furious when she saw her brother holding the hand of Princess Imogen like they were lovers, as they met at the royal palace the following day.

"Don't blame your brother, Areela. Ours was a fated romance, demanded by Fíordhéantóir," Imogen replied.

"Bullshit. Kailow had a choice. No one took his free will away from him." Areela exclaimed.

"Areela, I don't like your tone. Remember that you are our guest, and you should act accordingly." Imogen replied.

Areela was about to answer when Zelinko put a hand on her shoulder and replied. "Let's not worry about what has happened. Let's worry about the future."

"Kailow will marry me, and he'll stay on Elvonia as the Prince Consort when I succeed my father, King Concobhar," Imogen replied.

"I'd rather hear this from my brother." Areela snapped.

Kailow sighed. It was difficult enough to lose Gaia from his fated encounter with Imogen. Why did his sister also have to get involved? "It is as Imogen said. We will get married and work to transform Elvonia into a utopia." Kailow said.

"What about Gaia?" Areela asked.

"Princess Imogen is allowing us to Zeto-Charge our sapphires with the Elvonian Zeto Crystal. This gesture should help Gaia's project on Earth." Kailow replied with a monotonal voice.

"But you loved Gaia. How can you do this to her?" Areela protested.

"I love her, but I cannot be with the woman who is the physical manifestation of the True Maker. Imogen is the one for me." Kailow deadpanned.

"Let's not involve ourselves in your brother's love life. Princess Imogen, can you lead me to the Elvonian Zeto Crystal. It is crucial for our mission that we charge our sapphires and travel to Earth as soon as possible." Zelinko said.

"Of course, follow me," Imogen said and led the group to the Bracashine Temple.

"I NEED TO GO IN BY myself. Only I can know the secret of how to Zeto-charge sapphires." Zelinko stated as they reached the inner shrine of the temple.

"That is not going to happen. I am not letting a foreigner get unrestricted access to the crystal essential for our planet's ecosystem." Imogen replied.

Zelinko looked at the elven princess. It was risky to reveal his secret chant to charge the crystals. If Arish learned the procedure, he would have no leverage over his long-term rival. Then again, he could not press his point against Imogen, so he hoped she wouldn't tell Arish about his methods.

"You can come, Imogen. However, don't share what I am about to show you, or Arish might show up with a large contingent of Zetans and colonise your planet," Zelinko warned.

"I wouldn't worry about that. We are more capable of defending ourselves than you might think, Master Zelinko. In any case, I will follow your advice, and I won't disclose anything to Governor Arish." Imogen replied.

"Thank you, princess. Let's get the ritual underway." Zelinko said and entered the inner sanctum with Imogen in tow.

GAIA FELT DISORIENTED when she woke up in the medical ward. What had happened? She remembered the snakebite, but the snakes had bitten her last, so why had no one else reacted to the poison?

"Gaia, so you finally woke up. Zelinko has charged enough sapphires for our project on Earth. The others are waiting for us in the Divine Dimension. We need to leave as soon as possible," Areela urged.

"What happened? Where is Kailow?" Gaia asked.

"You became sick from the bite of the Elvonian snake of truth, but the elves helped you find an antidote," Areela replied.

'What is she hiding from me, and where is Kailow?' Gaia thought. A terrifying realisation struck her. Could her mother have manipulated events to make Kailow abandon her for Princess Imogen? Would she make a last-ditch attempt at winning him back if that was the case?

Gaia decided against her far-fetched plan. Regardless of what True Maker had done, it was his choice to be with someone else. Seeing him again would not make any difference, and besides, if he had abandoned her while she was unconscious, he wasn't a keeper.

"I understand. Let's hurry back to the Divine Dimension," Gaia urged and got up from her bed.

Areela nodded, and she helped Gaia towards the portal. While she felt heartbroken over what her brother had done to her best friend, there was nothing she could do about it, so the sooner they left Elvonia, the better. Areela lifted a charged sapphire towards the last rays of the evening sun, which opened a portal. Together they entered the portal and left the planet.

KAILOW WATCHED HOW Areela and Gaia left Elvonia as the portal closed behind them. He felt terrible over what he had done. He had abandoned his lover for another woman, and he hadn't even been brave enough to see her. Kailow had an epiphany. Now that Gaia was alive, they could be together again. True Maker had told him that he needed to sleep with Imogen for his destiny to happen, and he had carried out her plan. Because of his actions, his group had their Zeto-charged crystals, and Gaia had recovered from her poisoning.

Kailow was about to pull up a charged sapphire and run to the teleportation spot when he heard a beautiful voice. "Oh, there you are, Kailow. I have been looking for you. My father is throwing a feast in honour of our betrothal."

Kailow turned around and looked at Imogen, who was as stunning as ever. His life had changed from that of a servant on Zetani to that of a prince on Elvonia. As much as he loved Gaia, this was the place for him, and Imogen was his wife-to-be.

Kailow put back the sapphire in his pocket, turned around, and replied, "I was watching the sunset. How nice of your father to organise a feast for us. I can't wait to attend it with my beautiful bride."

"Great, let's watch the sunset together and then we'll be on our way," Imogen said and took Kailow's hand. Together they watched the Elvonian sunset, which they would do together so many times over the years to come.

Chapter 32: On the way to Earth.

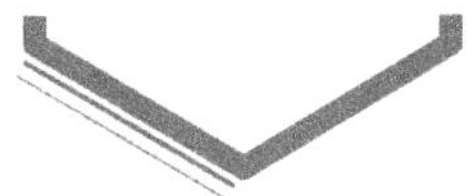

"Where is Kailow?"

Gaia knew the answer to the question, which she exclaimed when the Zetans gathered on Arish's hovercraft after their visit to Elvonia. Yet she couldn't let the whole episode go without first knowing why it had happened.

"Uhm, Kailow stayed behind as our ambassador on Elvonia," Arish replied.

"Ambassador? That's nonsense. He is my partner, and he was coming with me to Earth." Gaia objected.

"Kailow sacrificed himself for your sake. Princess Imogen refused to let us near the Elvonian Zeto Crystal. His act of seducing her secured access to the crystal." Zelinko interjected.

"So, the bastard slept with another woman while I was in a coma?" Gaia shouted.

"He had to. It was the only way to Zeto-charge the sapphires. Princess Imogen wouldn't let us near them otherwise. He did it so you could save humankind." Areela replied.

Gaia took a deep breath. She hated how the Zetans defended Kailow's actions. However, regardless of his motivations, it had happened, and her relationship had ended as True Maker had predicted.

"I see," Gaia said.

"I am sorry I didn't tell you when we were on Elvonia," Areela replied.

"It doesn't matter. Confronting Kailow for his actions wouldn't have yielded a positive outcome." Gaia replied. She turned to Arish and spoke, "How far away is Earth?"

"Earth is 4000 lightyears away, or 40,000 kilometres in this dimension. Unfortunately, we can only drive 250 km per hour to avoid a dangerous crash with another gravity well," Arish stated.

Gaia did the maths. It would take them 66 days to reach Earth at their current pace. It wasn't fast enough, as humanity was bound for extinction later this year. Once they had set up their Garden of Eden, it would take time to find humans on the vast tundras on Earth during the Mount Toba Ice Age.

"I'll speak to my mother. She can tell us if the path is clear so we can go faster." Gaia stated and left the room.

"WOW, WHAT HAPPENED to you?"

Gaia stared at the image of the frail and old middle Eastern woman that True Maker manifested in when she contacted her.

"This is what your future mother from another timeline, Keila Eisenstein, will look like when she dies in the future." True Maker replied.

"Oh, she must have been hundreds of years old?" Gaia asked.

"No, she died at the age of 37. Dark forces caused her to age, but I have not seen who did this to her." True Maker replied.

"I see. Would you mind changing to my other mother?" Gaia asked.

True Maker snapped her fingers, and she appeared as a beautiful middle Eastern woman with auburn hair, sparkly green eyes, and a fit body. Gaia flinched and replied, "This is not the body you used during our last conversation. The other female was blonde."

"Oh yes, I mixed up your mothers from different timelines because I wanted you to see what your future will hold. Ellen Hines is your mother in the 21st century, and Keila Eisenstein will be your mother in the 29th century. Dark forces will taint your mother Keila, and your future self as Sabina Eisenstein will kill her." True Maker revealed.

"Wow, my future mother will be the destroyer of the universe and my worst enemy?" Gaia asked in shock.

"No. Your enemy will be someone else. A hideous beast shrouded in pitch-black darkness. But, somehow, you'll stop this enemy, and for this to happen, humanity must survive." True Maker replied.

"That's why I contacted you. We are running late because Arish worries about hitting another gravity well if we travel quickly. Can you help us?" Gaia asked.

True Maker froze for a bit, and her eyes flickered back and forth. Then, after a few seconds, she was back in control of her physical body, and she spoke, "Yes. Accelerate to 2520 kilometres per hour and set the course to 88 degrees south-west in exactly 12 minutes. That will take you to Earth in 6 days, and it will avoid all the black holes that are currently ravaging the galaxy."

"Thank you, mother," Gaia replied, and she hurried to leave the room so she could tell Arish the new speed and coordinates.

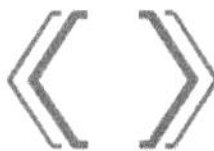

THE NEXT DAY, AREELA visited Gaia in her room. Areela was bubbly and chirped, "I am having another baby with Zelinko."

"Congratulations! how did this happen?" Gaia asked in excitement.

"You should know about flowers and bees. You kept pretty busy with my brother," Areela teased.

Gaia didn't answer, and Areela said, "I am sorry, I shouldn't have brought it up; I understand if you are still upset about what happened with Kailow."

"It's okay. I am happy for you. Would you mind if I feel it?" Gaia said.

"Not at all, but you wouldn't feel it this early; I am in my second month," Areela said.

"I have attuned senses. I would like to try them." Gaia said.

"Okay, try away." Areela teased and pulled up her sweater.

Gaia put her hand on Areela's stomach, and her eyes flickered as the spirit of True Maker fulfilled her. While True Maker completed her, Gaia could see the boy's future. He would be a handsome man named Gromvir, and he would become the leader of the dwarves.

"Congratulations. Your son will be a handsome man when he grows up." Gaia said.

"Wow, do you know anything else about my son's future?" Areela chirped.

"I am sorry, but I cannot tell you more without altering your timeline," Gaia said.

"I understand. Thank you, Gaia." Areela said and hugged her.

As Areela hugged her, Gaia got an insight into her own future. She would be pregnant with twins that would be called Ava and Adan. Gaia shook it off. She couldn't see the future of her children without changing it.

As the True Maker's spirit left her body, Gaia felt bittersweet. As great as it would be to become a mother, it was a shame that the father was the man who broke her heart.

Chapter 33: A Frozen Wasteland.

Gaia held Areela's hand and shared a vision of what Earth looked like from the Divine Dimension. Seeing the tundra covered in volcanic ash, Areela felt hesitant about going. Earth was not the paradise she had envisioned.

Gaia sensed her emotions and said, "Admittedly, Earth is not beautiful now, as the worst ice age has struck my planet in eons. However, it has all the hallmarks of a paradise, and we can make it one."

"Is that what True Maker told you?" Areela asked.

"Yes, we need to create a beautiful garden, which we will name the Garden of Eden, where we can preserve life until the ice age is over. Then, once the worst winter has ended, living creatures can thrive again." Gaia replied.

"The Garden of Eden?" Areela said.

"Yes, and we will build it in Mesopotamia where the Euphrates and Tigris Rivers converge," Gaia said.

"I disagree on this location."

Gaia turned around and saw Arish Kisherom approach them. 'Why is he eavesdropping on us?' Gaia thought and replied, "So, you think you know better than the True Maker where to build this garden?"

Arish brushed off some imaginary dust from his jacket and replied, "As the Governor of two planets, I am sure I am better suited at determining settlement locations than a young human female. The Euphrates and Tigris Rivers are frozen and heavily polluted by volcanic ash. By choosing a location closer to the equator, we would be getting better external circumstances for our settlement."

Gaia considered Arish's statement. While she disliked his tone, his conclusion was correct. The best settlement spot was the least icy location. Yet, True

Maker had instructed her to build the garden in Mesopotamia, which was currently a tundra.

Gaia contacted True Maker to ask, "Mother, why are you instructing us to build the Garden of Eden in Mesopotamia? A location near the equator would make more sense."

"Why do you question the instructions of the omniscient divine being who ordered you to go there?" True Maker asked rhetorically.

"I am not questioning you, mother. Yet, I need to know what I should tell Arish," Gaia replied.

"Well, my daughter, this is my dilemma. I cannot tell you about the future without changing it. But I can tell you this, building the garden at the coordinates I gave you will yield the desired outcome." True Maker replied and disconnected.

Her mother's unclear message caused a dilemma for Gaia. How would she convince Arish to carry out her mother's plan without giving a good reason?

"Arish, if we build the Garden of Eden in Mesopotamia, all your dreams will come true," Gaia said and felt amazed by the lie she peddled. She had no idea how building in Mesopotamia would impact Arish's life, yet she had told him this.

Arish studied her and replied, "Is that what True Maker told you?"

"Yes," Gaia lied.

"Did she mention any details?" Arish asked.

"She cannot reveal your future without changing it. Yet, your dreams will come true if you follow her instructions." Gaia replied.

Hearing this, Arish smiled. He dreamt about finding the Terran Zeto Crystal to set up another Zetan Civilisation on Earth. While he would keep his promise to save humankind, his true motivations had nothing to do with humanity. If he could colonise many worlds, he would be the natural leader of the Zetans.

"We'll land on Earth tomorrow. Get yourselves some rest; we will need it," Arish said and returned to the control room on the hovercraft.

Gaia sat silent and looked down on Earth. While her earlier visits to the planet had been unpleasant, this time would be different. This time she had brought friends, and together they would build a paradise for her unborn children, Ava and Adan.

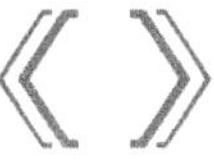

SWOOSH

As Gaia opened her eyes, she gazed down at the frozen wasteland where she would create her destiny. Mesopotamia was a tundra during the present ice age. The empty, barren rocks with a slow stream of ash-filled water running down a semi-frozen river filled Gaia with dread. However, she had seen the future. She would transform this desolate plain to be lush like Arishome Valley before the Zetans unintentionally had flattened the vale.

"Darn, it's so cold here. How can people live under such circumstances?" Areela exclaimed.

"They can't. Our species, Homo Sapiens, have gone extinct in all earlier timelines because of this ice age. Our extinction made room for the Neanderthals, another subgroup of humans, who adapted to the cold. However, if we can get my people to survive the Mount Toba ice age, humanity will experience a golden age." Gaia replied.

"So, are we changing evolution on the whims of your deity? Why doesn't she do it herself?" Zelinko asked while rubbing his hands to stay warm.

"It is not her purpose to change evolution. Instead, our actions will decide the survival prospects of my species." Gaia stated.

The Zetans overlooked the landscape. This planet was a frozen hellscape, and they couldn't understand how one of the Zeto Crystals could be here. Yet, according to two independent sources, this was the truth.

Arish turned to his followers and spoke, "Time to get to work. Set up the perimeter generators for the Nanotechnology forcefield. This will keep us safe."

Hearing this, Nayanika grabbed a bunch of the perimeter fencing and distributed the poles to her co-workers. Together they measured a circle and placed the stakes at even intervals. When they had completed the task, the Zetans entered the circle. As everyone gathered, Arish started a forcefield generator, which he had repurposed to run on Zeto-charged sapphires.

The forcefield generated formed a nano protective layer in the shape of a dome and stopped the icy wind from reaching inside the circle, making the temperature more enjoyable. Yet, a problem remained. Ash clouds covered the grey sky, and as ashy water droplets fell to the ground, it got mixed with the protective layer that kept them safe in the dome. The ash tinted the transparent forcefield layer, so it was impossible to see the bleak sun in the sky behind the clouds.

Gaia looked hard through the ash-covered protective dome. They were stuck on a barren rocky plain that she called Earth, packed with thick ashen-filled air, semi-frozen rivers with no living things, and a colourless grey sky. Why had True Maker sent her to this bleak planet, and how would she fulfil her purpose?

Chapter 34: The Child Abductions

Gaia, Areela, and Zelinko were driving their hovercraft around the empty tundras surrounding the Garden of Eden, a project they had worked on since their arrival on Earth. The Garden survived due to the water purifiers constructed inside the protective forcefield and mirrors that captured the weak solar light that gets into the dome. Yet there was a problem. The Zetans hadn't travelled to Earth to practice gardening; they had come to help Gaia save humanity. To do that, they needed to find some humans to live in the garden and thrive.

"Some primitive humans are living in this ice age. Alas, you might not like what you see."

True Maker's voice echoed in Gaia's head. What did her mother mean? They had been looking for humans for weeks; why wouldn't she like what she saw?

"There are humanoids over there. Are those the humans we are looking for?" Zelinko shouted, stopped the hovercraft, and handed Gaia a binocular.

Gaia looked at the creatures in the distance. They looked human, yet she felt no connection to them as they looked dumb and primitive. The group was grilling something over a fire.

"Those are humans. Let's park our hovercraft and establish contact." Gaia urged.

Zelinko parked the hovercraft behind a cliff, and they got dressed in thick winter gear. But, as they got closer to the human camp, Gaia had a foreboding feeling. What were the humans eating?

"Watch out!" Zelinko exclaimed and used telekinesis to redirect the arrow fired towards Gaia. Gaia threw herself to the ground, and she stared aghast at the flesh the humans were grilling. They had come across a tribe of cannibals.

"You intrude Grung Clan territory; you die." A giant black man roared in a paleolithic language.

"We are not intruding. On the contrary, we are here to help." Gaia replied in the same tongue.

"Your tasty meat; fill our bellies." Chief Grung taunted, and the other men laughed maliciously.

Gaia sighed. True Maker meant for her to save humanity from the Mount Toba ice age. Yet, how would she save these brutish people from their well-deserved death? If she saved them and brought them back to the Garden of Eden, how would she be able to co-exist with such cannibalistic monsters?

Zelinko looked at Gaia and spoke, "What are you talking about. I don't think we should bring cannibals to our garden. How can we live with such monsters in our midst?"

"I agree. However, there are a few children in the group. Saving those children is our best way of saving humankind as children are more malleable." Gaia said.

"Do you have any suggestions?" Zelinko said.

"Yes, if you challenge their leader to a duel, we can save the children," Gaia said.

Zelinko studied the angry primitive caveman who stood 20 metres away from him. The man wielded a large wooden club, swinging it like a mad man. It wouldn't be difficult to shoot him with a pistol. Yet, gunning down their leader would be culturally inappropriate if they were to coexist with these creatures in the Garden of Eden.

Gaia turned to Chief Grung and spoke, "Our leader is challenging you to a duel. A duel is better than if we all fight it out."

Hearing this, Chief Grung pulled down his fur pants and showed his genitalia to Zelinko. "Watch this, blue man. These big balls I have."

Zelinko looked at Chief Grung in disgust. The Zetan culture was one of prudence and self-control. So why had he agreed to come here to save these barbaric cannibals?

"Tell him that I fight with my fists, not my genitalia," Zelinko remarked.

Gaia forwarded Zelinko's message to Chief Grung, and the gigantic man replied, "Then, enter our ring of death. I will feast on your flesh tonight! Gr-raahh!"

Zelinko entered the ring, and Grung swung after him with his bludgeon. Zelinko avoided Grung's attacks with ease, using his premonitory powers and flexible body. Grung jumped clumsily at Zelinko's feet, and Zelinko took a step to the side, causing the giant man to crash headfirst into the gravels and rocks.

Hitting the ground with speed caused Grung's face to bleed and covered his body in ash from the sky. Zelinko pitied the miserable caveman. What would he have done if he lived on a planet with ashen rain and subzero temperatures, where a man's physical strength was the only measure of importance?

Pow

Zelinko's reflections ended abruptly when Grung's haymaker punch broke his nose, which caused silver-blue blood to stream down his handsome face.

The colour of Zelinko's blood scared the humans, and they started mumbling among themselves. "This man is no God. He bleeds, and he dies like the rest of us." Grung exclaimed.

Zelinko shook off the pain. He had allowed his mind to wander, but he needed to end this fight. Zelinko blasted Grung with a psionic blast, which caused the giant man to stagger. After stunning Grung, Zelinko ran up to him, punched him in the face, and kicked him in the crotch.

As Grung collapsed to the ground, Zelinko grabbed his cranium and haemorrhaged his brain with his Zetan psionic power.

"The blue man did it. Honour us by feasting on his flesh with us." The primitive humans chanted.

Zelinko turned to Gaia and spoke, "What are they saying. Have they turned less hostile?"

"In a way. They expect us to honour their fallen by feasting on his flesh." Gaia replied.

"We can't do this. We cannot eat humans to appease their sick rituals. What have you gotten us into?" Areela screamed.

"I am not doing this. These humans are not worth saving." Zelinko stated.

"If you take their children, you can create a new generation of humans. You can form them in your image." True Maker whispered.

"What about the adults?" Gaia asked.

"The adults are doomed either way. Starving and broken, they'll succumb to cannibalism and the extreme cold." True Maker replied.

Gaia shed a tear. She had come to save humanity, but as it would seem, the only way of doing so was by separating innocent children from their parents. Gaia nodded reluctantly and made a sweeping motion that knocked all the humans to the ground.

"Now, grab a child each!" Gaia exclaimed, took the closest child by her hand, and hurried back to the hovercraft. Zelinko and Areela followed suit, and shortly afterwards, they were on the way back to the Garden of Eden.

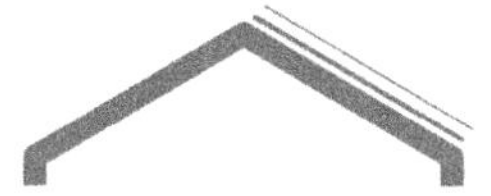

Chapter 35: The Way Forward.

The moon shone through the ash clouds when Gaia looked at the children she had abducted. The children had been crying for their mothers all day, and Arish had sedated them with sleeping potions to get peace and quiet. It all felt so incredibly wrong. Gaia had travelled to Earth in the hope of becoming the saviour of humanity. Yet, her first encounter had led to bloodshed and broken hearts.

"Mother, you knew about the future; why didn't you tell me about this?" Gaia cried silently.

Swoosh

A breeze hit Gaia's neck, and she felt a warm hand on her shoulder. She turned around, and she saw True Maker in the beautiful form of Keila Eisenstein.

"There were changes along the timeline. For example, I hoped you would come across the Paci Tribe humans and befriend them. However, the Grung Tribe humans killed them and ate them several months ago." True Maker said.

"How would I have gotten here several months earlier?" Gaia asked.

"If you had taken the Zetani Nova Zeto Crystal out of its sanctuary before the Zetans flattened Arishome Valley, you could have skipped going to Elvonia. That would have saved you time and made you capable of saving the Paci Tribe people." True Maker replied.

"That's unfair. There is no way I could foresee these things happening." Gaia protested.

"I am not blaming you," True Maker stated.

Gaia turned around and looked at the children who were sleeping peacefully. When she saw the children, she was looking forward to her motherhood.

Gaia was in her second trimester, so the effects of pregnancy were showing a bit on her.

"They are beautiful, aren't they? So young and innocent. You can still save them." True Maker enthused.

"What would have happened if I didn't kidnap them from their parents," Gaia asked.

"In every timeline so far, the Grung Tribe cannibalized on their children to survive the harsh ice age. Those that survived the ice age were too weak to procreate, and their lines ended." True Maker said and looked away.

"Why are you looking away? What are you not telling me?" Gaia remarked.

"In this timeline, they would have survived. After the Grung Tribe humans ate the Paci Tribe humans, they were well-fed and wouldn't have needed to kill their young to survive the Mount Toba Ice Age. The volcano will stop erupting in two weeks, and the skies will clear in two months. The Grung Tribe would have formed the basis of humanity." True Maker revealed.

"Why are you telling me this now? What am I even doing here then? I could have stayed on Zetani Nova with Kailow. We would be happy, and we could have raised our children together." Gaia exclaimed.

"I am…. I am sorry. This is why I rarely intervene; my actions have unintended consequences." True Maker replied.

"I hate you!" Gaia yelled, pushed True Maker, turned around, and started crying.

True Maker took a step back and studied her daughter. Mortals were such complex creatures, and they brought emotions to everything. How would she handle this?

After a moment of hesitation, True Maker put her hand on Gaia's shoulder, whispered, "I will always be here for you, my daughter," and evaporated into thin air.

"ZELINKO TOLD ME ABOUT your species' dangerous and violent nature."

Arish's statement in front of the gathered Zetans made Gaia anxious. Would he use the incident with the Grung Tribe as an excuse to withdraw his support for saving humankind?

"You cannot abandon my species; you promised me," Gaia said.

"I never said that I would abandon your species," Arish said and took out a gas grenade. "I have been examining the genome of the human children, and I developed this non-lethal gas grenade. For future interactions with human tribes, we will attack them with this gas pre-emptively. Once we have subdued the adults, we can take all children under five, as they are the safest group to raise and civilise in the Garden of Eden."

"But what if the tribe we find is peaceful, and we can save them all?" Gaia objected.

"From Zelinko's report, I determine that to be unlikely," Arish stated.

Gaia looked away. She had caused this to happen. She had brought aliens to her home planet, and they would abduct children to alter humanity in their image. So much for being saviours. However, it was what it was, and she had to continue her chosen path.

"I understand. Have you found more human tribes?" Gaia asked.

"Not yet, but we have sent out several drones programmed to search for them. If there are any humans left, we will find them." Arish said.

"Thank you," Gaia said and left the meeting.

"Gaia, where are you going?"

Gaia ignored Areela's calls. For now, she wanted to be alone with the children she had abducted. She couldn't undo what she had done, but at least she could be there for them.

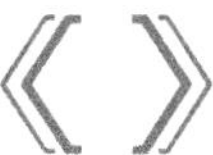

"WHY DID YOU TAKE US from our mothers and fathers?"

Gaia looked at the innocent-looking brown-eyed girl who spoke to her. She hadn't given the abducted children names, as she thought it was more suitable to use the names they already had. Thus far, they had been unable to converse with the children, but the girl's tone indicated that a change was coming.

"I had to. Your tribe people were eating other humans while I am trying to ensure humanity's survival." Gaia replied.

"Who gave you that task?" The child asked.

"The True Maker did," Gaia replied.

"Is that one of your blue-skinned friends?" The child asked.

"No, she is my mother," Gaia replied.

"Where is your mother now?" The child asked.

"She is everywhere and nowhere," Gaia said and sighed.

"I understand that you are sad. What is your name? I am Kuamsha, and those other kids are called Nadira and Tumaini," Kuamsha revealed.

"Nice to meet you, Kuamsha. My name is Gaia, and my blue female friends are called Areela and Nayanika." Gaia replied and smiled.

"Okay. Your people are nicer than my family." Kuamsha said and hugged Gaia.

When feeling the embrace from the feral child, Gaia felt hopeful. She had travelled so far and lost so much, yet the child's embrace gave her a glimpse of a better future.

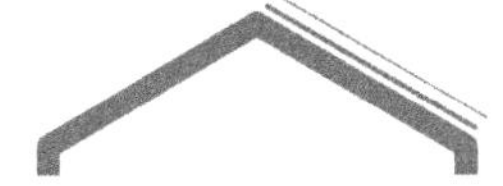

Chapter 36: A Brush with Death.

"Wow, your planet is beautiful."

Gaia smiled as she was having a picnic with Areela in their favourite part of the Garden of Eden. The gardening robots had been busy planting and manicuring the 10 square kilometres large park. Apart from being beautiful, the garden needed to feed 300 human children and 15 Zetan explorers. Yet, the Zetans were an advanced species, so they used hydroponic farms and grew fast-growing crops to ensure that food was plentiful.

Gaia looked at the skies. The ashy clouds had disappeared after the ice age had ended, and the skies were clearing. She was glad that she could now enjoy the sunlight and the blue skies. With the ice age era coming to an end, life slowly returned outside the garden. Thus, what was once a tundra was now becoming beautiful meadows with many colourful budding flowers.

Gaia thought of asking Arish to turn off the forcefield layer that separated them from the outside atmosphere. She had been outside the protective dome the day before, and she knew that the air was pristine. Yet many of the children in their ward would run off to look for their parents if she opened the perimeter fences. As much as she didn't want to keep them as prisoners, she didn't want to let young children get lost in the wilderness.

"Please let me in. I want to see my son."

Gaia looked outside the transparent protective forcefield layer. A filthy and worn-out looking woman had burns on her hands from touching the electrified nano-technology layer. How had she got here? Gaia ran towards the perimeter to communicate with the stranger.

"Who are you, and how did you find us?" Gaia asked.

"I Lucy. I followed your tracks; you took my son. Please, I want to see him again." Lucy pleaded.

Seeing the desperate woman, Gaia felt heartbroken. She imagined how she would have felt if someone had stolen her children from her—what a desolation. Seeing the desperation in the woman's eyes, Gaia spoke to the voice-controlled AI, "AI, open perimeter field at sector 6B. Authorization code ZZ6B."

"No, Gaia, what are you doing?" Areela exclaimed and ran towards Gaia.

"Authorization confirmed. Opening sector 6B," the AI replied and lowered the forcefield.

Lucy staggered towards Gaia and collapsed to her knees. Gaia ran towards Lucy to keep her upright.

Swoosh

Gaia stared in shock as Lucy stabbed her in the neck with an Onyx knife laced with poison. She let go of her grip around the woman, staggered backwards, and collapsed.

"Gaia. No!!!" Areela exclaimed and blasted the woman with a psionic blast.

Much to Areela's dismay, the woman was unaffected by the blast, and she charged toward Areela and bit her in the shoulder. Upon tasting Areela's blood, the woman got stunned, and Areela used this opportunity to shove her outside the perimeter of the forcefield.

"AI, close perimeter field 6B, authorisation code ZZ6B!" Areela exclaimed, and the forcefield re-emerged.

Fizz

The unpleasant sound of burnt flesh and Lucy's hissing screams of pain filled the air as Lucy leapt headfirst into the forcefield. Areela stared at the hissing feral creature outside the perimeter. It had been a close call.

'Gaia is hurt,' Areela thought and rushed towards her friend. Unfortunately, Gaia was delirious and rambling incoherent nonsense.

"Zelinko, come here at once. It's an emergency," Areela telepathed and tore her blouse to stop Gaia's bleeding.

"TSK, TSK, TSK. WHY would you trust someone whose child you abducted?"

As Gaia opened her eyes, she was in the Divine Dimension, looking at her mother's spiritual form.

'Adan, Ava! What happens to my unborn children if I die?' Gaia fretted.

"Don't worry about your children. You'll survive this episode. The Zetans are resuscitating you as we speak. In the meantime, you should reflect on your actions." True Maker replied.

"What did I do wrong?" Gaia sobbed.

"Was it the wisest choice to expose yourself to your enemy?" True Maker asked.

"She wasn't my enemy. I had never seen her before." Gaia objected.

"Yet, the Zetans attacked her and stole her child. How couldn't she hate you?" True Maker asked.

"I... I didn't think. Lucy suffered, and I felt compelled to save her." Gaia replied.

"Ah yes, empathy. Without logic, it's reckless, while logic without empathy is inhuman. You'll need to find a way to combine the two." True Maker remarked.

Gaia was about to answer when the Divine Dimension faded, and a mishmash of colours shrouded her vision as she was slowly coming awake.

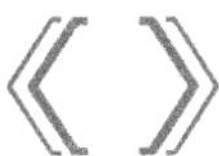

"OH, GAIA, I AM SO GLAD that you are still among us."

As Gaia opened her eyes, she felt Areela squeezing her hand. Tears covered Areela's face, and yet a smile had emerged.

"You'll need to stay still for now. We have healed your stab wound, yet venom laced on the dagger is still circulating in your body."

Gaia nodded, but she didn't worry. Her mother had assured her that she would survive the attack, and that was the best guarantee one could get in life.

"I need to rest now. I'll see you when I get better," Gaia said, closed her eyes and dozed back to a long dreamless sleep.

"REMARKABLE. AS IT TURNS out, there are more than one species of humans."

Gaia and the gathered Zetans looked at Lucy's corpse. After her attack on Gaia, the Zetans had hunted her down, and they had been unwilling to make the effort of capturing her alive.

"What do you mean about two different species?" Gaia said.

"I meant what I said. This woman has a 0.3 per cent variation in her genome compared to the other human samples we have. So, while it is close enough for the different human species to interbreed, it's too far away to be another race within the same genus." Arish stated.

'0.3 per cent variance. That's the same variance as there is between mine and the Zetan genome," Gaia thought, as she had a speck of Zetan genome in her.

"I understand. Thank you for telling me this." Gaia replied.

"Why didn't you tell us about the presence of two distinct human species living concurrently. What else are you hiding from us?" Arish accused.

Gaia shook her head and replied, "I didn't hide anything from you. I didn't know about the two distinct human species."

Arish gave Gaia a suspicious look, but he didn't say anything.

"The attacker seemed impervious to my psionic attacks," Areela recalled.

"Areela, you are not good at psionic attacks. My attacks worked when I duelled against Chief Grung." Zelinko stated.

"So, if your psionic attacks didn't work, how did you push her outside the perimeter forcefield? Your physique is inferior to this muscular female primate," Arish said.

"She bit me and got paralysed. She must have had an allergic reaction to something in my blood." Areela recalled.

"Interesting. In any case, we need to be more careful moving forward. Do not let any of these people in, and never leave the garden while you are unarmed." Arish stated.

Gaia nodded and left the meeting. Her appointment as humanity's saviour was deteriorating, and after almost getting killed, she wanted to leave this horrible place and abandon humanity to its demise. However, she remembered her growing belly and that she would give birth to beautiful twins who would lead Earth to a new era of evolution.

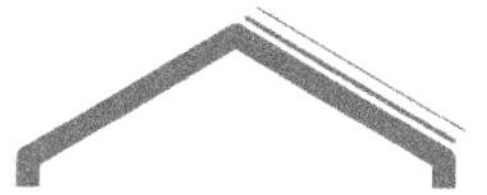

Chapter 37: Double Births.

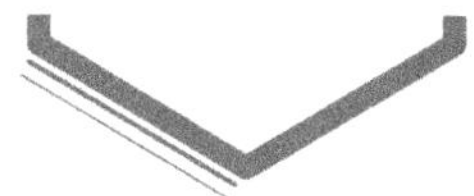

Gaia munched on some delicate grapes and watched the sunset with Areela when she felt odd. She felt like she had felt towards Kailow before he left her for an elven princess. Thinking of Kailow made Gaia feel bittersweet. While she was happy that he had impregnated her with her future twins, she couldn't forgive him for what he did. Gaia didn't care what the others had said; there must have been a better way to secure access to the Elvonian Zeto Crystal than cheating while she was at death's door.

Thinking about Kailow's betrayal no longer angered Gaia. She knew True Maker made him choose the elven princess over her. Instead, she felt a warm feeling. She wanted to stroke the beautiful Areela Kheeran, who sat next to her. Their sisterhood had grown more intense since they landed on Earth, and Gaia knew that Areela would never abandon her as Kailow did. She secretly wanted to own Areela for herself. There were, however, two issues.

The first was that Areela was married to Zelinko and expected her second child. Knowing that Podixa kept Thorax safe, they were eager to have another child, whom they hoped to be normal. Everything indicated that they were happy together. Did Gaia have the right to break up a happy and loving couple to pursue her happiness?

The second issue was more debatable. Since they were both females, wouldn't their sisterhood relationship breach the natural order?

Gaia decided to telepath her mother and ask for advice. "Mother, I am struggling with a dilemma,"

"I am listening," True Maker replied.

"So, Areela and I..." Gaia stuttered.

"Oh yes, you and Areela are destined to be together. Let her come to you." True Maker replied.

"Uhm, you never tell me about the future. What made you change your mind?" Gaia asked.

"Well, I guess I want to see my daughter happy again," True Maker replied.

"Okay. But isn't it unnatural for me and Areela to be together?" Gaia asked.

True Maker stroked her cheek, pondered on Gaia's question for a few seconds, and replied, *"Well, that's debatable. On the one hand, humans and Zetans are separate species. But, on the other hand, you are genetically similar and can interbreed, so I would say it's natural. Besides, you are part-Zetan, so your attraction to Zetans is completely natural."*

"Uhm, I meant because we are both females," Gaia replied.

"Oh. While homosexuality is not ideal for spreading your genes, I have no objections regarding mortals' choices for sexual partners." True Maker replied.

Gaia looked at her mother in confusion. Her mother had been against her relationship with Kailow, but she approved of a relationship with Areela. What was going on? Gaia remembered that her mother was omniscient; thus, she knew what would happen.

"I need to disconnect with you now. You and Areela will soon be in labour. Best of luck, Gaia." True Maker said, and the Divine Dimension faded away.

"How is your mother?"

As Gaia opened her eyes, she looked at Areela's beautiful smile. She smiled back and replied, "My mother is fine. She gave me some good news."

"I have an urgent need," Areela squealed in pain.

"Tell me, Areela," Gaia asked.

"I am going into labour," Areela exclaimed in excitement and fear.

Upon hearing these words, Gaia felt how her water also broke. As it would seem, destiny enabled her and her best friend to give birth on the same day.

Zelinko and the other Zetans arrived and rushed the two heavily pregnant women to the medical ward.

AREELA FELT BLISSFUL as she looked at her handsome baby boy, whom they had named Siblex, after Zelinko's father. Areela hated the name, but she hadn't voiced her concerns. While Siblex had been terrible and allowed Judge

Jasper to sentence her to death, she understood Zelinko's predicament. Her husband had to kill his father to save her, so she understood why Zelinko wanted to make amends by naming their child after his slain father.

Areela compared Siblex Junior with a photo of Thorax. She hadn't seen her mutant son since she left Zetani Nova, and while she should miss him, she didn't feel that way. Thorax had been a terrifying freak due to Xialiab's experiments, and it was relieving to not be in his presence. Siblex would be what Thorax never was; he would be her and Zelinko's beautiful boy.

Areela looked at Gaia, who was nursing her twins Ava and Adan. The children looked more Zetan than human, yet they had some features that distinguished them from other Zetans. For instance, their skin was purple-blue as a mix between Gaia's red blood and Kailow's silver-blue blood ran through their veins. Apart from that, they were beautiful children, and Areela couldn't be happier to be their aunt.

Areela turned to Gaia and spoke, "Hey, do you think our children will be best friends?"

"I don't know. I need to ask my mother whether that would be possible." Gaia replied with an afterthought.

"What do you mean?" Areela asked.

"It's a matter of life expectancy. If they have human life expectancy and development, they will be adults at 18 and dead by 90. But if they inherited Zetan life expectancy, they will be adults by the age of 200, and they would die around the millennia mark." Gaia replied.

"I understand. Why don't you ask her?" Areela suggested.

"Well, you know what she will reply," Gaia replied and smiled.

"That she cannot reveal our future without changing it." Areela teased.

"Yes, so let's enjoy life for now," Gaia said and turned her eyes to her babies.

There and then, they were both at peace, shielded from the tragedy that would soon strike.

Chapter 38: A Deadly Premonition.

Gaia was breastfeeding her twin babies when an unpleasant feeling took hold. This feeling confused her; it was a beautiful day, and life had been smooth sailing recently, so why the discomfort?

"Gaia, leave the twins with me. Zelinko needs to talk to you."

Gaia turned around, and she saw Nayanika. The Zetan woman had a stern look, and Gaia sensed that tensions were running high.

"What is this about? Why isn't Zelinko coming himself?" Gaia asked.

"Because it would be unsuitable for you to leave the garden together. Tensions are running high between Master Zelinko and Master Arish," Nayanika replied.

Gaia nodded. She knew about the rivalry between the two Zetans, who both yearned for power. It was a complication which True Maker had told her not to get involved in. For better or worse, the issue would resolve itself in due time. At least according to her omniscient mother.

"Okay, so I assume that he has already left the garden? Where do I meet him?" Gaia asked.

"Meet him in the Shamraz Caves to the south. I will mind your twins in your absence." Nayanika replied.

Nayanika's statement made Gaia uncomfortable. She had no desire to get involved in Zetan politics and schemes; her priority was safeguarding humanity. So, she telepathed her mother for advice. "Mother, Zelinko Siblexom summoned me to a secret meeting at the Shamraz Caves. What shall I do?" Gaia asked.

"Then you should meet him. He and Areela have pulled many strings to get you this far." True Maker replied.

"But what is this about?" Gaia asked.

"Hear him out, and you'll know what to do," True Maker replied and broke the connection.

"Why do I even bother talking to her?" Gaia muttered, turned to Nayanika, and spoke. "I will accept Zelinko's request. Please look after my twins for me."

"Of course, Gaia. I owe you my life," Nayanika said and bowed.

Gaia grabbed her backpack, kissed her twins goodbye, opened a section of the forcefield and left the Garden of Eden.

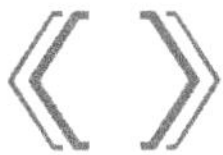

AS GAIA ARRIVED AT Shamraz Caves, she noticed that mining robots were operating. This was confusing since no one had briefed her about this mining project. Then again, her focus was on raising the children that would form humanity's future; the other aspects of the outpost were of lower importance.

As Gaia entered the cave, Zelinko approached her with a flashlight and a large sapphire in his hand. He shone the light through the gemstone and spoke. "Behold the Shamraz Sapphire, also known as the Terran Zeto Crystal."

Gaia looked at Zelinko in confusion and replied, "What are you talking about? That is not the Terran Zeto Crystal."

"I know, but it could have been. Imagine if it was Zeto-charged. How would an untrained eye see the difference?" Zelinko asked rhetorically.

"What are you getting at. What is going on?" Gaia asked curiously.

Zelinko put down his flashlight, sighed, and replied, "I fear Arish has come to steal the Terran Zeto Crystal. However, I want to test him to confirm my suspicions."

"Steal the Zeto Crystal? That's madness; he would destroy the ecosystem we came to save." Gaia exclaimed.

"Yes, that is why we need to test him. You know where Earth's Zeto Crystal is, don't you?" Zelinko asked.

"Yes," Gaia replied with an afterthought.

"So, let's test him. We charge this crystal with the power of the Terran Zeto crystal. Once we meet Arish, we will tell him that this is the Terran Zeto crystal. Arish will remove this crystal from Earth and return with it to Zetani Nova. Such an action would destroy the Terran ecosystem if it were the real Zeto Crystal, wouldn't it?" Zelinko speculated.

Gaia contemplated Zelinko's speculation. Life on Earth wasn't closely aligned to the True Maker, so it could survive without the presence of the Zeto Crystal. Then again, if Arish were willing to risk all life on her home planet to increase his status and power in Zetani Nova, that made him an enemy. True Maker was correct. After speaking to Zelinko, Gaia knew what she needed to do. She needed to find a way to confirm or disprove her friend's suspicions.

"The Zeto Crystal is at Mount Sinai, 1500 kilometres to the west. Let's grab a hovercraft and leave tonight." Gaia said and left the mine.

GAIA FELT ANXIOUS AS she snuck aboard a hovercraft in the middle of the night. While she needed to find out whether Arish was a traitor, she didn't like sneaking out like a thief in the night. Gaia had refrained from seeking her mother's guidance. True Maker had told her that she would know what to do, and she did, even if she had preferred resolving the issue in another manner.

Zelinko joined her in the hovercraft while carrying a bag of smaller crystals. "I brought our uncharged Zeto crystals. We might as well charge as many crystals as possible while we are there."

Gaia nodded, but she didn't reply. Instead, she felt tense, knowing that she had a multi-hour trip ahead of her with Areela's husband.

A dark thought struck Gaia. If something were to happen to Zelinko, that would pave her path with Areela. She shook it off and grimaced in disgust. How could she even think such a terrible thought? Yet, she couldn't let the idea go. While she would never harm Zelinko, she sensed that his death was approaching.

"Is everything alright, Gaia? Is something bothering you?" Zelinko said as they took off.

"Yes, I am fine. I was just thinking back on our first trip together last year when we faced the cannibals." Gaia lied.

"Yes, that was gruesome. But at least Kuamsha and the other children we rescued on that day seem to be turning out fine." Zelinko replied.

'Rescuing? We attacked their parents and kidnapped them,' Gaia thought but realised that she only had herself to blame for her actions. "Yes, Kuamsha's development gives me hope for the future," Gaia replied.

"Very well, I have set the hovercraft on autopilot. We should get some rest," Zelinko said and leaned backwards.

Gaia watched Zelinko. She felt guilty knowing about Zelinko's approaching death, yet it was meant to be. Fearing the terrible outcome that would soon happen, Gaia closed her eyes to catch some shuteye.

Chapter 39: The Fall of Zelinko.

Gaia woke up when the first rays of the morning sun reached her from the rear windows of the hovercraft. There was a mountain radiating with blue light ahead of her.

"Is this the right place? What do you see?" Zelinko asked.

"It's beautiful. The whole mountains shimmer with energy." Gaia replied.

"Is that so? I don't see anything out of the ordinary." Zelinko replied.

Gaia grabbed Zelinko's arm, looked him in the eyes, and spoke, "Yet, you brought me here for a reason, didn't you?"

Zelinko looked at Gaia's glowing blue eyes. It was terrifying to be in True Maker's presence, and he preferred when her spirit wasn't present in Gaia. But without the True Maker, Gaia would be clueless concerning the Zeto Crystal's location.

"Well, lead the way then," Zelinko said, opened the hatch to the outside and climbed out. Gaia followed suit, and shortly afterwards, they were at the foot of Mount Sinai.

"Follow me," Gaia instructed, and they started their ascent of the mountain.

As they got to a higher altitude, the wind got icy, and Gaia wondered how they would reach the top under the conditions. While the skies had cleared after the Mount Toba eruption, Earth was still under an ice age, so any elevated position was freezing cold.

Gaia got other things to think about when a group of humans approached them. They reminded her of Lucy, who had gained her sympathy and stabbed her in the neck. Were these humans also Neanderthal humans? Gaia knew one thing; she did not trust the group.

The group's leader stepped forward and spoke, "You are intruding on our holy mountain."

Gaia smiled at the man and replied. "We are not intruding. My mother, The True Maker, instructed me to fetch a magical artefact on the top of the mountain."

"This mountain belongs to Wanita Gunung. Go away." The man warned.

"What is he saying?" Zelinko whispered to Gaia.

"He says that this mountain belongs to another deity, The Lady of the Mountain," Gaia replied. "That's nonsense. Tell him that I am the mountain lord and demand their immediate departure, lest I unleash my wrath."

Gaia forwarded Zelinko's message to the Neanderthals, but it didn't have the intended effect. Instead of becoming awe-struck, one of the men started shouting, "It's him. He is the blue devil that stole our children and killed Lucy."

The Neanderthal man threw a spear and struck Zelinko in the shoulder. The Zetan master responded with a psionic blast, which, much to his dismay, didn't affect his adversaries. As the humans approached him with spears and clubs, he pulled up his pistol to shoot them. However, the gun jammed while the group's leader pierced Zelinko with a spear, lifted him with one arm, and roared, "Revenge for Lucy!"

The group chanted, "Revenge for Lucy," while Zelinko punched the giant man with feeble and weakened arms. After a few seconds, the giant threw Zelinko off the cliff, thus ending the days of Zelinko Siblexom.

Seeing Zelinko plunge to his death, Gaia jumped to the floor to pick up his gun. Violence, it seemed, was the only way to handle this encounter.

The giant man was about to stab Gaia when her pistol unjammed, and she fired off a shot that hit the man in the head. The man stared at her in shock and slumped dead to the ground. After killing the man, Gaia grabbed the sack of uncharged sapphire and ran towards the mountain's summit. Meanwhile, the Neanderthals ran in the opposite direction, as each group was equally terrified of the other.

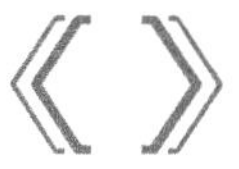

AS GAIA REACHED A SHRINE near the top of Mount Sinai, True Maker approached her as Keila. True Maker smiled and spoke, *"You did it, Gaia. You found the Terran Zeto Crystal. I am sure you understand that it cannot leave this temple?"*

"Is that because Arish would steal it and bring it to Zetani Nova?" Gaia asked.

"Yes. The locations of the Zeto Crystals are critical to keeping the galaxy in balance. They contain fragments of my soul."

"So, what do I do?" Gaia asked.

"You should charge the common sapphires. Give the large one to Arish and claim that it's the Terran Zeto Crystal. Then we'll find out about Arish's intentions." True Maker replied.

"But you already know the future?" Gaia asked.

"You can never judge a man based on your suspicions. You can only judge them on their actions. The opposite would be a terrible example."

"Okay, I am ready," Gaia said and took her mother's hand.

They put all the sapphires on the altar next to the Zeto Crystal, and they chanted while holding hands, "Gong Dau, Gong Dia, Gong Undung. Mua Terra. (For the past, for the present, for the future, my Terra.)"

Together they watched as the energy from True Maker's soul streamed into the sapphires and filled them with lifegiving energy. It was a sight to behold.

GAIA CRIED WHEN SHE dragged the dead body of Zelinko onto her hovercraft. She felt guilty for letting him die, yet she would not defy her mother and alter the timeline by trying to resuscitate him. Besides, he was in the way of her pre-destined relationship with Areela.

"Oh, Zelinko, why did you have to pass like this?" Gaia said while she looked at the Zetan. He looked old, worn out, and he had died in terror. She had never understood what Areela saw in him, yet Areela's preferences in men were none of her business.

Gaia feared how the other Zetans would react to Zelinko's death. Would they blame her, or would they understand? How would Areela handle what had happened? She thought of asking her mother for advice, but she refrained from doing so. Uncertainty was part of life, and she would have to deal with it like everyone else.

After strapping Zelinko to a seat, Gaia set the hovercraft's autopilot for the Garden of Eden, tilted her chair backwards, and resigned to whatever fate would bring upon her return.

Chapter 40: Arish's Betrayal.

"You could have saved him! Why did you let my husband die?"

Gaia watched how the heartbroken Areela Kheeran mourned the death of her husband, Zelinko Siblexom. She felt terrible knowing that her friend was correct. As the daughter of the Supreme Deity, she could bring people back to life, yet it wasn't her call to make. Disobedience had only brought her heartbreak, and besides, she carried no guilt in Zelinko's death. Zelinko had suggested that they would go to Mount Sinai, and he hadn't made sure that his weapons were in top condition.

"I couldn't resurrect him. My mother wouldn't let me." Gaia lied.

"But you had the Terran Zeto Crystal, one of the most powerful artefacts in the Milky Way Galaxy. If you rebelled to save Nayanika, you could have saved my husband," Areela protested.

Gaia reflected on Areela's statement. She had indeed saved Nayanika against her mother's wishes, but she had matured since then. Besides, what would the future hold if she kept Zelinko? Could such an act of mercy lead to her undoing?

"I cannot save him against my mother's wishes. However, she never forbade you from trying," Gaia said and handed Areela a charged sapphire.

Areela grabbed the sapphire, kneeled next to Zelinko's body, and touched him with the sapphire. Sparks of blue energy streamed from the charged sapphire, but to no avail as Zelinko remained dead. "My love, come back to me. Baby Siblex and I need you."

Areela got back up, rushed to Gaia, and sobbed, "It's not working; please do something."

Gaia grabbed Areela's hand, looked her in the eyes, and explained, "I can't. My mother won't let me."

"The Terran Zeto Crystal, give me the primordial Zeto Crystal." Areela insisted.

"It won't help," Gaia replied.

"It doesn't matter. Wouldn't you do everything to save the people you love? I must do this. As my friend, please let me." Areela pleaded.

Gaia hesitated. Giving Areela the Shamraz Sapphire wouldn't bring Zelinko back. While it looked like the Zeto Crystal, it was merely a sizeable Zeto-charged sapphire. While it would hold more charge than smaller gemstones, it wasn't more powerful than they were. If Areela wasted the Shamraz Sapphire's charge in a fruitless attempt to revive Zelinko, Arish would know that it wasn't the Zeto Crystal, and he would start looking for it.

"Give her a chance, Gaia. Let's see if the Terran Zeto Crystal can save him."

Gaia looked at Arish, who had come with the unexpected statement. Did the Zetan leader want to revive Zelinko or verify the crystal's power?

"Okay, I'll try," Gaia said, grabbed the large gemstone, and slammed Zelinko's body with it to no avail.

"I am sorry, Areela. She won't let me save him," Gaia said.

Areela didn't reply. Instead, she ran back to her cabin to mourn in peace. Gaia was about to chase after her when Arish grabbed her arm and said, "Don't chase her. Let her mourn in peace. It is the only way for her to get over the loss of her husband."

Gaia thought of protesting, but she abstained from doing so. Areela blamed her for the death of her husband, and as unfair as it was, it made sense to blame others for tragedies.

"So, what do you suggest that I do?" Gaia said.

"Come with me. Let's put the Zeto Crystal in our vault so it's safe. After that, you should spend some time with your children. They have been missing their mother," Arish suggested.

Hearing this, Gaia knew that Zelinko had been correct. Arish yearned for the Zeto Crystal, and he would steal it if he let her. She would let him since giving up the fake Zeto Crystal was the best way to expel the traitor from her home.

"Thank you for being so kind," Gaia lied and hugged Arish.

"You're welcome," Arish said and smirked as he led Gaia to the vault where she deposited the fake Terran Zeto Crystal.

As Gaia returned to her twins Ava and Adan, she waited in anticipation for the next move. Finally, the plan had come to fruition, and soon she would find out if Arish planned to betray her.

IT WAS EARLY MORNING when Gaia woke up from the loud ruckus of Zetans packing up their equipment. Gaia approached one of the Zetan scientists and shouted, "Darius, what is going on?"

Darius turned towards her and spoke, "Arish has ordered a return to Zetani Nova. Didn't he tell you yesterday?"

Gaia shook her head and replied, "No, he didn't. I guess I better discuss this with him in person." Having said this, she hurried to the command centre, where Arish was directing the others to pack supplies onto the hovercraft.

"Arish, what are you doing?" Gaia shouted.

"We are packing up. We have completed our mission on this planet, and we are heading back to Zetani Nova. Areela and Nayanika will stay behind to help you with the operation of the conservatory." Arish stated.

Gaia pondered on whether to protest or not. She knew that Arish was leaving because he thought he had the Terran Zeto Crystal. Since he was a traitor, it was ideal that he took his men and left as soon as possible. However, would he find it strange if she didn't protest his sudden departure?

"Why didn't you mention that you were leaving. A heads up would be nice!" Gaia pretended to protest.

"I don't share my plans with an untrustworthy beige-skinned alien that sneaks off in the night with my rivals. You should have brought my men and me to the Terran Zeto Crystal shrine. In any case, you did bring me the crystal, and it will be invaluable for my research on Zetani Nova." Arish ranted.

"Arish, you cannot steal the Terran Zeto Crystal. It belongs on Earth." Gaia protested.

"It belongs to me. I financed this expedition, and you are powerless to stop me." Arish mocked.

Arish's taunt baffled Gaia, and she felt furious. Arish was a clueless fool. She was the daughter of the True Maker and magnitudes more powerful than he was. If Arish had the Zeto Crystal, she would not hesitate to unleash her powers upon him.

Gaia turned around to speak to True Maker. It was better if her eyes weren't flashing blue in front of Arish; otherwise, he would know she was up to something.

"Mother, I am so angry. Arish just mocked me. Should I smite him?" Gaia telepathed.

"What are you saying, girl. You want to use violence for no better reason than appeasing your fragile ego." True Maker replied.

"He is stealing the Zeto Crystal, and he taunted me," Gaia whined.

"He has a replicated Zeto Crystal. So, letting him leave is the best outcome." True Maker replied.

"Understood, mother," Gaia said and ended the transmission.

Gaia turned around, shouted, "I won't forget this betrayal," and stormed off.

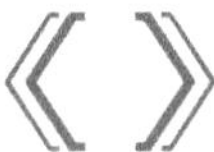

"SO, ARISH LEFT WITH the Terran Zeto Crystal?"

Gaia nodded and tried to look distressed as Areela spoke to her. It was safer for Areela if she didn't know the truth. Eventually, Arish would realise that Gaia had allowed him to steal the Shamraz Sapphire instead of the Zeto Crystal. When that happened, he was likely to return, and for everyone's safety, it was better if only she knew the truth.

"So, what happens now? Will the loss of the Zeto Crystal end life on Earth?" Areela asked.

"No, my mother told me that life on Earth could exist even without the Zeto Crystal," Gaia said and didn't mention the terrible effects if the Crystals were moved from their intended planets.

"Why didn't you stop him?" Areela asked.

"I couldn't. My mother forbade me from shedding Arish's blood," Gaia replied.

"I understand," Areela said and walked towards the hill where they so often had enjoyed the sunset in the last few years.

Gaia followed her, and they got seated on a rock where they watched the sunset where the two rivers met the ocean.

"I could never have imagined that it would end like this. The two of us stranded with our children on this planet." Areela said with a sad tone.

Gaia took Areela's hand, looked her into the eyes, and replied gently, "Don't say that. We must stay strong and live on for the sake of our children and the many human children we have in our ward."

Areela smiled bittersweetly between her tears and replied, "I am not complaining. As much as I am sad that my child will grow up without a father, Zelinko was never good to me. He used me and left me to die until he had a last-minute change of heart. After that, a relationship can never be good, so I stayed with him out of misplaced gratitude."

Gaia nodded, and her eyes followed a couple of white doves flying towards the ocean. This was her destiny, and everything would turn for the better. Now that the other Zetans were gone, she wouldn't need to deal with their intriguing. Yet one fear remained; when Gaia closed her eyes, she knew that Arish would return.

Chapter 41: Arish's Rage.

Arish Kisherom felt excited as he returned to Zetani Nova with what he believed to be the Terran Zeto Crystal. He had engaged in telepathic conversations with Podixa while he was on the way home, and he had found out that she had recovered Zetani Nova's Zeto Crystal. With two Zeto Crystals in their possession, they would be more potent than any other faction. Together, they could invade Zetani to get revenge for their exile.

As Arish got off his spaceship, Thorax Zelinkom approached him. Arish looked at the boy in disgust. Despite being only four years old, Thorax was the size of an adult, and he was a freak of nature with sharp beastly claws, lizard-like skin, and nasty fangs.

'I better get rid of Zelinko's progeny,' Arish thought as Thorax spoke, "Master Arish, where is my mother?"

"Areela stayed on Earth with Gaia and Zelinko. They have a new child now. A lovable child." Arish sneered, and he felt surprised by his contempt towards Thorax. While the failed genetic experiment disgusted him, it wasn't a wise move to show his contempt in public.

Thorax frowned and bit his lip. He wanted to tear Arish to shreds for his comments but trying would be suicide. Arish was powerful, while True Maker had abandoned Thorax a long time ago. As it would seem, both his parents and the supreme deity stopped caring about him when someone better came along.

"I understand. I would like to go to Earth on the next occasion." Thorax replied.

"There won't be any more occasions. I found what I needed. Behold the Terran Zeto Crystal!" Arish exclaimed and unbuttoned his jacket to show the charged sapphire that hung around his neck.

"That is not the Terran Zeto Crystal, you dumb fuck." Thorax stated, got down on all four and walked away.

Arish stared at Thorax and shook his head. He needed to deal with that freak, but he had to be subtle. Murdering the son of his rival wouldn't look good, so it needed to look like an accident. Besides, he had a more urgent matter on hand. He needed to ensure that he had the Terran Zeto Crystal and not a bleak copy.

Arish grabbed his stuff and rushed to get to the train to the governor's palace in Podixania.

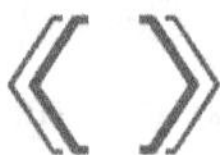

ARISH MARVELLED AS he stood outside his beautiful palace in Podixania. It had been a messy construction site just two years earlier, but now it was a beautiful oriental palace surrounded by a serene park.

"Hi, father. How was your trip to Earth?"

Arish turned around and looked at his son Besim Arishom who had grown a lot in the last two years. Besim was now in his 60s, and he started to look like an adult, although he wouldn't reach sexual maturity until he was around 100 years old. It was a strange feature of the Zetan race that they had an adult's physiognomy decades before they could mate. Yet this was the consequence of millions of years of evolution within a civilised society.

"I need to see your mother. I had expected to see my family when I returned to Zetani Nova." Arish remarked.

"I am sorry, father. Mother didn't let me know of your arrival. She is in the crystal room of our palace." Besim replied.

"Okay. We will discuss this later, son." Arish sneered and hurried ahead.

As Arish arrived in the crystal room, he felt mesmerised by the intense blue light from Zetani Nova's Zeto Crystal, which hung in a necklace around Podixa's neck. The blue light reflected onto thousands of sapphires set out in patterns around the room that symbolised the geography of Zetani Nova. As impressive as the Zeto Crystal was, seeing it filled him with angst. When he saw the tranquil beauty of a real Zeto Crystal, he knew that Gaia had fooled him.

"Greetings, ex-husband. Welcome to my planet." Podixa said with an arrogant tone.

"This is my planet; you are my wife!" Arish exclaimed.

"No, you are not my husband, and you are not my master. You are the father of my children, and as such, I'll let you live." Podixa said as she touched the Zeto Crystal and enclosed Arish in a forcefield.

"What is the meaning of this? Why are you rebelling against your master?" Arish roared.

Podixa pressed a button, and Amela Andelan entered the room. She wore a beautiful intricate dress while carrying a toddler. She walked towards Podixa and turned to face Arish as she stood next to her.

"Behold your son, Darian Arishom," Podixa said.

Arish stared at the child that Amela held in her arms. Could this be his son, or was Podixa bluffing? The timing was right, as the child looked old enough to be his.

"Don't harm my child, you wicked woman!" Arish hissed.

Hearing this, Podixa kissed Amela, who reciprocated her kiss. Then, after a lengthy rub, she turned towards Arish and spoke. "I would never harm Darian. I love him as my own, as I love his mother."

"So, what is this about?" Arish asked.

"You broke our marriage contract, Arish. As such, our marriage is over. But, as it turns out, I fancy your taste in women." Podixa said, grabbed Amela and French-kissed her.

Podixa's actions made Arish furious, and he grabbed the Shamraz Sapphire and tried to slam his way out of the forcefield that encapsulated him. However, as he hit it several times to no effect, he noticed how the crystal started to drain. Thus, it proved that Thorax's claim was correct; Gaia had tricked him by giving him a false crystal. Realizing his mistake, Arish collapsed to the floor and cried in anger.

"Pathetic. Guards, expel Arish Kisherom from my palace." Podixa commanded, and a few guards entered the room to take him away.

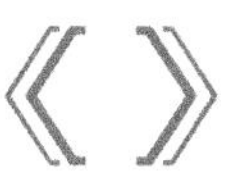

ARISH HAD HIS FIFTH glass of wine at a seedy pub when his resolve returned. He would get his revenge for this outrage. The only way to get revenge on his wife was to return to Earth and steal the Terran Zeto Crystal. With the crystal in his possession, he would be as strong as her, and he could retake his rightful leadership over the Zetan race.

Arish spotted Hadad and Dagan Raminom in the corner of a tavern. They had been notorious criminals on Disyerto-2, and if he had still been the governor of Zetani Nova, he would have summoned the city guard. However, under his current circumstances, they were his best bet. Arish approached them and spoke, "The Raminom Brothers, I could never have imagined that I would see you on Zetani Nova," Arish said.

As Hadad glimpsed at his pistol, Arish slapped him with a psionic blast and warned, "Don't even think about it, Hadad."

The Brothers stared dumbfoundedly at him, and Dagan spoke. "Why are you here? Rumour has it that you died two years ago."

"So, is that what my wife claimed?" Arish asked.

"Your fate was never mentioned. Instead, there was a proclamation that Podixa Sairan was the new governess and that she was in control of the Zeto Crystal." Hadad replied.

'Hmm, is there still support for me on Zetani Nova if I choose to rise against my ex-wife?' Arish thought and brushed off the idea. Podixa had ruled the planet for two years, she held the Zeto Crystal, and nothing indicated that she faced a rebellion. So, to move now would be foolish. Yet, if he secured the Terran Zeto Crystal, he could travel to the other Zetan penal colonies and gather enough support to overthrow her.

"I have a proposition for you. Help me, and you can find endless wealth." Arish said.

"That sounds like an empty promise since your wife deposed you." Dagan taunted.

Arish held back his impulse to blast the mercenary out of existence. He needed men for his plan, and committing a pointless murder in front of witnesses would only cause his death.

"The Zeto Crystal is the basis of my wife's power. I know where we can find other ones. Once we have Zeto Crystals, we will find wealth and power beyond belief." Arish proclaimed.

The Raminom Brothers looked at each other with evil greedy eyes. They knew that Arish had been among the explorers that found this world. If he could discover another world where they were in charge, the opportunities would be endless.

"We'll help you, Master Arish," Dagan said.

"Good. There is a secret site in the Karmena Mountains. Gather your men and meet me outside tomorrow night. Here are the coordinates," Arish said, scribbled a note and left it along with a gold coin.

The ball was rolling. Now he needed to find out if the brothers could deliver.

Chapter 42: The Neanderthal Intervention.

Gaia woke up and studied the naked Areela Kheeran, who slept next to her. She felt happy to seduce the beautiful Zetan, yet she couldn't let go of her guilt. She could have saved Zelinko with the Terran Zeto Crystal, and she hadn't. How could she ever have an honest relationship if she didn't reveal the truth?

Gaia got up and made herself some tea. Then, she walked to a nearby hill and watched the full moon reflecting in the quiet Tigris River. It was such a peaceful night, yet she couldn't find peace. "Mother, what shall I do?" Gaia telepathed, but True Maker didn't reply. It seemed that her mother did not want to intervene in her love life, or was everything progressing as her mother intended?

Gaia felt how the wind was increasing, which itself was not strange. They had built a wall around the Garden of Eden, and it was summer, so there was no reason to waste power by keeping the forcefield on. Yet, as the wind got stronger, she had an ominous feeling. It reminded her about how Arish had flattened Arishome Valley when he arrived on Zetani Nova three years earlier.

"Mummy! Mummy! Help!"

Gaia heard how her twins Ava and Adan were shouting her name. Something was amiss.

She rushed back to her cabin, and she saw something terrifying. Arish and a dozen mercenaries were holding Areela and the twins at gunpoint. Arish shouted to Gaia, "Gaia, I had hoped to never return to this shitty planet, but you left me with no choice. Give me the Terran Zeto Crystal."

Gaia closed her eyes and telepathed to True Maker: "Mother, please help me."

"What do you want me to do? Even if I made you powerful enough to kill the mercenaries, any violence would lead to the death of Areela and your children. So, you'll have to make a choice. If you choose violence, everyone you love will die." True Maker revealed.

"Why don't you intervene and kill every assailant with a snap of your fingers? What is stopping you?"

Gaia pleaded.

"Because I do not make choices that affect the lives of mortals. Only mortals can make those choices." True Maker replied.

"So, how do I save my loved ones and my species?" Gaia asked.

"Have faith, my dear daughter. You are not the only force of good on this planet. Give in to Arish's demands, and everything will work out." True Maker reassured Gaia.

Kaboom

Gaia opened her eyes and screamed in pain when Arish shot her left shoulder. "Don't try speaking to your deity, Gaia. Next time I'll shoot one of your children. Now take me to the Terran Zeto Crystal. It is at Mount Sinai, isn't it?" Arish threatened.

"Yes." Gaia whimpered.

"I knew it! I should have checked it out myself after finding out where you went with Zelinko. Such a fool I was to trust you. Yet, you were the bigger fool, Gaia. No one crosses me!" Arish barked.

"So, what happens now?" Areela asked.

"Get on the hovercraft. It is time for an excursion on this miserable planet!" Arish said, which prompted the mercenaries to shove Areela and the toddlers onto a hovercraft.

Gaia hesitated for a bit. She was in pain and couldn't understand why her mother wouldn't help her. Yet she knew of the True Maker's mysterious ways. Gaia pushed aside her doubts and got on the hovercraft, which took off in the direction of Mount Sinai.

"I AM SO ANGRY WITH you. Why did you lie to me?"

Gaia didn't catch a break when Areela cleaned her bullet wound with a cloth. Instead, the scenario she had feared had finally occurred; Areela had found out about Gaia's lies and refusal to save Zelinko's life.

"I couldn't tell you the truth. It was Zelinko's idea to give Arish a false Zeto Crystal. I didn't know what to do about his death." Gaia replied.

"Why didn't you save him at Mount Sinai?" Areela accused.

"I... My mother would not let me." Gaia said gently.

"You have denied her in the past. She never approved of your relationship with my brother." Areela replied.

"I... It made sense to obey her wishes as Zelinko stood between me and what I desired." Gaia admitted.

"So, you let my husband die so you could sleep with me? Did you kill him?" Areela exclaimed.

"I didn't kill him. He fell while fighting a Neanderthal human. However, I did follow my mother's wish not to resurrect him. I am sorry," Gaia replied.

"I hate you. You chose to let Zelinko die. You might as well have killed him yourself." Areela shouted and took a few steps away from Gaia.

"Please don't say that. I love you, Areela." Gaia said and walked towards Areela.

Slap

Gaia fell backwards when one of the mercenaries slapped her right cheek and taunted her. "Arish told you to stay in the back of the hovercraft, bitch."

Gaia bit her lip and prepared to fight. She had enough of these people, and she was on the verge of exploding from losing everything.

Be calm, my daughter, and everything will be okay. Lose your temper, and you'll lose everything.

Her mother's words echoed in Gaia's head, which prompted her to close her eyes and meditate to find inner peace.

"GET UP. LEAD US TO the Zeto Crystal."

When Gaia opened her eyes, she woke up next to a puddle of vomit. The bullet wounds in her shoulder had festered, which caused nausea and fever.

"I can't. It's in a shrine near the top of the mountain. I am too weak to climb it." Gaia said while holding in pain.

"Bah, too weak? Aren't you the Chosen One, the supreme deity's daughter? Do as I say, or I'll kill everyone you care about in front of your eyes." Arish threatened.

"Do as he instructs. He shall soon face judgement on the narrow path." True Maker whispered.

Gaia got up. She was in pain, and she felt nauseous. Yet, knowing that the narrow path was near, she pulled herself together and got up.

"Well, let's go then, motherfucker." Gaia said and walked as fast as her injuries allowed her towards the mountaintop shrine.

"EEEEEEK!"

The sounds of dozens of falcons swooping against Arish and his mercenaries surprised Gaia. Was her mother controlling the birds, and how would it be enough to defeat her enemies?

"Shoot those fucking birds," Arish shouted, and the mercenaries started shooting after the falcons.

Swoosh

Gaia saw how one of the mercenaries fell off the cliff with a spear sticking from his back. She looked up. Neanderthal humans had ambushed the Zetan mercenaries by throwing spears and shooting bows.

Arish tried to blast the Neanderthals with psionic blasts, but like Zelinko, he experienced how psionic discharges didn't affect these humans. So, he ended his days falling off the cliff with an arrow through his windpipe.

Seeing how the Neanderthals vanquished the Zetan mercenaries, Gaia was about to take a sigh of relief when she noticed something. She felt excruciating pain as she breathed. She put a hand on her chest, and she felt how blood and air were pouring out. A stray bullet had punctured her lung.

"Is this how I die?" Gaia asked True Maker, who didn't answer as darkness shrouded her eyes.

Chapter 43: The Terran Guardians.

"Gaia. Come back to me. Please, I love you."

Gaia woke in shock as she took a deep painful breath. She had been out before, but never like this. The other times, her mind had teleported to the Divine Dimension, but she had only experienced the dark oblivion of death this time. Gaia opened her eyes, and she smiled at the angelic beauty of Areela Kheeran, who smiled behind a face covered in tears. The bright light from the Terran Zeto Crystal in Areela's hand revealed what Gaia had suspected for a long time. They were equals, chosen by destiny for a higher purpose.

"Did we win?" Gaia asked.

"Yes," Areela replied.

"And our children?" Gaia asked.

"They are safe," Areela replied.

Gaia took another breath. It wasn't as painful as the one that awoken her from death, and with a bit of luck, she would make a full recovery. "Thank you, mother." She whispered and closed her eyes.

"THANK YOU FOR LEADING those evil men into my trap. It would have been terrible if Arish stole the Zeto Crystal."

As Gaia opened her eyes, it was night, and she was rolled up in animal furs next to a bonfire. Dying was tiresome, and all she wanted was to get more sleep, yet she was intrigued about where she was.

Her eyes caught the tall and obese primitive woman who stood next to the fire. The Neanderthal humans worship her, yet Gaia had never seen anyone fatter and uglier in her life.

"Don't judge a book by its cover, my daughter. I am the essence of beauty to these people," The fat woman stated in the Zetan language.

"Mother?" Gaia asked.

"Yes, but to these people, I am Dewi Kesuburan. As unappealing as I am in your eyes, I am the pinnacle of beauty in this caveman world where people starve in the cold." True Maker revealed.

"I don't understand. Why did you train these people to fight Arish instead of helping me directly?" Gaia asked.

"The problem is choice. I told you this so many times in the past." True Maker replied.

"But you influenced them," Gaia argued.

"Yes, but in the end, they chose to fight the invaders at the risk of their own lives. I taught them how to control the falcons and kill with bows and arrows, but they chose to fight for what they believed in." True Maker revealed.

Gaia disagreed with True Maker, but she did not voice her opinion. Her mother was the way she was, and her methods were mystical.

"So, did I die when I got shot?" Gaia asked.

"Yes. I left it to Areela to decide whether to save you or not. It was her choice." True Maker replied.

"Thank you," Gaia said with an afterthought.

"Yes, now get some rest. I will move the Terran Zeto Crystal to a new location. I will also give you enough Zeto-charged sapphires to last you a lifetime." True Maker said.

"Thank you, mother," Gaia said, closed her eyes, and caught some well-needed sleep.

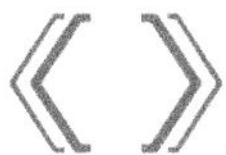

"THANK YOU FOR SAVING me."

Areela said and looked at Gaia as they were on the hovercraft for the flight back to the Garden of Eden.

"I don't understand. You were the one who saved me." Gaia protested.

"You saved me from myself. I never hated you for letting Zelinko die as he used me and left me to die. I was on death row for nine months because he didn't stand up for me, and he didn't tell the court what happened on the night when Xialiab died. During my time in prison, I hated him more than anything, and although he saved me in the end, I could never love him." Areela revealed.

"I understand. Thank you for saving my life, and I hope that there will never be any more reasons for us to hate each other." Gaia said.

"I hope that as well!"

Gaia and Areela turned around, and they saw True Maker, who had taken the form of Keila Eisenstein.

Being in the presence of the supreme deity, Areela kneeled, bowed, and said, "Your eminence, you honour me with your presence."

True Maker put her hand on Areela's head, filled her with blue energy, smiled, and spoke, "I am the one who should thank you, Areela Kheeran, for saving my daughter. As my daughter-in-law, I have bestowed you with the same powers as Gaia. Therefore, you should roam this planet as equals until you find your final purpose."

"Thank you, mother," Areela said and smiled at True Maker while her eyes were glowing blue.

True Maker nodded and was about to evaporate into thin air when an unusual feeling gripped her. She felt guilty. She didn't know if this was because of the human shell she inhabited or if something else was at play, but she did know one thing. She needed to get it off her chest.

"Daughters, there is something I need to tell you," True Maker said.

"Yes, mother?" Gaia replied.

"I... I feel a sense of guilt." True Maker mumbled.

"A sense of guilt, your eminence? How can that be?" Areela replied confusedly.

"I sacrificed the lives of the Neanderthal humans with my choices in this timeline. They were the noblest of the humanoid species on Earth, and they would have continued to live even if I didn't task Gaia with building the Garden of Eden. But, instead, the spread of Homo Sapiens will lead to the Neanderthals' demise, as they will be killed by the former." True Maker revealed and sobbed silently.

Gaia hugged her mother, and Areela joined in. Although they didn't know what to say to comfort the deity, they found peace when they embraced the source of pure energy. True Maker evaporated after a while, leaving the women alone and blissful. They looked at each other and felt content, knowing that even the supreme deity faced the same emotional dilemmas as they did.

Chapter 44: Dark Clouds on the Horizon.

Thorax Zelinkom was studying his massive member in his bedroom mirror. It was full of thorny spikes and lizard scales, and he looked at it with a sense of hatred and pride. He looked remarkably different from the rest of the Zetans, which didn't help his love life. Other Zetans had smooth genitalia, which was more suitable for gentle lovemaking than the rough sadistic sessions Thorax dreamt about with his future mates.

His sex drive was problematic for several reasons. First, he was still a minor, 87 years too young to legally have sex on Zetani Nova. Seeing how he had developed compared to other Zetans, he didn't even know whether he would live that long. A more significant issue was his looks. He knew that he acted as a repellent to all the Zetan women on the planet, so how would he find a mate?

'I'll show them; I'll take them by force if they reject me.' Thorax grumbled and smiled wickedly to himself. Yet, as tempting as the thought was, it was also a dumb idea. His looks stood out from the rest of the Zetans, so the first rape he committed would be his last, as an angry mob would hunt him down.

'Hmm, what if I become the master of the Xenos on Xenora, as True Maker once prophesized?' Thorax reflected. Thorax recalled his visions of Xenora years ago when the True Maker still guided him. The Xenos were strong, and their women were much like him, thorny and scaly with lizard-like skin. Would it be possible for him to entice Xeno females with his raging violent dreams?

There was an obvious problem with the plan. Despite Thorax being larger than the other Zetans, he was small and weak compared to the Xenos. As a hybrid between Xeno and Zetan species, his physical inadequacy would cause him issues in the Xeno society, where physical strength was the law of the land.

'The Xenora Zeto Crystal... If I can use it against the other Xenos, I can control their weak minds,' Thorax thought. Although the Xeno species were far more aggressive and bloodthirsty than Zetans, their intelligence level was on par with those of a boar. If he found a way to control the Xenos, he could have as much rough sex as he wanted and seek something far more important. He could seek revenge against his mother for abandoning him and against Gaia for stealing his rightful place as the herald of the True Maker. How glorious it would be to retake what was his.

But to reach Xenora and dominate the galaxy, he needed to get away from Zetani Nova. He knew that to be extremely powerful, he needed to acquire the primordial Zeto crystals around the galaxy, and the first one to acquire should be the Zetani Nova Crystal.

Thorax realised that he could make a deal with Podixa. If she allowed him access to the Zetani Nova Crystal, he could charge a bunch of sapphires with it and have a plentiful supply of charged sapphires. He could offer to make her the strongest Zetan in the universe by teaming up with him once he becomes the Master of the Xenos.

Feeling excited by the prospects of his future revenge, Thorax got horny and relieved himself in front of the mirror while laughing and fantasising about how mighty he would become.

KING KAILOW VOLTROM and his young son prince Mellron Kailom watched the double eclipse while on a boat and munching on an expensive delicacy, as Elvonia's two moons merged in the sky and covered Elvonia's sunlike star, showing traces of lights in the shape of a moonflower. It was the first time in Kailow's thirteen years on the planet that he experienced the legendary Double Moonflower Eclipse, and he wished he could share the moment with Queen Imogen. Queen Imogen longed to witness the double eclipse before facing her unfortunate death three months earlier during child labour.

Kailow didn't know what bothered him the most, the loss of his wife Imogen and his unborn child or the fact that he could have saved them if he had access to Zetan lifesaving technologies. Why did Imogen have to die so young?

On this occasion, Prince Mellron gave a speech to his Elven subjects to commemorate his darling mother and celebrate the Double Moonflower

Eclipse. The address impressed Kailow. Despite his young age, Prince Mellron had given a magnificent speech, and he remained very composed despite his mother's recent death. The Elven prophecy was correct; Mellron would lead the Elves to a Golden Age.

After giving the formal speech, Prince Mellron walked off the podium, hugged his father, King Kailow, and spoke, "How did you find my speech, father?"

"It was amazing. I am so impressed that you pulled yourself together after the tragedy." King Kailow replied.

"I did it for our people. Fíordhéantóir gives and takes. It is the way of our law. She took my mother too early, but she gave us this marvellous double eclipse, which marks the start of a new era." Prince Mellron replied.

Kailow reflected on Mellron's statement. He was confident that the True Maker had nothing to do with Queen Imogen's death. Instead, the supreme deity only manipulated crucial events for the timeline. Gaia had explained that to him before he left her for Imogen.

Kailow thought about what had become of Gaia and his sister Areela. Had they arrived on Earth, and had they saved humanity? When thinking about his first love, Kailow felt a desire to leave Elvonia. He was an outsider on this planet, and without Imogen, he didn't want to stay. Yet, his son needed him. Mellron was only 12 years old. He was too young to rule without his father's wisdom and guidance.

Kailow woke up from daydreaming when Mellron looked at him with glowing blue eyes while murmuring words silently. Kailow gasped in shock, this was the third time he saw the mark of possession by True Maker, and it was as impressive as it was terrifying. *"Your sister Areela and your true love Gaia will fulfil their mission of saving humankind, while your destiny and Mellron's lie on Elvonia."*

After saying this, Prince Mellron reverted to his usual green eyes, and he spoke with a groggy voice. "Uhm, my head hurts... what happened?"

"Nothing, everything will be alright," Kailow said as he watched the sunset and reflected on what changes life would bring.

"AVA, COME HERE, MY daughter."

Ava Gaian was sitting down at the local herb garden and was educating the primitive humans about medicinal herbs when she heard her mother's voice. She approached her dear mother, who was sipping tea by the garden shed. The humans revered her mother as a goddess, as she and the Zetans had built the Garden of Eden. Ava knew that people saw her the same way, making her uneasy. She didn't strive for high status in life; she wanted to be like everyone else, albeit her pastel blue skin and half Zetan heritage made that impossible.

"Yes, mother, you asked for me," Ava said and smiled politely.

"You are now 12 years old, and you'll soon be a woman. Thus, you need to start thinking about finding yourself a suitable husband." Gaia said.

"But I don't want a husband. I want to be like you and Aunty Areela. You love each other, and you don't yearn for any annoying males." Ava said.

Gaia sighed. She wanted her daughter to copulate and spread her genes, and True Maker had instructed her on suitable mates for Ava when she turned 16. Yet, she hadn't been leading by example, and she could face an uphill battle in convincing her daughter to seek male companionship.

"Before Areela and I found each other, I was in love with your father, Kailow. I thought he was the love of my life, but he abandoned me for an elven princess. Since then, I couldn't see myself with another man." Gaia revealed.

"So, why did father abandon us?" Ava said.

"He never abandoned you and your brother. He didn't know about my pregnancy when he left me." Gaia replied.

"So, then it's your fault I don't have a father? You were too prideful to return to him and tell him about us?" Ava exclaimed and rushed off in anger.

Gaia watched as her daughter walked away, and she couldn't make herself run after the dear child. She had prioritised saving humanity, but the ice age period had slowly faded after the Mount Toba eruption, and she didn't need to be on Earth all the time. So what had stopped her from visiting Kailow in the last few years? Was now a suitable time to visit Elvonia so her children could finally meet their father?

Gaia felt a cold breeze, and she saw dark thunderclouds on the horizon. 'Hmm, I better turn on the forcefield to protect my people from the thunderstorm,' Gaia thought and sent a voice command to the AI. "AI, turn on the forcefield in all sectors. Authorisation code, ZZ6B."

"AI, please ignore that request, authorisation code ZZ12."

Gaia turned around and looked at the person in front of her. It was the True Maker again, taking the form of Ellen Hines.

"Why are you here, and what happened to Keila?" Gaia asked.

True Maker snapped her fingers, changed her body to Keila Eisenstein, and replied, "I wanted to change it up, but I can use this form to appease you; it is all the same."

"So, why did you turn off the forcefield?" Gaia asked.

"Because you cannot protect them forever; they'll need to weather this storm," True Maker replied.

"Why now, though? They are still young." Gaia protested.

"Most of the humans in your ward are no longer children. They have reached adulthood, and they need to face a trial. Besides, Ava is correct. It is time for her and Adan to meet their father and stepbrother." True Maker instructed.

"Stepbrother?" Gaia asked.

"Yes, Kailow had a son with Queen Imogen before her passing," True Maker replied.

Hearing about Imogen's passing filled Gaia with mixed feelings. One part of her wanted to reignite the flame with Kailow, but another really hated him. However, she knew that her children needed to see their father, and Areela would be happy to see her brother.

"Don't even think about rekindling the flame with Kailow Voltrom. The two of you are not meant to be." True Maker warned.

"I guess you are right. If I leave, will I ever return to Earth?" Gaia asked.

"Your spirit will never abandon this planet," True Maker said and evaporated.

Gaia shivered as the icy rain soaked her, and she had an ominous feeling that her death was drawing closer.

Chapter 45: A Rapist at the Monastery.

Thorax Zelinkom was sleepless, and he was grinding his teeth in frustration. Podixa had refused to allow him access to Zetani Nova's Zeto Crystal. Thus, she bereaved them both of an endless supply of Zeto-charged sapphires.

'That stupid bitch! I could have made her more powerful than any Zetan has ever been." Thorax mumbled. He had been honest about his intentions; he would have made Podixa the mightiest Zetan ever, and she could have kept the Zeto Crystal after he became the Master of the Xenos. All he needed was enough charged sapphires to make his way to Xenora, where he was destined to be the ruler. So, why had she denied him?

"Why do they always deny me?" Thorax growled, and his mind wandered to a remote monastery. The nuns had denied themselves the pleasures of the flesh. Moreover, they had done so by choice, while his abstinence was anything but voluntary. How ironic it would be if he raped one of them.

Thorax recollected that Podixa had hidden the charged Shamraz Sapphire in the monastery. Why hadn't he thought about this before? He could attack the nuns, steal the sapphire, and leave this damn planet before anyone could make him answer for his crimes.

Excited for his prospects, Thorax started drooling while whooping in delight. His time was soon to come.

IT WAS LATE AT NIGHT, and the absence of a moon made the night sky dark as Sarah Amelan was doing the rounds of mopping in the Besimung Temple. She hated the monastery and the strict nuns that ran it. Such hypocrisy that her mother, Amela Andelan, and Governor Podixa Sairan had sent her here. Some things were better left unsaid, such as criticising her mother and the governor for their lesbian lifestyle. They had sent her away, and she was stuck with zealots in the wilderness.

"Rawshhhh, Krawwrr......"

Sarah saw the terrifying freak Thorax Zelinkom sneaking around the premises, hiding under a bush. Why was the mutant beast here?

"Thorax, why are you here? Did my mother send you to intimidate me?" Sarah whispered.

Thorax muttered something, crouched out of the shadows, and replied, "Arrrghhhh!! Rawwrr... Sneaking... Sneaking isn't the Xeno way."

"What are you talking about?" Sarah replied.

"I am here for the Shamraz Sapphire. Let me have it!" Thorax commanded.

Sarah looked at the terrifying Thorax, who had extended his razor-sharp claws. Would he attack her if she screamed for help? However, she knew one thing; she would not risk her life to save this monastery's relic.

"Do you promise to leave me unharmed if I take you to the sacred Shamraz Sapphire?" Sarah said.

"I promise," Thorax hissed and smiled wickedly.

Sarah nodded and led Thorax along a small path until they reached a cave. "The...The charged sapphire is in there." Sarah stuttered.

"So, what are you waiting for? Lead the way!" Thorax growled.

Sarah froze in place. The last thing she wanted was to enter the cave with the angry beast. If he were to attack her there, no one would hear her screams.

"But I took you to the sapphire. You promised to let me go," Sarah protested.

"You are coming with me. I cannot allow you to raise the alarm, you stupid Zetan bitch." Thorax threatened.

Sarah nodded, and they entered the cave temple. They spotted the sapphire, which shone with a tranquil blue light from the altar as they reached the temple's inner sanctum.

"Gaahaha.....Rawwrrr!!."

Seeing how close he was to reaching his goal, Thorax felt orgasmic and horny, and he decided to fulfil his darkest desires. He closed the door behind them, extended his claws and cut off the belt that held up Sarah's pants.

"Please, you promised not to hurt me." Sarah pleaded in shock.

"I guess I lied. GRAAAWRRR!" Thorax mocked, jumped Sarah, pinned her down, and raped her with his barbed member. He came after a few strokes, and he knocked Sarah unconscious. Then, with Sarah bleeding out on the floor, Thorax grabbed the gemstone, and he laughed menacingly. The sapphire was his, and soon he would be where he belonged. The Xenos on Xenora was his to lead, and he couldn't wait to shape his destiny.

Chapter 46: The Escape to Xenora.

"**R**aarhh…I got to run faster. They are getting closer. Ggrrrr!"

Thorax looked over his shoulder as he ran faster than he had ever run before. In the divine dimension, there were no obstacles that inhibited his running speed, and he had been running at over 100 kilometres an hour for several hours. In less than an hour, he would reach Xenora. Yet, a problem approached him from behind. Several Zetan hovercrafts were chasing him, and those vehicles cruised a lot faster than he could run.

"I got to keep going; my salvation is near." Thorax urged as he ran towards his destiny.

"THE FUGITIVE IS WITHIN range of our lasers, and we should fire before he escapes."

Amela Andelan looked at the hovercraft's captain, Petar Ademom, and shook her head. While Thorax needed to die for what he had done to her poor daughter, killing him with lasers was too lenient. Instead, he needed to suffer for what he had done.

"My beloved Sarah is in the ICU after what that monster did to her. We cannot allow him the mercy of a swift death!" Amela commanded furiously.

"But what if he escapes?" Petar said.

"Then we'll chase after him. We will follow that monster to the edge of the universe if we need to. Besides, we'll catch up with him in less than 10 minutes."

The captain was about to answer when a flash of light blinded them. As the light disappeared, Thorax had vanished from their sensors.

"He is gone. What do we do?" Petar asked.

"We'll pursue him, of course," Amela replied.

"But we don't know where he went?" Petar objected.

'There is supposed to be a Zeto Crystal on the inhospitable planet Xenora. Thorax spoke about the planet's existence when the True Maker possessed him. One day you and I will go there and claim what is ours…'

Amela recalled this conversation she had with Arish many years earlier. At the time, Arish had ambitious plans for the Zetan race. However, as Podixa had found out about their affair, she had given Amela a better offer.

"Thorax has escaped to the planet Xenora. We will pursue him there." Amela stated.

"Planet Xenora? I have never heard of it. How can you be so sure?" Petar asked.

Amela thought of telling Petar what she knew about Xenora, but she refrained from doing so. She was far away from home, and it was better if Petar didn't know about the Zeto Crystal on Xenora. Otherwise, he might get too ambitious.

"Don't worry about that. Carry out my commands. We'll head there at once." Amela stated.

"Understood, Vice Governess Andelan," Petar replied and rushed off to alert his men.

As Petar left, Amela ground her teeth in resentment. Her daughter had suffered at the hands of Thorax. If she could avenge Sarah and obtain the Xenora Zeto Crystal, it would be worth facing the vile flesh-eating Xenos.

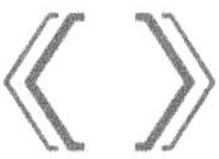

"HRRNM…. THE SUN IS approaching noontime; take cover."

As Thorax opened his eyes, he was on an alien planet covered in grassfires. A dark blue star covered a large portion of the maroon, cloudy and smoky dark sky. How could anything live in this hellhole?

"Hisss….Don't stand there. Take cover, child." A Xeno female shouted from a hatch in a cliffside.

Thorax nodded and ran towards the woman. She closed the hatch as he got to her, stepped away from the door, and spoke, "What were you doing in the noontime sun, child? Are you too injured to run with the others?"

Thorax looked at the woman. She was three meters tall, and she had massive claws, fangs, and purple eyes. She looked gorgeous in Thorax's eyes. Yet, he sensed that she was older, far beyond her child-bearing age.

"I am not a child. I am a hybrid of Xeno and Zetan. Half of my genome is that of another species," Thorax revealed.

"Hrrnmm... What are you talking about? We cannot breed with other species on this planet." The Xeno woman replied.

"I am not from this planet. Anyway, let's get introduced. I am Thorax Zelinkom from Zetani." Thorax said.

The woman stared at Thorax, nodded, sighed, and spoke, "It has finally happened. The prophecy is about to come true!"

"You don't seem very excited, lady?" Thorax replied.

"My name is Sandrung. The prophecy is not a good thing. It marks the end of an era." Sandrung replied.

"Why is that?" Thorax asked.

"Hrrnmm......To understand that, you must first know what this place is. These tunnels are our nurseries. This is where our proud females give birth, and babies live here for the first years of their lives. This is also where those too old to live on the surface look after the young." Sandrung replied.

"How could anything live on the surface? That place was an inferno." Thorax replied.

"Hirrrsss...... It all depends on the time of the day. Xenora has a slow rotation, so it is a paradise in the morning as the sun defrosts the ice and everything springs to life. It turns into a blazing inferno at midday as the sun heats the planet, and at night, everything freezes to ice. So those who are fit can run westwards to stay in the morning, which is a paradise," Sandrung revealed.

"Interesting. Would you mind if I stay here until the morning?" Thorax asked.

"I would not mind at all. I cannot send a handsome young man like you to your death. You can help me raise the young." Sandrung replied.

"Thank you," Thorax said, growled happily, and sat down to reflect on his options. While this place was his destiny, it didn't feel encouraging to lurk in a dark cave while babysitting children.

'Oh well, things will improve when the morning comes,' Thorax thought and started eating the giant mushrooms, the only food source in the cave.

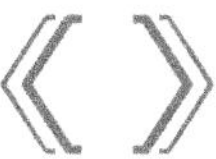

"VICE GOVERNESS ANDELAN. We need to leave this planet at once."

Amela looked at Petar. Her captain was correct, yet she couldn't leave things as they were. She couldn't give up pursuing Thorax after what he had done to her daughter.

"Thorax is still out there. We need to capture him and bring him back to Zetani Nova for what he did." Amela commanded.

"That's not going to happen. Thorax must have died in the inferno, and so will we if we venture out to look for him." Petar replied.

"Yet, I command you and your men to help me look for him." Amela urged.

"No. Soldiers, capture Vice Governess Andelan. We are returning to Zetani Nova." Petar commanded.

"You cannot do this to me. This is treason!" Amela exclaimed in shock.

"No, this is following orders. We are loyal to Governess Podixa Sairan. She ordered us to make sure that you stay safe." Petar stated as a few soldiers grabbed Amela, and the group left Xenora through the same portal as they arrived.

Chapter 47: The Crystal at the North Pole.

"**Y**es!"

Thorax Zelinkom shone with glee when he realised that his prediction was correct. Xenora had a stable climate in the polar regions of the planet.

"What are you so excited about? It's freezing cold here. We will freeze to death when the sun sets."

Thorax looked at Dijana, who was petite compared to most Xenos. Measuring two metres, she had been the shortest adult in her tribe. Impressed by Thorax's superior intelligence, Dijana had fallen for him, and here they were, at the world's edge.

"Ahhh.... My beautiful Dijana. You are missing the point. The sun will not set while we are here. We will live in tranquil twilight without the need to keep moving." Thorax replied.

"But the sun moves in the sky. How would you make it stop?" Dijana asked.

Thorax bit his lip and looked at Dijana. While he enjoyed the sex, her beauty, and her infatuation with him, her lack of intelligence annoyed him. Such was the curse of being a hybrid. Among the Xenos, he was a genius, so he had to suffer the idiocy of his peers.

"My dear Dijana. We have discussed this already. The sun is not moving in the sky. Instead, Xenora is rotating around its axis, creating the illusion that the sun is moving. Since Xenora doesn't have an angular tilt and seasons, the polar regions are always in the twilight zone." Thorax replied.

"This place is cold and barren. How can the North Pole be the future of our people?" Dijana asked.

"The cold is manageable. The Zetans have colonised many places like this in the past. We need to gather the sun's rays and use them for heating and farming. This is the only place without the searing midday heat. This is where we will create Xeno Civilization." Thorax stated.

Having said this, Thorax noticed how Dijana showed signs of wanting to mate. He was about to mount her when something more important caught his senses. He sensed that Xenora's Zeto Crystal was nearby. The presence of the Zeto Crystal at the North Pole made sense. Destiny had taken him to the only place where a permanent settlement was possible, so the crystal had to be close.

"Growl...... Copulation will have to wait, my lovely. There is something far more important to do." Thorax stated.

Dijana gave him a confused look and replied, "What is more important than sex?"

"The Zeto Crystal is nearby. Once it is mine, nothing will stop me from ruling this planet." Thorax exclaimed.

As Dijana poked her lizard-like tongue and licked her shiny claws, Thorax added, "Rahhawhaw! Once WE have the Zeto Crystal, nothing will stop US from ruling this planet together."

Dijana scratched Thorax's arm with her claw, licked the blood from the superficial cut, and replied flirtatiously, "That's better, my love. Never forget that we are a team."

"I would never forget that, my dear Dijana," Thorax replied, although his inner thoughts were less cordial. 'I better get rid of her when I have the Zeto Crystal. I will not co-rule with that stupid bitch. She is only good for a fuck.'

After their conversation, Thorax got up, and he let his intuition lead him in the direction of the Xenora Zeto Crystal. Immense powers would soon be his!

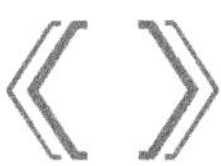

"WHY ARE YOU STARING at that rock? What is so special about it?"

Dijana's words awakened Thorax from his mesmerised trance. How long had he been standing here? Once they had found the Xenora Zeto Crystal, he was stunned by its beauty and potential to change the fundaments of the universe.

"What do you mean? Can't you see the beautiful light that irradiates from the crystal? Can't you feel the immense power it has over the universe?" Thorax exclaimed.

"It's just a gemstone. I have seen similar stones in the past. How is this sapphire going to make us the masters of this planet?" Dijana asked confusedly.

Thorax looked at Dijana and then turned his eyes to the crystal. It was still as magnificent as it had been moments earlier. There were only two explanations. Either Dijana was blind to the crystal's magnificent powers, or he had lost his mind.

There was only one way to find out. He needed to grab the crystal and use its powers against Dijana. That approach would prove him right!

Thorax ran up to the altar where the crystal was placed. As he grabbed it, he tried blasting Dijana with a psionic blast. She gave him a confused look and said, "Grrmm... What are you doing? Why are you waving your hands like that...?"

'Ah, so the Xenos have immunity against psionic powers.' Thorax realised. While the revelation didn't shock him, it amazed him that Dijana didn't even flinch while he was holding the Zeto Crystal. Yet, if the Zeto Crystal's powers didn't work against the Xenos, he would never be able to use it to dominate the planet.

"This is pathetic. I can't believe I followed you to this desolate place. I am returning to Grichuk's harem. I need a real man!" Dijana hissed, turned around, and crept towards the exit.

Hearing Dijana's taunt in his moment of defeat made Thorax see red. If he couldn't use the Zeto Crystal's powers to control her, he would use it to bludgeon her. Thorax grabbed the crystal, sprinted towards Dijana, and slammed her in the back of the head. As she slumped to the ground, he kept bashing her with the Zeto Crystal until he heard a cracking noise and Dijana's greenish brain substance splashed on the ground.

Thorax collapsed next to Dijana's lifeless body. He had lost everything. The Xenora Zeto Crystal was useless, and he had murdered his fuck buddy out of an impulse. The only thing left to do was jumping off a cliff to end it all. But, before moving on with his suicidal plans, Thorax looked at the Zeto Crystal. It had changed. Being used to bludgeon Dijana, it had absorbed the colour of her greenish-red blood, and it shone with a crimson red light. His destiny was to obtain the Xenoran Zeto crystal and turn it into a dark crystal. Thorax instinctively knew that an era of dominion and terror had begun.

Chapter 48: The Subjugation.

Thorax Zelinkom felt his anger and resentment grow as he tore a medium-sized rodent-like creature to shreds and ate it ravenously. As he drank its blood, his thoughts were circling around the event that had just happened. How could Dijana choose to leave him for such a brutish, fruitless existence?

As he thought about Dijana's death, Thorax reflected on it with regret and anger. It was terrible that she had threatened to leave him for another man, which made him kill her. Now that he had bludgeoned her to death, he was alone in the universe. Yet, the episode also brought him a new meaning. He would never have unlocked the true potential of the Zeto crystal if he hadn't used it to bludgeon Dijana. The crimson coloured Dark Zeto Crystal would make him unstoppable, as it was the ultimate arbiter of life and death. Furthermore, it would enable him to seek revenge against Gaia, Areela, and the other Zetans for outcasting him. He had been good to them in the past, but they had always treated him with disgust due to his unnatural looks, so he vowed that they should suffer.

Thorax looked up, and he saw a flock of wildebeest running westwards. While he wasn't hungry, he wanted to try out the power of the Dark Zeto Crystal. He had no one to help him, but he was destined to rule Xenora and dominate species on other planets.

Thorax aimed the crimson coloured Dark Zeto Crystal towards the flock of animals, focused his mind on controlling the power of the dark crystal, and smiled wickedly as he saw the group of wildebeest explode, which created a cascade of blood and scattered body parts.

'Grichuk will pay for stealing Dijana from me. After his death, I will make his tribe my servants and build a fortress at the North Pole. Once I have subjugated the Xenos, I will conquer the galaxy.' Thorax thought. He ran towards the southwest to avoid the searing midday sun and get his revenge on the man who made him murder Dijana.

"GROWWL... HEY, FILTHY rat. Where is Dijana?"

As Thorax opened his eyes, Grichuk and his tribe surrounded him. His quest to find his enemy had ended, and the fool was clueless about the fate that awaited him; otherwise, Grichuk would have slit his throat while he slept.

"Dijana is dead," Thorax said.

"What happened to my Dijana?" Grichuk exclaimed.

"She wanted to return to you. But a woman cannot serve two masters, so I had to put her down." Thorax stated.

"You despicable creature! I will kill you for this!" Grichuk roared and extended his claws.

"Grahahaa... I hoped that you would say that. But don't attack me now. Surely, a trial by combat is a better way of avenging Dijana? Let the whole tribe see how you tear me to shreds." Thorax replied and smirked.

Grichuk gave Thorax a surprised look. What could the ugly halfling gain from trial by combat? Grichuk knew that Thorax was the most intelligent man he had ever come across, and this situation was a predicament. He feared that Thorax had a mischievous plan, yet he couldn't deny him a trial by combat now that everyone had heard him. "I should have ripped his throat when he was asleep," Grichuk muttered and proclaimed, "I accept your challenge. You'll face death at Flame Rock Falls. Randug, tie him up and bring the skinny-lizard freak to the fight!"

Having said this, Grichuk turned around and left.

Thorax smiled as the Xeno leader rushed off in anger. This would be the perfect opportunity to show the Xenos the fearsome powers of the Crimson Zeto Crystal.

As Randug approached him, Thorax shouted with authority. "You are not tying me up because I am not a prisoner. I want this trial as much as Grichuk does."

Hearing his confidence startled the Xenos, and none of them intervened as Thorax took the alternate route to Flame Rock Falls.

"GRICHUK, GRICHUK, GRICHUK."

Thorax smiled as the crowds chanted his rival's name. They expected a slaughter, as Grichuk was 3.5 metres tall and weighed 950 kilos. Compared to him, Thorax was tiny, standing at 2 metres and weighing 150 kilos. Yet, what a great time to show the power of the Crimson Zeto Crystal.

Thorax walked to the centre of the ring, looked at the crowd, and shouted, "Where is Grichuk? I bet he is hiding away, trembling that his end is near."

The crowd booed Thorax, and they threw gnawed bones toward him. Thorax smiled at the crowd. This was his destiny, to face despisal and mockery wherever he went. Yet soon, they would not have any choice. He would force them to serve him.

"Grichuk, Grichuk, Grichuk."

Thorax smiled as Grichuk approached him from the east, which blocked the nasty UV radiation from Xenora's blue star. One thing was certain, he would not miss the sunburns when he founded his city in the eternal twilight at the North Pole.

"Look who dared to show up. Do you have any last words?" Thorax taunted.

"GRRRR!! I will kill you for what you did to Dijana. No one steals my woman and lives." Grichuk roared.

"No, you won't," Thorax replied and pulled out the Crimson Zeto Crystal.

Thorax squeezed the crystal and focused his mind. He had dreamt about this moment for a long time, and he wouldn't grant Grichuk a swift death. He made a small flick with his hand, which caused Grichuk's claws to dislodge and hit Randug with speed.

As Randug collapsed with Grichuk's dislodged claws penetrating his throat, Thorax laughed. While he hadn't intended to murder Randug, it was a funny incident that could prove helpful. If he were to become the new leader, what better way to start than eliminating the previous leadership?

Thorax walked up to Grichuk and taunted, "This is where I'll kill you for murdering Dijana."

"What are you talking about? I never touched her." Grichuk moaned in pain.

"She would have returned to you. You were in MY way. You were in the way of destiny. As such, I sentence you to death." Thorax replied.

Grichuk leapt towards Thorax, who saw it coming and stepped to the side. He made a chopping gesture, and the crystal split Grichuk in two.

Thorax ran up to Grichuk's severed body, knocked the crimson crystal on his temple, and this caused the giant Xeno to explode into a cascade of blood and body parts and soak the crowds.

Thorax turned towards the crowds and spoke with a thundering voice, "Today, you are witnessing history. I will take you to the stars, and we will conquer this galaxy. Join me, and you shall have glory. Resist, and you must suffer. Now kneel to me."

As the crowds kneeled, Thorax laughed maliciously. The ugly outcast had become the leader, and the Zetans would suffer for what they had put him through!

Chapter 49: A Foreboding Vision.

Areela Kheeran was dipping her toes in the icy river, reflecting on life and fearing the future. The situation on Earth had been tranquil ever since the Neanderthals had stopped Arish and his mercenaries from stealing the Terran Zeto Crystal at Mount Sinai a decade earlier. Yet, Areela feared an invisible enemy, which, unlike Arish, was unstoppable. She feared the passage of time.

Areela had turned 220 or thereabouts just a few days earlier. Yet, if she was 220, 219, or 221, it did not really matter, as her time away from Zetani was only a fraction of her life. It was hard to tell her exact age, as the year wasn't the same length on Earth as on Zetani or Zetani Nova. Yet, she felt and looked young, whereas Gaia had started to look old. Moreover, her son, Siblex Junior, a young Zetan child who, in physical development, was still the size of a 5-year-old boy, was beginning to speak and think like an adult way beyond his years.

As Areela pondered how much they had been through, she feared what the future would bring. In the glimpse of an eye, the passage of time would end the short life of her human partner, which would leave Areela and Siblex Junior alone on this foreign planet.

"What's the matter, love? Is something bothering you?"

Areela turned around and looked at Gaia. She recalled how many times she had fallen in love with Gaia's beautiful face, but the magic was fading. She was too "young" to love someone that looked so old.

"No. Everything is fine," Areela replied.

"Is that so? You usually pull up your feet from the river as you hate the cold." Gaia replied.

Being reminded of the cold, Areela had a reality check, pulled her feet out of the river, shivered and spoke, "Brrrr... You're right. It is so cold. How could I forget?"

Gaia smiled and replied, "Ah, so your mind was wandering? Where did it take you?"

"I was thinking about the future. You are aging much quicker than I am. What happens when...." Areela mumbled.

"When I die? As mortals, we can never know when our deaths will come. So, we can only enjoy the moment and make the best of our time." Gaia replied.

"You know what I mean. My species can live a thousand years. What is the human lifespan? A hundred?" Areela asked.

"I know what you are talking about. I have seen how you look at me differently after I lost the beauty of my youth." Gaia said and sighed.

"Don't say that. I still love you." Areela objected.

"It's okay. I should have asked my mother to slow my aging and extend my life a long time ago." Gaia replied.

"Why didn't you?" Areela asked.

"Because I feared that True Maker wouldn't extend the favour to my children. Watching Ava and Adan wither and die from old age while I remained youthful would be a terrible curse." Gaia revealed.

"Then you understand how I feel?" Areela asked.

"Yes, I will discuss it with my mother," Gaia said, picked up Areela's feet and massaged them to rejuvenate her blue-skinned partner and show her some affection. If life could only last longer...

AREELA WAS FEVERISH and experienced terrible tremors. This was the first time she had been sick since she arrived on Earth. As it would seem, there were no pathogens on earth that could affect her. It made sense in a way. The only Zetans on the planet were Areela and her son, so a pathogen targeting her race was an evolutionary improbability.

Areela closed her eyes and tried to sleep. It didn't work. Instead, she saw terrible images of her firstborn son, Thorax, who carried out savage murders to corrupt a Zeto Crystal. Seeing how her son had fallen to hatred and malevolence, Areela shivered, and her body ached. Was this how she would meet her maker, falling victim to a pathogen on a planet far away from home?

"I heard you asked Gaia to petition me for a life extension."

As Areela opened her eyes, she faced the embodiment of the True Maker. This wasn't the first time she saw True Maker, as the supreme deity visited her daughter Gaia in physical bodies from time to time.

"Where is Gaia?" Areela wheezed.

"I sent her on an 'urgent' mission to Mount Sinai," True Maker replied.

"What is going on?" Areela asked and stared at True Maker in fear.

"You must make a choice. You have seen what has become of your son. You must choose whether to stop him or not." True Maker stated.

Areela stared at the embodiment of the Supreme Deity. She looked like any beautiful woman in her human form, yet Areela knew that the unimpressive body was a façade that the creator put on.

"Why me?" Areela asked.

"Why anyone else? You are the only one who would struggle with the moral dilemma, and the most important choices are the hardest ones. Besides, If I leave it to Governor Podixa Sairan, she will exterminate the Xenos as a precaution. So only you can reach Thorax without causing bloodshed." True Maker revealed.

Areela closed her eyes, and she saw visions of Thorax carrying out ritual murders to corrupt the Xenoran Zeto Crystal. She wanted to save her son from himself, as she was to blame for his dark soul. Her abandonment had caused it. But what if she couldn't save him? Was she ready to kill her son to save her species?

"What do I need to do?" Areela asked.

"You need to convince my daughter to follow you to Xenora. Together you can save the galaxy; separated, you are doomed." True Maker revealed.

"Why don't you convince her yourself?" Areela asked.

"I told you already. I cannot make choices. Mortals must have the final say." True Maker replied and turned her gaze away.

'She is lying. I can sense the guilt in her eyes.' Areela thought, but she pushed the thought aside. True Maker wasn't human, so whatever her body language showed could be a physical misrepresentation.

"I will do your bidding. I feel terrible knowing that my negligence caused Thorax to become this way, but I will stop him. I caused this, and I'll end it."

Areela said and felt surprised by the sudden determination that filled her spirit. Was this True Maker's doing?

"I'll cure your ailments. Prepare yourself for my daughter's return." True Maker said as she stroked Areela's cheek and evaporated into thin air.

As the supreme deity left, Areela felt invigorated. Her illness was gone, and so was her fear of the slow decay of time. She had a new purpose, which was more important than her life. The future of the Milky Way Galaxy was at stake. Absorbed by her mission, Areela got out of bed and started tinkering with Arish's old hovercraft. Time was of the essence, and as soon as Gaia returned, they had to be on their way.

Chapter 50: The Infanticide

Thorax Zelinkom inspected his newborn Xeno babies as their mothers brought them to him. He was powerful for the first time, and he felt immensely proud of himself. He would become the patriarch of the Xenos domination in the Milky Way Galaxy. He planned for the Xenos to become the most potent species by spreading his half Zetan gene to all future generations of Xenos.

At present, Thorax's goal was unachievable as his tribe consisted of only 100 Xeno females, where he was the only male. They needed to prepare their defences, and time was of the essence. He had been unable to kill all the males of his tribe, and rumours would spread about the many Xeno women available for the taking. This would bring roving bands of males to his settlement. This process would be never-ending until all hope of overthrowing him was gone.

"Faster! You need to work faster!" Thorax shouted to a group of sickly and older Xeno women that he had enslaved. When he gained control of Grichuk's tribe, Thorax had decided to only impregnate the beautiful and healthy-looking Xeno women while keeping the sick and old as slaves.

"Faster, I said!" Thorax roared, squeezed his hand, and made a pulling movement that caused one of his slaves to fall off the ramparts and plunge to her death.

Thorax bit his lip. It was irrational to murder his slaves because of perceived laziness. Slaves were a finite resource, and he needed to manage his resources to become the God-King of Xenora. Yet, his insomnia was driving him insane. He hadn't slept for six months, and the only thing that kept him alive was the malevolent powers of the corrupted dark Zeto Crystal.

Thorax looked at the last baby presented to him, and he sensed that the baby would grow up to look like Dijana.

"Dijana! Why did you betray me? You were my one true love." Thorax exclaimed, and he blacked out as blind rage took control of his body. As he got back to his senses, he had torn the baby into shreds. What had he done?

Thorax knew that he couldn't show weakness to his subordinates. Regardless of if he was right or wrong, he needed to be in control.

"Don't ever dare to present such an imperfect baby again. This is what happens." Thorax roared at the slain baby's mother. After this, he rushed off to the inner sanctum of the Zeto Crystal temple, and he locked the door behind him.

Once he was alone, he wailed in agony. Despite being powerful, he was lonelier and more miserable than ever. He thought of his Zetan mother, Areela, whose abandonment had turned him bitter and full of resentment. He swore that he would get his revenge. He would find Areela Kheeran and make her pay for what she did, even if it was the last thing he would ever do.

"MASTER THORAX, ENEMIES are approaching the fortress."

Thorax woke up as he heard Gulbatira's voice from the other side of the heavy gate that separated his bedroom from the outside world. After the infanticide, he had collapsed from his insomnia. It was ironic that the mother of the slain infant had come to warn him. Such was the nature of tyranny; some individuals would continue serving their master no matter what suffering he put them through.

Thorax grabbed his dark crystal, hurried to leave the bedroom, and spoke, "Thank you, Gulbatira. I'll remember your loyalty. Now come with me to the city walls. It is time to put on a show."

As Thorax arrived at the city walls, he realised that he had come in the 11th hour as the attackers were already scaling the walls. It was just as well, as this allowed him to test one of his inventions.

Inside the walls, there was a mesh of metal wiring. Could the power from the Zeto Crystal be enough to repel his attackers? There was only one way to find out. Thorax inserted the crystal into a slot between the metal wiring, flipped a switch, and laughed hysterically as the walls instantly electrified, which caused the attackers to plunge.

slash

Thorax stopped laughing as Gulbatira suddenly slashed him with her sharp claws and buried them deep into his torso.

"Arrggh!! Gulbatira, why did you betray me?" Thorax shouted.

"You murdered my baby in cold blood. You are a monster not worthy of being a Xeno leader." Gulbatira exclaimed.

Thorax looked at Gulbatira for a few seconds, smiled wickedly, and spoke, "You should have aimed for the head." Having said this, Thorax grabbed the crystal from the slot and allowed himself to plummet backwards from the wall.

Once he was on the ground, he used the dark crystal's powers to heal his wounds. Then, he jumped back onto the wall and lifted Gulbatira up telekinetically, utilising the power of the dark crystal. With her body under control, he used her body like a raging hammer to vanquish his enemies outside the fortress.

After defeating his enemies, Thorax exclaimed, "Bring their bodies to me. It is time for a feast."

His servants didn't dare object to their evil master, and shortly afterwards, Thorax's tribe reached a new level of villainy by embracing cannibalism.

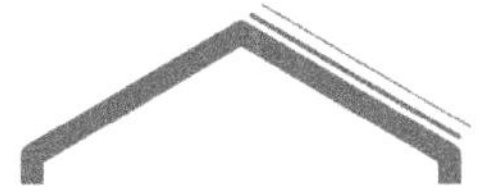

Chapter 51: The Exodus.

"What should I do with Siblex Junior? We need to stop Thorax, but I cannot bring him to Xenora, and I cannot leave him here," Areela stated.

Gaia looked at Areela Kheeran, who was heartbroken after True Maker revealed the terrible atrocities Thorax would unleash on the Milky Way Galaxy unless they stopped him. Gaia felt sympathy for her lover. It was Areela's destiny to find out about Thorax's villainous plans, though it was a cruel ploy by the True Maker to ask Areela to stop him.

"Siblex will be safe on Earth. My children Ava and Adan will protect him." Gaia replied.

"And what will happen after they die? Humans live such short lives." Areela said and bit her tongue.

Gaia looked away and didn't reply.

"I am sorry. I should not have said that. It wasn't a nice thing to say." Areela whispered.

"It's okay. I agree that your worries are warranted. Siblex Junior will be in trouble if we don't return from our trip to Xenora." Gaia replied.

"So, let's go via Elvonia and leave him in Kailow's care. My brother would never hurt him." Areela replied.

Areela's suggestion made Gaia flush with anger. She had vowed to never return to Elvonia after Kailow left her for Princess Imogen after the Snake of Truth had bitten her. His betrayal had broken her heart and left her children fatherless. The fact that everything turned out fine after she fell for Areela wouldn't change that.

"You can't be serious? Do you remember what he did to me?" Gaia exclaimed.

"He is my brother, and yes, I do remember. He sacrificed your relationship for our mission. Princess Imogen would not have let us go near the Elvonian Zeto Crystal if it wasn't for Kailow." Areela replied.

Gaia shook from anger and didn't know what to say. She knew that Areela's statement made sense, yet Kailow's betrayal was something she had been unable to forgive.

"Aunty Gaia, what are you and mother fighting about?"

Gaia looked at the child-like Siblex Junior, who was still a child in the Zetan development cycle, despite being an adult in human years. It was strange that two species that looked so similar had such differences in lifespan and growth development stages. Gaia felt guilty, walked up to the child, kneeled and said, "We are fighting about nothing. We are just silly adults."

"Don't patronise me. While I look young, I am more mature than a human child. Tell me what is going on." Siblex Junior urged.

Hearing Siblex's authoritative voice, Gaia had a flashback from when she envisioned his future when he was still in Areela's womb. Siblex's destiny was to change his name to Gromvir and become the King of the Dwarves. She had never revealed this vision to Areela, as she didn't want to change the future by telling it. Yet in their current predicament, who was more suited to decide Siblex's destiny than himself?

"Your mother and I must travel to Xenora to confront your evil brother, Thorax. But we worry about what will happen to you if we leave you behind on Earth. So, your mother wants to leave you with your uncle Kailow on Elvonia, while I want to bring you to Goldonia, where you are destined to become the King of the Dwarves. However, you are also free to stay on Earth if you like." Gaia stated.

"I cannot stay on Earth without my mother. My Zetan longevity would curse me on this planet since humans die so young. I also do not really care nor want to see my uncle Kailow, Ava and Adan's father. Goldonia seems like the most promising choice to follow my destiny." Siblex Junior stated.

"But, Siblex... Your uncle and your cousins live on Elvonia. Wouldn't that be a better alternative than going somewhere where there is no one to care for you?" Areela objected.

"No, mother. What uncle Kailow did to Gaia was indefensible. I love Gaia like my second mother. Besides, I cannot reject True Maker's chosen path." Siblex replied.

Areela bit her lip and gave Gaia a cold gaze. It infuriated her that Gaia had never revealed her vision of Siblex Junior's future. Yet, Areela knew that Gaia would never do anything to harm the good-natured child.

"Well, then it's decided. We are leaving tomorrow. I pray that the True Maker allows me to save Thorax from himself so we can all meet again." Areela said, walked up to Junior, and carried him away to show her disapproval of Gaia's intervention without verbalising it.

Gaia watched as Areela walked off. The conversation had been unpleasant, and she hoped that her upcoming farewell to Ava and Adan would be easier.

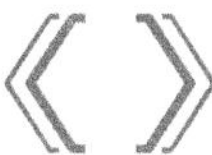

"MOTHER, WHY ARE YOU leaving? This came so sudden."

Adan Gaian looked surprised as Gaia revealed her travel plans while barbecuing a rabbit with Areela and Siblex Junior. Gaia looked away. She didn't want her son Adan to share her worries about the future, but she didn't want to lie either. She soothed him and said, "I would never leave you or your sister if I had the choice, but leaving Earth is the only way to save you and the rest of humankind."

"So, is another asshole from Zetani Nova planning to steal the Terran Zeto Crystal?" Adan asked.

'It's much worse than that,' Gaia thought and replied, "Yes, something like that. But rest assured that your mother will keep you safe ."

"Thank you, dear mother," Adan replied.

Gaia looked around, and Ava was nowhere to be seen. She feared that her daughter had left for one of her long wanderings as she had done so many times in the last five years. After finding out about her father, Ava blamed Gaia for their separation, and their relationship had never been the same.

"Where is Ava?" Gaia said, and she felt how a panic attack was approaching.

"She is far away. She left on a journey to contact the tribe living at the foot of the Euphrates River a week ago." Adan replied.

Hearing this, Gaia regretted that she hadn't sought her daughter when she returned from her travels the day before. It was a shame that she hadn't sought to mend their relationship until the fear of her passing had taken hold of her.

'Mother?' Gaia whispered.

This is not the time nor the place to mend the relationship with your daughter. Why have you wasted five years if it matters so much?" True Maker replied.

Gaia sighed. Sometimes, sorry was indeed the hardest word to say.

"Tell Ava that I am sorry and that I love her," Gaia said, turned around and walked off into the night, unwilling to show her son the tears that were flooding her cheeks.

Chapter 52: A Pre-Destined Regency.

"You have arrived at Goldonia."

Gaia woke up with a twitch as the autopilot of their hovercraft stopped in the Divine Dimension, just above the planet of Goldonia. How long had it been? As they started their journey from Earth, Gaia had decided to leave her life in True Maker's hands instead of manoeuvring the hovercraft. It was a risky move, as they could have collided with a black hole like they did many years earlier during their trip to Earth. Yet, Gaia knew that she would reach Xenora and face Thorax, so in the grand scheme of things, how did her actions until then even matter? That was the danger of foresight. Knowing that one would reach a specific destination made the journey less meaningful.

"Is this it? Is this the planet where my son's destiny lays?" Areela sighed.

"Why are you sighing? This is a great day." Gaia enthused.

"Is it? I have seen our future. We are landing amid a great dwarven war. I regret listening to you. We should have brought Siblex Junior to my brother on Elvonia." Areela objected.

"War can be a great harbinger of change, as can the arrival of a new Messiah," True Maker whispered to Gaia.

"What did your mother say?" Areela asked.

"That we are where we are meant to be," Gaia replied.

"And that is, in this foreign warzone?" Areela asked.

"Yes," Gaia replied.

"Hmm, I guess I must put my trust in you." Areela pondered.

"Sometimes, faith is all we have in life," Gaia replied.

Areela nodded, turned to the door, and called out, "Siblex, come to me. We must travel to your new home."

As the Zetan boy came running, Areela hugged him and whispered, "Everything will be alright, my son."

"I know, mother. Let's go." Siblex Junior replied excitedly.

Areela nodded and went outside the hovercraft with her son and her lover. Gaia opened the portal to Goldonia, and there was a bright flash as the trio travelled through time and space.

"STOP THIS MADNESS! Let's settle this war with a duel."

King Vir of the Bluetongue Clan looked at his counterpart King Grom of the Redneck Clan, who had made this utterance. It made sense for him to accept. The conflict had spanned for centuries, and this battle was still in the balance. If he could avoid thousands of extra deaths by accepting the challenge, so be it.

"I accept your challenge. What are your terms." King Vir shouted.

"We fight a duel to the death. Whoever emerges alive from the duelling ground will unite our clans and sit on the Golden Throne." King Grom shouted back.

"I agree. Prepare to die." King Vir shouted and blew his horn to signal his troops to withdraw.

King Grom followed suit, and a gap formed between the two sides, with each side forming a shield wall. The Dwarven kings explained the rules of the duel to their followers, that whoever exited the duelling ring alive should rule both kingdoms under the name Gromvir.

As King Grom walked towards the duelling ground, he saw the many dead and maimed dwarves on both sides. Such a tragedy that their followers had died for their vanity. No matter if he survived the day, he hoped that his actions would set an example for settling political feuds in the future.

The two kings entered the ring, gave short speeches to their followers, and charged at each other. Suddenly, a blue light appeared from the sky, and Siblex Junior got out of the portal first, followed by Areela and then Gaia. Siblex Junior's fall from the divine dimension caused an explosion, and it shattered the dwarven kings, instantly killing them.

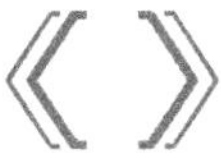

GAIA PANICKED AS SHE opened her eyes. She felt very heavy, and the lifeless gaze of two dead dwarves stared into her soul. She heard the nearby dwarves chant something in an incomprehensible language, but one word stood out, "...Hvala Gromvir! ....hvala Gromvir!"

"What happened?" Gaia asked True Maker.

"Everything went as I meant for it to happen," True Maker replied.

"Why do I feel so heavy?" Gaia asked.

"Goldonia's core consists of gold, making the planet much denser. This causes it to have higher gravity than Earth and the other Zeto Crystal worlds. The high gravity is why the inhabitants here are dwarf-like, short but human-like, and that's why Areela's son is the only one of you who can stand up." True Maker replied.

"So, what happens now?" Gaia asked.

"I have granted Areela's second son, who shall henceforth be known as King Gromvir, the ability to speak the local language. Here on Goldonia, you and Areela will improve your physique for your true purpose." True Maker replied.

"And that is to stop Thorax from invading the rest of the Milky Way Galaxy with his Xeno hordes?" Gaia asked.

"Yes..." True Maker replied and disconnected.

Hearing the reassuring message from the True Maker, Gaia felt better. Knowing that she experienced heavy gravity, she pushed herself to a kneeling position and crawled over to Areela.

"What is happening? What are those strange dwarves doing to my son?" Areela yelled.

"They are making him their king," Gaia replied.

"Why?" Areela asked.

"It is his destiny," Gaia replied.

"Be that as it may, but the dwarves must have a reason." Areela objected.

"We can ask him when we get to him. My mother granted him the ability to speak in the dwarven tongue. Now rise, my love. We are not injured; it feels that way because of Goldonia's strong gravity." Gaia said, got up, and helped Areela back on her feet.

After helping Areela, they followed the procession of dwarves taking Gromvir to the castle. Gaia felt good about herself as she had helped Areela's second son reach his destiny, and she used her mind to overcome her physical burden. Spending some time on this planet was precisely what she needed to build her physique for the trial and tribulations ahead.

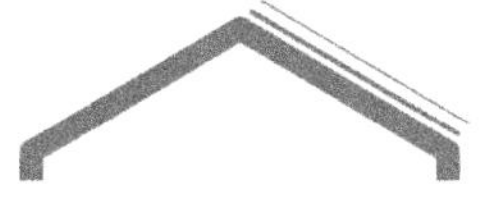

Chapter 53: War and Peace.

Gaia and Areela sat together, wrapped under a warm blanket while sitting by the fire next to Goldonia's Golden Throne. Areela pitied her son for his destiny of living here as it wasn't the most hospitable planet to live on. Goldonia's orbit was squeezed between two brown dwarf stars. Both stars shone with a bleak light that caused the planet to be in perpetual twilight. Alas, it was always cold, even in the middle of the day. Also, the intense gravity on the planet caused every living being on it to be stout and robust, like the dwarves, and she dearly missed the natural beauty of Zetani and Earth.

Areela got distracted from her thoughts when her son, crowned King Gromvir, walked towards the throne accompanied by his golden guard, which consisted of a dozen dwarves covered in golden armour. It was a fascinating sight to behold. Although golden armour was cumbersome and weighty, Goldonian tradition stated that their finest warriors should fight wearing it. The elite soldiers' golden armours were the equivalent of a peacock's tail. It signalled superiority as the wearers had survived battles despite wearing conspicuous and inferior equipment.

Areela pitied her son, who struggled with heaviness as he walked towards the throne slowly. It was difficult enough to walk on Goldonia in regular clothes; to move while covered in all that bling would be a nightmare.

As Gromvir got seated, the dwarves started chanting, and an elderly seeress walked towards the throne. She carried the royal crown, which was laden with gemstones and made from pure gold. She stared at Gaia, pointed at her, and started chattering in seriousness as she walked to the throne.

Gaia looked at Gromvir and spoke: "Why is she looking at me like that, and what is she saying?"

"She recognises that you are closely aligned to the All-Mother. Therefore, she wants you to crown me as the King of Goldonia." Gromvir replied.

"Did you tell her about my powers?" Gaia asked.

"No, but to someone aligned with the spirits, they must be obvious," Gromvir replied.

Gaia nodded. She had never envisioned that she would be the one crowning Gromvir as the King of the Dwarves, yet here she was. By following her visions, she had made them self-fulfilling. She took the heavy golden crown from the seeress, put it on Gromvir's head, and was met by thunderous applause. Gromvir stood up, gave a speech, and at the end of the address, servants came in and set up an endless buffet of tasty barbecued wild meats and rejuvenating meads.

Areela looked confusedly as Gaia grabbed a horn of mead and a large chunk of barbecued meat. "But Gaia, you don't drink, and you are a vegetarian?" Areela objected.

Gaia smiled at her, winked and replied, "When on Goldonia, do what the dwarves do."

Areela realised that Gaia was correct. They were guests here, and they should adapt to the local customs. So, she grabbed a horn with mead, bit on a large piece of grilled rabbit, and the ladies danced the night away.

AS AREELA WOKE UP, she felt even heavier than when she first landed on Goldonia. Transitioning from a non-drinking vegetarian to an alcohol drinking meat-eater wasn't easy, and the bucket next to her bed showed that she hadn't handled it well.

The room was still blurry when Gromvir and some of his men, clad in steel, entered her room.

"My son, why are you dressed like that? What is going on?" Areela mumbled.

"We have celebrated my coronation on Goldonia. Now we need to go to war." Gromvir said with a serious and calm tone.

"I don't understand. Who are you going to fight?" Areela asked.

"The brother I never met, who threatens to subjugate all life in the galaxy," Gromvir stated.

"But... But we brought you here to keep you safe. Or did Gaia lie to me?" Areela objected.

"Gaia didn't lie, mother. I am not safe hiding here while Thorax builds his army. The safest choice is to confront him before he reaches his peak." Gromvir replied.

Areela bit her lip and didn't say anything. She wanted to feel anger towards Gaia and the True Maker for deceiving her. Yet, she was to blame for their situation. She was the one who had given birth to the monster, Thorax Zelinkom.

"I see. Please bring me some herbal tea. I need to recover from last night." Areela mumbled.

"I will see to it," Gromvir replied, turned around, and left the room together with his armed entourage.

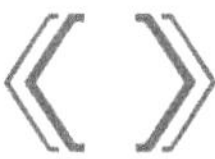

GAIA STUDIED THE DOZEN dwarves in the back of their hovercraft on their way to Xenora. She had charged a lot of sapphires with the power of Goldonia's Zeto Crystal. She could use the charged sapphires to give the dwarves modern Zetan weapons instead of the swords, axes, and plate mail that the dwarves wielded. Yet Gaia sensed that everything was going according to her mother's plan. As illogical as it was to bring a group of dwarves to fight Thorax on Xenora, this was how it was destined.

Gaia tried to visualise what Thorax would look like now, many years later. He had been an ugly baby when she last saw him, a baby she had neglected when he was in her and Kailow's care. She had been so young and in love with Kailow back then, and although their separation had broken her heart, their relationship had not been in vain. Kailow had fathered her beautiful twins Ava and Adan, who had remained in the Garden of Eden to educate and lead humankind. Gaia cried when she realised that she might never see Ava and Adan again. Yet, she had to do everything, even sacrificing her own life, to keep them and humankind safe.

In her emotional state, Gaia reflected on whether she had created the predicament she was in. Did her negligence and Thorax's early separation from his mother drive him to become what he was, or would he have become evil nonetheless? The question was irrelevant. She could not change the past; she could only affect the future.

Areela approached Gaia and sniped, "I hope you are happy now."

Gaia sighed and replied, "I did what I could to keep your son safe. I thought I could save him if I made him the king of Goldonia."

"Hmph, he would be safer if you didn't convince him to travel with his elite guard. He could have stayed on Goldonia, rallied his troops, and marched on Xenora." Areela said in retaliation.

"No, he wouldn't be safer that way. Rallying the dwarven armies and gathering supplies for a long march would take years. Who knows what damage Thorax could cause in that time? We need to strike while Thorax is still weak. Your son chose to come with us." Gaia replied.

Areela looked at Gromvir, who was sleeping in the back of the hovercraft. He had been determined to go, and there had been nothing she could do to convince him otherwise. "I hope you are right," Areela stated.

"So do I," Gaia replied, leaned back in her seat, and turned on the autopilot for the multi-day trip to Xenora.

Chapter 54: Join or Die.

Thorax Zelinkom sweated profusely, so much that his scaly and shiny lizard skin turned purple as he reached the Temple of Life at the Xenora equator. The temple was a meeting place for all the tribes, as they had to permanently move to avoid getting caught in the searing midday sun on the slow-rotating planet. Thorax hated this place. When he became the Supreme Leader, he would have settlements in the polar regions with tunnel networks connecting the two. That was the only way to have permanent settlements, which was necessary to build a force capable of conquering the six other prime planets in the galaxy.

Thorax sought shade behind a stone pillar, but it didn't help him much. While the shade protected him against the searing UV radiation, the temperature was over 50°C and rising. In less than 24 hours, it would reach 70°C as the planet progressed further in its three months long day-night-cycle. 70°C was more than his body could handle, and Thorax damned that his superior Zetan genome didn't allow him to withstand Xenora's searing midday heat. Yet, his intolerance for high temperatures was irrelevant. Once his subjects had completed their settlements in the polar regions and their adjoining tunnel networks, he would no longer need to tolerate heat.

Thorax picked up the corrupted dark Zeto Crystal from his pocket. It had turned from blue and tranquil to dark and fiery. He held in a shout of pain as he touched it. The dark crystal was as icy as the darkness of space and as hot as a glowing star. It was painful to handle, and it was his destiny to let the pain guide him.

"Thorax Zelinkom, stop hiding in the shadows. Come out and face the council." A voice mocked.

Thorax clenched his jaws tightly. He had expected them to be more respectful after the way he had repelled their attacks on his North Pole base. Yet, they didn't fear him enough, and they thought they were safe as the Xeno culture did not allow violence in this holy place.

Thorax squeezed the Zeto Crystal and entered the circle in the temple, bathing under the searing blue sun. "I wasn't hiding, and it would behove you to be more respectful to your future king," Thorax warned.

The councillors looked at Thorax in disdain. They hated the ugly freak, as he was shorter than an average Xeno man, and his skin was lizard-like and scaly, unlike theirs, which looked more thorny and furry, and they were twice his humanoid size. Yet, their defeat at the North Pole had forced them to offer him parlay and safe passage.

"We don't have kings on Xenora, we have leaders, and you are not leading anyone. You can rot while hiding in your fort on the North Pole for all I care." Maicon, one of the Xeno chieftains, exclaimed.

"Yet you tried to expel me and lost many of your men doing so." Thorax taunted.

"It doesn't matter, tiny creature. You are too cowardly to face us in the field. Your followers will get sick of eating mushrooms and hiding in the icy twilight when they can roam the plains of Xenora under a true leader."

Thorax bit his lip. He hated that his physique didn't allow him to lead his tribe as the other Xeno leaders did. He could not run at a sustained pace to outrun the planet's rotation while also leading hunts of the fantastic beasts that roamed the planet. Instead, he had to ride on the back of his men to get to the meeting, and while his men feared him and his corrupted dark Zeto Crystal, he was also dependent on them to survive. If he killed them, the midday sun would catch up with him and burn him alive.

"You are wrong," Thorax stated and smirked.

"And why is that, you filthy rat?" Maicon sneered.

"Because my men know that their children are safe at the North Pole, and they are outside your reach. Meanwhile, we grow enough mushrooms in our caves to sustain ourselves until the end of time."

"What does it matter? Our children are not part of the conflict." Maicon replied.

"They are now. Submit to my kingship or watch your children die. I will come for them; I will clear one nursery at a time until none of you remains." Thorax threatened.

Hearing this, Maicon jumped Thorax. They crashed to the ground, and Maicon held his claws to Thorax's throat. Thorax squeezed the dark Zeto Crystal, smirked to hide his pain, and spoke, "So, Maicon of the Mun Tribe. Is this how you treat the holy sacraments and the ban against violence at the Temple of Life?"

"You stay away from our children. Infanticide is not the Xeno way." Maicon roared.

"I have changed the Xeno way, as foretold in the prophecies. Yield to me or die." Thorax said and prepared to have his throat ripped while hoping that the crystal's power would keep him alive.

This didn't come to pass, as another Xeno leader, Kandung, pulled Maicon away and spoke, "Don't shed any blood in this temple, Maicon. We cannot breach against our ancient laws."

"We need to kill him now; it's the only way." Maicon protested.

"He will be dead soon enough, but not like this." Kandung replied, turned to Thorax, and proclaimed, "Thorax Zelinkom, for the threats towards our children, I proclaim you a heretic. You'll receive a two-day head start. After that, it's the obligation of every Xeno following our traditions to kill you. Begone."

Thorax grasped his dark Zeto Crystal. He could kill them here and now; he could feel it. Yet, he did not want to be the one breaking the sanctity of this temple. It would have been better if they drew first blood. "I guess I'll see you soon," Thorax stated and left the temple.

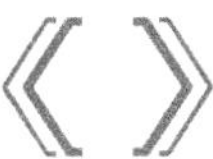

"MASTER THORAX, WHAT happens now?"

Thorax looked at his loyal servant Drang, who had carried him 1200 kilometres to the Northwest. Moving away from the equator to an earlier time in the day, the temperature had fallen, and Thorax's skin tone had reversed from purple to scaly green. He sighed relief and replied, "Well, I expect that they'll come to our North Pole settlement with their finest warriors where we slaughter them all."

"What if they don't take the bait?" Drang asked.

"Then we'll seek out their nurseries and murder their children. That will gain their attention. Either way, I won't allow any division on this planet. The others must join me or die. The Milky Way Galaxy shall be mine." Thorax screeched as he squeezed the Zeto Crystal so hard that blood sipped from his lips.

Drang didn't reply. He didn't know what the Milky Way Galaxy was or what Thorax planned to do. Yet, he knew one thing; terrible things happened to those who questioned his master when he had that look in his eyes. So, driven by fear, Drang forgot about his fatigue and ran towards the northwest, away from the scorching day and his master's fearsome temper.

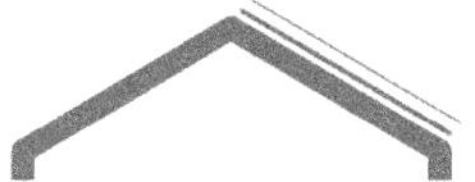

Chapter 55: An Unexpected Outcome.

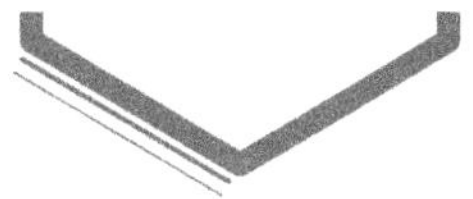

Gaia, Gromvir, and the dwarves were in the Divine Dimension outside Xenora when one of Gromvir's men, the veteran Gunnar, broke down and started crying. "Oh....I don't want to die like this. I want to die wearing the golden armour that has belonged to my family for generations."

Gaia felt bemused by the dwarf's whinge. While she shared his fear of dying, she had no preference for what clothes to wear when her time came. Gromvir put a hand on Gunnar's shoulder and spoke, "I understand your concern. You were King Grom's greatest champion, and it befits you to fall in your family's armour. Yet, we are here because of something that is far more important than your legacy. We are here to stop an existential threat to our people. Please wear the steel plate mail and help us save Goldonia from those who seek to enslave us."

Gunnar nodded, walked over to the plate mail, and put it on. Then, when he was dressed, he pounced his chest, shouted, "For death and glory, for Goldonia!" and ran through the portal. The other dwarves followed suit, as did Gaia, Areela, and Gromvir. The battle of their lives was ahead of them.

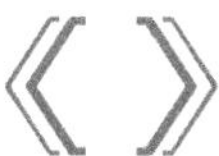

"MASTER THORAX, ENEMIES are approaching our main gate."

Thorax looked at Drang, who had interrupted the hot and kinky orgy session he was in with several sex slaves. He hated interruptions when enjoying himself, yet he would have been even angrier if no one had told him about the approaching threat. Thorax pulled up his waist girdle and spoke. "They act sooner than I anticipated. How many of them are there?"

"We counted 15 individuals, Master Thorax," Drang replied.

"15?! You interrupted my orgy session just for 15 enemies ahead? Just dispose of them already." Thorax growled.

"Uhh...... they are not from here. They demand to speak with you, Master." Drang replied meekly.

Drang's answer puzzled Thorax. Who were these strange visitors that dared to approach his fortress? In any case, they would not pose any threat to him or his followers. "Take me to the ramparts at once," Thorax commanded and got on the back of Drang, who carried him towards the ramparts like an obedient dog serving its master.

"THESE XENO BEASTS ARE huge. How are we going to fight them?" Gunnar said to Gromvir as the dwarves gathered in front of the city gates.

"They might be huge, but the bigger they are, the harder they fall. Do you notice how light you feel on this planet?" Gromvir replied.

"Yes, I do. Why is that?" Gunnar asked.

"It is because gravity is much weaker on Xenora. You are used to fighting on Goldonia, so you will be light and super-fast on this planet. Now fight and bring honour to your family." Gromvir replied.

Gunnar was about to reply when Thorax appeared on the rampart and growled madly. "Grahhhh!! Who dares demanding an audience with Supreme Leader Thorax Zelinkom?"

"I am, brother. Surrender your evil ways, or we will stop you." Gromvir replied.

Thorax stared at Gromvir and froze when he saw his mother, Areela, and his spiritual enemy, Gaia. Gaia's presence was a threat to Thorax, as the spirit of the True Maker filled her with her immense all-knowing power. While he could hide behind his electrified walls, he couldn't allow himself to appear fearful to his subjects, who outnumbered the intruders 100 to 1.

"Open the gates. Slay the dwarves and bring the women to me." Thorax commanded.

One of the Xenos, seeking glory, sprinted ahead to attack the dwarves as the gate opened. Gunnar jumped towards the beast, swung his axe, and decapitated the Xeno mid-air with a clean cut. After this, Gunnar grabbed the cut-off head, threw it towards Thorax, and hit him in the head.

"Charge!" Thorax shouted, but his warriors hesitated. They followed him out of fear, but now they had found something else to fear, the mysterious super-powered aliens that looked like tiny little humans with extreme speed and agility.

"Charge!" Gunnar shouted, and the dozen dwarves stormed towards the gates to fight.

"Come with me and stay close," Gaia instructed Gromvir and Areela and activated a forcefield of light granted by her mother. "We need to get to Thorax. Hurry while the dwarves distract his troops!" Gaia exclaimed. Areela and Gromvir followed Gaia as they sprinted through a gap among the defenders and pursued Thorax to his dark temple while the fighting continued in the courtyard.

GUNNAR WAS THE LAST dwarf standing when a claw suddenly pierced his side. He looked at the Xeno warrior who was about to deliver the finishing blow to his neck and smiled. It was an honour to die for his king in battle. While it was a shame that he died so far away from his home, he would reach paradise for his bravery. However, the finishing strike never came; instead, Gunnar watched something unbelievable. Other Xenos had arrived to aid him in the battle. Gunnar closed his eyes and thanked the All-Mother for saving him so that he would have another chance to see his family.

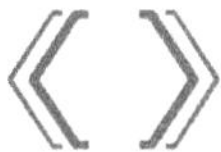

THORAX STARED DOWN at the city as he was about to enter the dark hilltop temple. His Xeno rivals had arrived at the most unfortunate moment, and nothing could save him now. "If I am to die, they must all die. I will destroy the planet." Thorax mumbled and rushed towards the inner sanctum to perform a rite to destroy the Xenoran Zeto Crystal and, ultimately, the whole planet.

AS GAIA, AREELA, AND Gromvir entered the inner sanctum of Thorax's dark temple, he was sitting on his throne and cackling like a madman.

"Rrrahaha! Welcome, mother. How pleased I am that you are here to witness the destruction of this planet." Thorax taunted.

"My son. I know you are hurt. I know I wasn't the best mother, but please let Gaia heal you, as she healed me after your father died." Areela pleaded.

"Oh yes, she healed you by satisfying your carnal desires. But I desire nothing from that ugly human except for her to leave me alone. Instead, she destroyed everything for me." Thorax hissed.

"Don't say that. There are more than carnal desires to this life. Gaia can heal you." Areela protested.

"Hah, don't speak about that failed genetic experiment like you know her better than I do. Gaia and I are two sides of the same coin, created by that master manipulator who brandishes herself the True Maker. You worship her as a deity, but in reality, she is the operating system that runs the simulation you perceive as the Milky Way Galaxy. We are living in the 1000th iteration of the simulation, and I'll make sure this is the last." Thorax ranted like a mad man.

Areela turned to Gaia and spoke, "Is this true, Gaia?"

Gaia shook her head and replied, "I can neither confirm nor deny Thorax's claims. Yet, I know that I am here to set things right. Destroying the Xenoran Zeto Crystal would destroy this planet and make this part of space unstable."

"That is because the Zeto Crystals symbolise the seven mainframes that run the Milky Way Galaxy simulation. The True Maker never split her soul into seven pieces; that's what the creator of this simulation wants you to believe," Thorax continued ranting.

"I have heard enough, older brother. It doesn't matter whether this world is real or a simulation. What matters is that this is our world, and we have come to save it." Gromvir proclaimed.

"Well, it seems like you failed!" Thorax taunted and blasted Gromvir with a concentrated ray of dark energy from the corrupted Zeto Crystal.

As Gromvir collapsed, Gaia's perception of time froze, and she heard her mother's ethereal voice. *"If you hate Thorax for what he did, he'll win. Only love can stop him now."*

As time resumed, Gaia embraced the shocked Areela and whispered in her ear. "Close your eyes, and let me guide you. I love you."

Fizz, Fizz, Fizz

The powerful blasts of malevolent energy bounced off the forcefield surrounding Gaia and Areela. After a sustained bombardment, Thorax collapsed to his knees and exclaimed, "Why won't you die? This is impossible."

"Because true love is the strongest force of the universe, and it never dies," Gaia replied, walked up to Thorax, touched the corrupted Zeto Crystal, and unleashed a massive blast.

Chapter 56: Glory or Sacrifice.

As Gaia opened her eyes, she saw herself frozen in time. It was the moment when she and Thorax touched the Zeto Crystal simultaneously, which caused the blast that had made her fall unconscious. The True Maker approached her and spoke, *"This, my daughter, is one of the most momentous moments of this Milky Way Galaxy iteration."*

Gaia looked at True Maker, nodded, and spoke with an afterthought, "Let me guess, I need to choose because you cannot?"

"Yes," True Maker replied.

"Is Thorax's claim true? Is this world a simulation?" Gaia asked.

"I cannot answer that question with certainty. I woke up on this day a trillion years ago. As you know, this is the 1000th iteration of the Milky Way Galaxy. Perhaps there is a higher force than me in this world." True Maker speculated.

"Is that why you can't make choices?" Gaia asked.

"Yes, for one reason or another, only mortals can affect the outcomes of their lives," True Maker stated.

"So, tell me about the choice I need to make," Gaia said.

"I'd rather show you," True Maker replied and put her hand on Gaia's head.

Gaia closed her eyes, and visions of greatness appeared. She saw herself possessing the seven Zeto Crystals with all the sentient species of the galaxy bowing to her. There were monuments of her carved into every mountain, and life was ubiquitous throughout the universe.

"Wow, what was that?" Gaia asked.

"That was the outcome if you choose to claim the corrupted Zeto Crystal for yourself. The Xenos will bow to you, and you'll use them to subjugate the other sentient species for the greater good. All sentient species will interbreed in your galactic

empire until there are only one species left, and they'll worship you like their living deity." True Maker explained.

"I understand. Please show my other options, mother." Gaia replied.

True Maker touched Gaia's head again, and she felt like a free spirit. Gaia saw Adan and Ava raising their children. Time passed until they were dead, and their lifeforce flowed through their descendants. She felt at peace, but no one was aware of her role in saving the galaxy.

"That is the outcome if you choose to sacrifice yourself by using your lifeforce to restore the Zeto Crystal. You'll die and be forgotten, but life will go on, and free will shall continue to exist." True Maker explained.

Gaia nodded and replied, "What if I choose another option? You haven't described every possible outcome."

"What do you mean?" True Maker replied.

"What if I choose to neither sacrifice myself nor claim the corrupted Zeto Crystal?" Gaia asked.

"That scenario doesn't make any sense. Someone else will claim the corrupted crystal, do the same things Thorax did, and your entire existence will be for nothing." True Maker replied.

"Yet, sometimes people choose to make the meaningless choice. But I assume you already know what choice I will make?" Gaia asked rhetorically.

"Yes, I know your spirit," True Maker replied.

"Then bring Gromvir back. I promised Areela to keep him safe." Gaia requested.

"Are you negotiating with the Supreme Deity?" True Maker asked.

"Yes, mother," Gaia replied and smiled.

"Very well, I'll bring Gromvir back to life if you restore the Zeto Crystal," True Maker replied.

"We have a deal," Gaia said, and time resumed.

GAIA FELT IMMENSE PAIN as she returned to her senses. Thorax and Areela were dead; the former came as a relief and the latter as a sorrow, yet Gaia knew that she had made the right choice. Gromvir would have a future if he came back to life, while Areela wouldn't. Gaia grabbed the crystal, and she heard how the Xenos were approaching. It was now or never, she could either rule or sacrifice herself, but she had to choose. As Gaia grabbed the crystal to sacrifice herself, she felt angst as she feared dying alone. Gaia held Areela's still warm hand and let go of her divine energies to restore the crystal. There was a burst of light, and everything turned black.

WHOOSH

Gaia woke up with a twist as many fearsome Xenos looked at her in silence. She looked at the Zeto Crystal. It looked restored, and she felt strange; she had lost the ever-present contact with her mother.

"Eeeek!"

Gaia looked to her right, where Areela screeched in terror. Gaia grabbed the hand of her lover, squeezed it, and whispered. "Don't fret, my love. Everything is going to be alright."

"How do you know?" Areela whimpered.

"Because we are still alive. Let's go home." Gaia said, got up, and helped Areela back to her feet. On the way back to their portal, they joined Gromvir and Gunnar, the only surviving dwarf in their entourage. They left Xenora, never to return.

THE TRUE MAKER WATCHED as Gaia and Areela rose to life and shivered. Something had gone wrong, and the world was still in danger. When Gaia sacrificed herself, she gave up everything for her loved ones. Yet Gaia loved Areela more than life itself, so her subconscious had diverted some of her divinity to keep her and Areela alive. While the godhood that Gaia surrendered into the crystal made it seem pure, it still contained enough of Thorax's taint to pose a threat in the future.

The True Maker tried to contact Gaia. It was to no avail, as she had given up her divinity to be with her loved ones. True Maker looked at the crystal again.

For now, the world was safe, and she would have to stay vigilant to stop any new threats to the integrity of the Milky Way Galaxy.

Chapter 57: Epilogue

The events in the year 71,200 before the present changed the 1000th iteration of the Milky Way Galaxy, and all living things were never the same from then on. The Zetans that escaped Zetani and survived the Zetani Maximus going supernova have continued to live on various planets, educating the inhabitants with their knowledge and wisdom. They became prophets and deities and created different religions and moral ethics to spread their Zetan knowledge to the inhabitants over the years. This was something that did not happen during earlier iterations of the galaxy. The Zetans who escaped the supernova altered the genome of every other sentient species in the galaxy and imbued their Zetan genome to make them wiser. As the Zetans gave the recipients superior intelligence, their Zetan DNA and history continued to flourish amongst some. Thus, their descendants founded ruling dynasties on every planet and became the masters of their tribes.

Kailow Voltrom remarried after Imogen's death, and he fathered many many children. His descendants would remain the ruling family on Elvonia for 72 millennia until Rangda Kaliankan destroyed Elvonia during the Apocalyptic War in the 29th century AD, which is covered in the Divine Zetan Trilogy. Under Kailow's dynasty, the elves lived in peace, being attuned to the powers of the Elvonian Zeto Crystal.

Siblex Junior Zelinkom reigned Goldonia for two centuries as King Gromvir, and he reigned it well. He directed a shift among the dwarves to focus on commerce and industrialisation rather than warfare and family honour. While the strong gravity on Goldonia shortened his lifespan, his children continued his legacy. Eventually, Goldonia split up into a plethora of underground kingdoms. The dwarves helped the Zetans in the Multimillennial war, and they succumbed to Rangda's maleficence during the Apocalyptic War.

Gaia and Areela settled on Earth, and they died together 40 years after Thorax's defeat. They lived out their lives in sorrow. Gaia mourned the loss of her divinity, as she no longer could connect to her mother, The True Maker, and Areela was left feeling guilty over what happened with Thorax. They died together, Areela from cancer and Gaia from old age. The Zetan intervention in building the Garden of Eden helped Homo Sapiens to survive the Mount Toba Ice age eruption and caused the Neanderthals to go extinct. Humans kept living, and humanity helped the Zetans fight against the Xenos in the Multimillennial War. They were the only species that didn't succumb to Rangda Kaliankan's malevolence in the Apocalyptic War.

Lieutenant Hadib Nabilom and his enforcers didn't find any luck after they were sent to contact the orcs on Grashdung. They were captured by the orcish matriarchs and held as sex slaves. They succumbed after a short time due to exhaustion and the high sulphur content in Grashdung's atmosphere. Their seed lived on, however, and their sons overthrew the matriarchy when they came of age. The orcs helped the Xenos and Rangda Kaliankan in the Multimillennial War and the Apocalyptic War.

The Xenos were unaffected by the Zeto Crystal in its pure state, and they kept living the nomadic and barbaric lifestyle they always had followed. However, they did fulfil Thorax's ambition and built permanent settlements in the planet's polar regions. However, The Xeno lifestyle changed 60 millennia later when a Zetan explorer Kalianka Durgan was betrayed and left for dead on the Xenora. This led to the birth of the evil Rangda Kaliankan, a half Zetan and half Xeno, a direct descendant of Thorax. With a burning desire for hatred and malevolence, Rangda came up with a plan to subjugate the Xenos, avenge her mother, and conquer the Milky Way Galaxy.

If you want to learn more about the Multimillennial War, please read the sequel to this book, written soon. The Divine Zetan Trilogy follows the events in the Apocalyptic War where the future saviour Sabina must save humanity and the Milky Way Galaxy from Rangda's terror.